WARD D

FREIDA MCFADDEN

For my patients

ALSO BY FREIDA MCFADDEN

Never Lie

The Inmate

The Housemaid's Secret

The Housemaid

Do You Remember?

Do Not Disturb

The Locked Door

Want to Know a Secret?

One by One

The Wife Upstairs

The Perfect Son

The Ex

The Surrogate Mother

Brain Damage

Baby City

Suicide Med

The Devil Wears Scrubs

The Devil You Know

1

PRESENT DAY

Dear AMY BRENNER,

You have been assigned to overnight call
tonight on our primary locked psychiatric unit,
Ward D.

In preparation for your assigned shift, please
observe the following guidelines:

- You will be given a numerical code that
  can be used to leave Ward D. Except in the
  case of an emergency, you MAY NOT exit
  the unit during your shift.
- Do not divulge any personal information
  to your patients. This includes details
  about your personal life or your home
  address.

- The following objects are prohibited on Ward D: alcohol, flammable liquids, thumbtacks, pens, needles, staples, paper clips, safety pins, nail files, tweezers, nail clippers, tobacco products, electronic cigarettes, plastic bags, razor blades, weapons, or any items that could be used as weapons.
- Do not expect to sleep during your shift.

The on-call attending physician tonight is DR. BECK. Please report to the attending physician on arrival at Ward D.

Sincerely,
Pauline Walter
Administrative assistant to the Chief of Psychiatry.

Mrs. Pritchett can't sleep.

Or at least, she couldn't sleep the last time she was here at the psychiatry outpatient office where I have been doing a medical school clerkship for the past two weeks. I am working with a psychiatrist named Dr. Silver, who I have nicknamed Dr. Sleepy (at least in my head) because eighty percent of the patients he sees are here for sleep problems. The medical school psychiatry rotation that I'm on is supposed to expose me to a general outpatient practice, with a mix of depression, anxiety, psychosis, etc., but it's really just sleeping problems here. And I'm fine with that.

I still have the notes I took in my little spiral notebook from Mrs. Pritchett's last visit. I hadn't realized until this very second how illegible my handwriting has become. Aside from her age of sixty-four years old, I can only make out two sentences:

Can't fall asleep.

And:

Cat

I underlined "cat" several times, so it must've been important, but I can't read anything I wrote below that word. Something about cats, presumably. Maybe her cat was sitting on her face when she was attempting to fall asleep. That happened to me once.

Mrs. Pritchett is perched in the exam room, her chin-length gray hair combed into a neat bob, her big pink purse clutched in her lap. Unlike most exam rooms I have seen, this one doesn't have an elevated examining table. It's just a room with two wooden chairs in it. Mrs. Pritchett is sitting in one, I will sit in the other, and then when Dr. Sleepy comes in, he will take the second chair and I will stand, hovering over them awkwardly.

"Amy!" Mrs. Pritchett exclaims when I walk into the room. "I'm so happy to see you, dear!"

"Oh?" This is different from the usual bleary-eyed greeting I get from patients. "How are you sleeping?"

"So much better—thanks to you!"

"Really?" I try not to sound too astonished, but it's hard not to blurt out, *But I did absolutely nothing.*

"Yes!" She beams at me. "Everyone else just prescribed a bunch of sleep medications, but you actually talked to me. More importantly, you *listened*. And that's how I realized the reason I couldn't sleep was that I was missing Mr. Whiskers so much since he passed on six months ago."

Oh, *cat*. Now it all makes sense. "I'm so glad I could help."

She smiles tearfully. "And that's why after talking to you, I went out and I got a brand new kitten. Ever since I took home Mr. Fluffy, I have been sleeping like a log. It's all because of you. Because you took the time to listen."

What can I say? As a medical student, I don't have much knowledge, but I have lots of time to spend with patients. And it's a good thing, because Mrs. Pritchett proceeds to show me about five billion Polaroid photos of her brand new kitten.

"Also," she says when we finish looking at the photos, "I got you a thank-you gift!"

A thank-you gift? Seriously? Wow, this is the most exciting thing that's happened to me in about two years.

However, some of my excitement wanes when Mrs. Pritchett stands up from her chair. And I would say it vanishes entirely when she grabs a giant painting that I hadn't realized was in the back of the exam room. The picture had been turned to face away from us, but now I can see it clearly.

It's a portrait of a cat.

And it is almost as big as I am.

"This is a painting I had commissioned of Mr. Whiskers," Mrs. Pritchett says proudly. "And I would like you to have it."

"Oh," I say. "Um. Thank you!"

A black cat is prominently featured in the giant portrait. Clearly, this is larger than life, unless Mr. Whiskers was a bobcat or perhaps a small lion. And why does he look so *angry* in the painting?

"Doesn't it look realistic?" Mrs. Pritchett says.

Yes. He truly looks like he is about to leap out of the painting and maul me.

I lug the painting out of the exam room, unsure where I am going to put this thing in my tiny little apartment. For now, I leave it in the hallway.

Dr. Sleepy is working in the office next door to where I had been sitting with Mrs. Pritchett. This other office has a desk and a computer set up on top of it, and Dr. Sleepy is tapping away at the keys when I rap my fist against the open door. When he looks up at me, he pushes his half-moon reading glasses up the bridge of his nose and gives me one of his mild smiles.

"Hello, Amy." Dr. Sleepy always speaks in a calm voice that is close to a monotone. I'm pretty sure he could lull most of his patients to sleep with just his voice. They probably leave the appointment and immediately drift off in their cars, possibly while driving. "Are you ready?"

"Yes," I say.

"Well then. Tell me about Mrs. Pritchett."

I go through the information about Mrs. Pritchett on my little notepad. Dr. Sleepy takes it all in quietly, making slight grunts at appropriate moments. I mention the cat portrait, hoping he might offer to take it off my hands, but no such luck.

"Anyway," I say. "That's all."

Dr. Sleepy rubs his white goatee thoughtfully. "And how are *you* doing, Amy? You don't look like you've been sleeping very well either."

He's right—I didn't sleep well last night. I'm sure I have massive bags under my eyes. "I'm just a little nervous because I'm rotating on Ward D tonight."

"Ah, that makes sense." I'm not sure how disturbed to be by the fact that he thinks it's normal that I have spent half the night awake worrying about my overnight call on the locked psych unit. "It can be challenging on Ward D. But I think you'll learn a tremendous amount tonight. Who is your attending?"

"Dr. Beck."

He nods in approval. "One of the finest psychiatrists I've known. And an excellent teacher. You'll have a great experience tonight."

I highly doubt that.

"There's nothing to worry about," he says in that calm, reassuring voice of his. "Remember, you will have the code to exit the unit. You can leave at any time."

Right. There's apparently a keypad with a six-digit code that controls the locked door to the psychiatric unit. But I can't memorize a phone number, and that's only one digit more. What if I forget the code and I'm trapped? *What then?*

He smiles soothingly. "You have done such a great job here the last two weeks, Amy. All the patients tell me you are a wonderful listener. A lot of students seem to forget that psychiatric patients are human beings, just like you and me. They just want to get better, and part of your duty as a physician will be to give them the best possible care."

"I know."

He cocks his head to the side and looks at me in the thoughtful way he often does. "What are you so worried about, Amy?"

"It just seems like it could be... dangerous."

"You'll be fine." He levels his watery blue eyes at me. "All the patients are very well controlled on their medications. There's nothing to worry about."

That sounds like a lie. If they were well controlled, the unit wouldn't have to be locked, would it?

But that's not the real reason I am dreading my night on Ward D. I can't tell Dr. Sleepy the real reason I was tossing and turning last night. I can't tell anyone the real reason I'm desperately terrified of Ward D.

"Listen." Dr. Sleepy glances down at the gold

watch on his wrist. "Why don't you let me finish up with Mrs. Pritchett, and you can take off early? Take a little Amy Time before you head over to Ward D."

A little Amy Time sounds fantastic. I don't get much of that anymore.

"Thank you so much," I say.

He winks at me. "No problem. And don't worry. Once you get to Ward D, you'll see it's not so bad. I promise."

I hold my tongue to keep from telling him the truth. The truth is, I've already seen Ward D. I visited it once before, nearly a decade ago.

Back when my best friend was a patient there.

I still remember her matted hair and wild eyes when I came to visit. She didn't look like my best friend anymore—more like a wild animal closed up in a cage. But the thing that sticks with me most—the thing I will never forget—are the words she spit out at me just seconds before I ran out of the unit, swearing to myself I would never return ever again:

You should be the one locked up here, Amy.

2

I am going to be spending the next thirteen hours of my life in a locked psychiatric ward.

I try not to think about that fact as I sit in the passenger seat of my roommate Gabby's third hand gray Toyota. (It was her dad's, then her brother's, and now it's hers—any day now, it will be the junkyard's.) She has kindly offered to give me a ride to the hospital for my night shift, which is starting in exactly twenty minutes. It feels like a countdown to my execution.

"Stop freaking out, Amy," Gabby tells me. She's been working on Ward D during the days for the past two weeks, and she doesn't understand my concerns. She's even rotated with Dr. Beck the first week and absolutely adores him. "It will be fine."

Of course, at this moment I am freaking out a bit more about the fact that Gabby just zipped through a stop sign without so much as pausing. Gabby is probably the second-worst driver on Long Island (the first being me, of course). Then again, if Gabby wraps the car around a tree, I will have a free pass to get out of this shift. For once, I'm hoping we get in a terrible crash.

Well, maybe not *terrible*. But something just bad enough to require a visit to the hospital. Maybe a broken bone—an unimportant one like my pinky finger.

"Who are you on-call with tonight?" Gabby asks me.

"Stephanie."

"Oh!" She brightens. "Stephanie is awesome. That's so perfect."

I have to agree with her about that. Stephanie Margolis is one of my more level-headed classmates. She is the kind of person you want to be studying with the night before a test, because she always knows her stuff, but she's not obnoxious about it. She's a calming presence in any room. Knowing she will be with me tonight makes me feel a little better about the whole thing.

Gabby runs a hand through her black curls, but her hand gets stuck and for a moment, I am seriously scared I'm going to have to take the wheel and steer the car myself while she disentangles her fingers using both hands. But then she gets it under control.

My phone vibrates against my thigh. As I pull it out, I cringe at the sight of my badly chewed finger-nails—I would be chewing them right now if there were anything left to chew. The name Cameron Berger is staring back at me from the screen of my phone. Followed by a text message:

Hey.

I thought nothing could make me feel worse right now, but there it is. A text message from my ex-boyfriend, who recently broke up with me in a very humiliating way.

"What is it?" Gabby asks me.

"Cameron," I say.

She makes a face. Gabby was the one handing me the tissues after our break up, and she even helped me build a little boyfriend bonfire to rid myself of all Cam's belongings that he left behind at my place. "What does that jerk have to say?"

"He said, 'Hey.'"

"How dare he!" She lays a hand on the horn, probably startling the guy driving the car in front of us, who is doing absolutely nothing wrong. "I hope you're not answering him."

"Of course not."

"I don't know why you don't just block him!"

She's right—I should block him. And I will.

Maybe tomorrow.

We turn a corner and the hospital comes into view —it's a new structure built in a circular shape so that the inpatient units form a loop. It was built to have an ultra-modern appearance, like we're living in the not-too-distant future. For the last two years, I've been taking classes at the hospital: anatomy, physiology, pathology, microbiology, etc. But now we're finally using the hospital for the reason it's intended: to see patients and learn how to become doctors. This is what I have been dreaming about for my entire life.

Although I *never* dreamed about becoming a psychiatrist. Of all the specialties I have been considering, that is the only one that has never crossed my mind.

Gabby skids to a sickening halt in front of the busy entrance to the hospital, narrowly missing a man in a wheelchair. "Here we are!"

"Here we are," I echo, clutching the brown paper sack on my lap, containing my American cheese sandwich and a bag of chips I found in one of our cupboards. The sack crumples under my hands.

"Don't worry," she says. "You'll be fine."

"I'll text you when I get inside." I want to add: *If you don't hear from me every hour, send help.*

"Actually…" Gabby twirls a lock of black hair around her finger. "The reception isn't great there. It's actually sort of… nonexistent."

I gape at her. I didn't think it was possible to feel worse about tonight, but there it is. "You didn't tell me that!"

"You were already so upset. I didn't want to make you feel worse!"

I lean my head back and pout. "At least I could have *prepared* myself then."

"Look," she says, "if you go into the staff lounge and hold the phone right up to the window—like, actually touching it—you can get a couple of bars."

Apparently, I am going to spend most of tonight in the staff lounge, with my phone pressed against the window.

"I'll pick you up in the morning," Gabby says. "Seven o'clock sharp. We'll go get pancakes."

I feel bad dragging Gabby to the hospital at seven on a Saturday morning, although to be fair, it was her bright idea to attempt to carpool this year. So far, it feels like a mostly failed experiment, but we're still trying to make it work. And anyway, the thought of jumping into Gabby's car tomorrow morning and driving to the local diner for pancakes will give me something to look forward to.

"Okay," I say, except I don't get out of the car. I don't budge from the passenger's seat.

"Amy." She frowns at me. "You need to calm down. What are you so worried about?"

It's the same question Dr. Sleepy asked me. I open my mouth, wishing I could tell her everything, but also knowing that I can't. Only one person knows the truth, and that's Jade. I can never tell anyone else. Not my parents, not Gabby... I couldn't even tell Cameron before I found out what a jerk he was.

"What if," I say quietly, "at the end of the night, they get confused and think that I'm one of the patients there and they don't let me out?"

For a moment, Gabby stares at me with her pale

gray eyes. But then, after a few beats, she breaks out into loud laughter. The kind of boisterous Gabby-laugh that usually makes me want to join in, but not today. "Oh my God, Amy. You are *so* funny."

She thinks I'm joking.

I raise my eyes to gaze up at the fifteen-story hospital looming above me. Even though it's July, there must be rain coming because the sun has already dropped in the sky and heavy gray clouds are forming along the roof of the hospital, giving it an ominous appearance. I've never dreaded anything quite so much.

But I'm just being silly. What happened was a very long time ago. It's a distant memory, really.

This will be fine.

3

EIGHT YEARS EARLIER

I love this sweater. Like, so much.

I've never been much of a sweater person. But the shade of pink perfectly complements my skin tone. And when I run my hand over the soft fabric, it feels like I'm touching a cloud. I turn this way and that, admiring myself in one of many mirrors of Ricardo's—a busy clothing store at the mall.

"That looks *amazing* on you."

I jump slightly at the sound of my friend Jade Carpenter's voice. It's funny because she is one of the loudest people I know with one of the biggest personalities, but sometimes she can sneak up on you like a stealth ninja. I turn around and she is standing behind me, leaning precariously against a row of size two blue jeans that would probably be too big on her.

"You think?" I say. I run my hand over the fabric again.

"Yes!" Jade tucks a strand of her pin-straight blond hair behind one ear. She put on far too much eye makeup this morning, and it's caking on her eyelashes. "You never get new clothing for yourself, Amy. You always wear the same stuff."

That's not an entirely untrue statement. Yes, I can usually be found in blue jeans and oversized hooded sweatshirts. But I *like* hooded sweatshirts. They're warm and cozy, and if it rains, you can put up the hood. They're like the perfect clothing!

"Buy it," Jade says. "Trust me."

With those sage words, Jade wanders off to do her own shopping. Jade will leave the store with at least one new outfit, maybe two. And some jewelry. She always does.

For once, maybe I should do the same. My mom gave me some money—two crisp twenty-dollar bills which I broke on a bottle of peach iced tea (my absolute favorite drink in the universe), but the remainder is still sitting in my wallet. I could buy myself a sweater. I could have something nice to wear that isn't a hooded sweatshirt for once in my life. It would be fun to show off the sweater at school on Monday.

I grab the price tag hanging off the sleeve of the sweater. And my mouth falls open.

Okay, I will *not* be buying this sweater today.

I shrug off the sweater, replace it on the hanger, and stick it back in the rack of clothing, trying to squelch my feelings of longing. How could a stupid sweater cost that much money, anyway? It's just a bunch of yarn, isn't it? I need to walk away before I develop some kind of dangerous attachment here.

While I'm standing in the middle of Ricardo's, trying not to stroke the forbidden sweater, I notice a little girl standing on the other side of the clothing rack. She is about six or seven years old, wearing a pink dress that is the same color as the sweater, and with blond curls around her face. She is adorable, especially when she offers me a gap-toothed smile.

"That sweater would look pretty on you," she says in her sweet little girl voice.

"Oh, thank you," I say.

"You should buy it."

I smile regretfully at the little girl. "Unfortunately, it's a little too expensive."

The girl looks up at me. Her eyes are very blue, like two little pools of perfect ocean water, rimmed with long dark eyelashes. "You should take it then," she says.

What?

I stare at the little girl, thinking I must've heard her wrong. I wonder where her parents are. A girl that young shouldn't be all alone, should she? "Excuse me?"

The little girl flashes her gap-toothed smile again. "Nobody will see," she says. "It's a big store. They won't miss it."

She's right. Ricardo's is huge. And there are very

few salespeople working on the floor. If I stuffed the sweater into my backpack, nobody would notice. I could walk out of here with the sweater and it wouldn't cost me a cent.

But I couldn't do that. That would be stealing! I've never stolen anything in my life, not even a pack of gum. I couldn't steal a whole sweater.

Before I can explain to this little girl that stealing is not okay, a hand closes around my forearm. Jade is standing next to me, a wild look in her blue eyes that are flecked with bits of yellow. She shifts her trademark red purse on her shoulder.

"Hey, Amy," she says. "I'm ready to go. Let's get out of here."

Before I can protest, Jade is pulling me in the direction of the exit. It's for the best, though. The thirty-seven dollars and change in my wallet won't be enough to get me anything I really like here.

"Do you want to hit up Sally's next?" I say as we weave our way through the clothing racks to get to the exit. "They have cheaper stuff."

"Sure. Maybe."

"Or maybe I can grab another peach iced tea?"

Jade laughs. "I'm pretty sure that if I cut you open, your blood would be like ninety percent peach iced tea."

Well, what can I say? I love peach iced tea. There are worse vices.

Jade still has her skinny fingers wrapped around my wrist when we get to the store's exit. As we walk through, a deafening alarm goes off. I freeze, surprised, and Jade's grip on my arm tightens.

"*Run*," she instructs me.

Before I can even think about it, Jade and I are running. A voice behind us yells for us to stop, but it's obvious at this point we can't stop. We run through the mall, stepping between families with little kids in tow, and I nearly trip over a stroller at one point. Jade almost mows down a woman with a cane. But after we turn two more corners, Jade pulls me into a little nook, and we finally stop running.

Jade is breathing hard, but also laughing. Her cheeks are bright pink, and her bleached white-blond hair is wild. "Oh my God," she says.

I hug my arms to my chest, massaging a stitch in my side. "What was that?" I ask, although I'm afraid I already know.

Jade pulls open her red purse. I peer inside, and there it is: a shirt stuffed inside with the tags still attached.

"Jade!" I cry. "I can't believe you did that!"

She shrugs. "That store was *so* expensive. I didn't have a choice! Anyway, it's not a big deal."

Jade and I have been best friends since the very first day of kindergarten, when we discovered we were wearing the exact same dress—white with a pink and purple heart on the chest. We had sleep-overs every weekend from ages nine through eleven, she knows about every single crush I've ever had, and she swore she'd keep my secrets to the grave. I'll never have another friend as good as Jade Carpenter.

But lately, I feel like I barely know her anymore. She used to be more like me: liked to go to school, liked to read, and followed the rules. But over the last year or so, she seems to get all these wild ideas about things she wants to do. For example, last week she called me at two in the morning and asked if I wanted to break into Mrs. McCloskey's pool and go skinny-dipping! No, I did not.

"You shouldn't steal, Jade." I don't want to sound lame and give her a lecture about how stealing is wrong, so I just say, "What if you get caught?"

She waves a hand like this doesn't concern her in the slightest. It concerns *me* though. Next year, we're going to be applying to colleges. I don't want to have to explain a shoplifting charge on my application.

"Everyone does it." Jade gives me a pointed look. "You should have taken that sweater. It looked great on you."

I snort. "You know, that little girl was telling me I should take it. Can you believe that?"

Jade pulls the shirt out from her bag and holds it up, admiring the glittery lettering on the front. "What little girl?"

"The little blond girl who was standing next to me."

"I didn't see a little blond girl standing next to you. What are you talking about, Amy?"

I roll my eyes. Jade's powers of observation are

not exactly stellar. How could she not notice that little girl? The girl stuck out like a sore thumb in her frilly pink dress, all alone like that. And she was right next to me.

Wasn't she?

4

PRESENT DAY

HOURS UNTIL MORNING: 13

The psych ward is on the ninth floor of the hospital.

I stand in front of the set of heavy metal elevator doors, not sure if I want them to come faster or slower. If the elevators don't come soon, I'm going to be late. But on the other hand, every moment I stand here waiting for the elevators is a moment when I won't be in a locked psych unit. So there's that.

While I'm waiting, my phone buzzes inside my scrub pants pocket. The thought of not being able to use my phone soon is nothing short of terrifying. It's like having my arm amputated. Granted, this may indicate an unhealthy relationship with my phone, but

I don't care. I *need* my phone. What sort of place doesn't have cell reception? It's inhumane.

I dig my phone out from the deep pocket of my blue scrubs, hoping it's a call from Pauline, the psych administrative assistant, saying they don't need me to cover Ward D after all. But of course, it's not. It's my mother.

Great.

My mother is the last person I want to talk to right now, but if I don't answer and my reception goes out, she's going to panic. So it's better to take the call now and get it over with.

"Hi, Mom," I say, just as one of the elevator doors finally opens. I'll let this one go.

"Amy," she says. "How are you doing?"

"Busy," I say. "I'm going to be studying tonight."

Okay, I haven't exactly told my mother about my evening on Ward D. As anxious as I am about the experience, she will be even worse. It's not so much that she worries a lot in general, but she knows Jade was a patient here. She knows that entire history.

She won't want me returning to Ward D.

"How is psychiatry going?" she asks me. In the background, I can make out the evening news playing on their small television that was purchased about twenty years earlier. My father watches every night without fail. You could set a clock by it.

"It's fine," I tell her. "Easy."

"You're not interested in—"

"No," I cut her off. "I'm not interested in psychiatry as a career. Definitely not."

I would take anything else. Surgery, internal medicine, OB/GYN. I'll even be that kind of doctor who does nothing but look at rectums all day, because that's an important job and I could do that. But I can't treat people with psychiatric disorders. It's the one thing I'll never do.

"I wonder how Jade is doing," my mother blurts out.

"I'm sure she's fine," I say, even though I'm sure of no such thing.

"Do you ever hear from her?"

A couple of years ago, I got a Facebook friend request from Jade Carpenter. And not only did I not accept the request, I blocked her. "Not really."

"I haven't seen her since the funeral…"

I get a stab of guilt. Two years ago, Jade's mother died of a drug overdose. Apparently, she had been popping narcotics, and one day she took too many and stopped breathing. The funeral was on the same day as my first big anatomy exam, so I skipped it. I figured Jade wouldn't even notice I wasn't there, considering how long it had been since we last talked.

Except part of me thinks she definitely noticed. And she was *pissed*.

"Mom." I look down at my watch and then at the heavy elevator doors in front of me, which slide open with a dull thud. "I have to go."

"Okay, good night then, sweetheart. I love you."

"Uh-huh," I say, because I always feel weird saying "I love you" on the phone in public. Except then after we hang up, I feel bad. Why didn't I tell my mother that I love her? It would have been easy enough to say.

After all, what if that phone call is the last time I ever speak to her?

I push that morbid thought out of my head as I shove my phone back into my pocket. A wave of nurses in flower-printed scrubs sweeps me through the elevator doors, and I end up pushed up against the corner, which is just fine. Two nurses are chatting right next to me, and one of them is smack in the middle of describing a bad date last night in her loud, Long Island accent just as the elevator doors slam shut again.

Here we go…

I watch the buttons light up as we move from floor to floor. *Three, four, five…* The elevator seems to almost be moving in slow motion. Shouldn't a hospital elevator move quicker than this? What if we had an emergency? What if I were in *cardiac arrest*? I would be dead by the time we got to the Cath Lab.

Not that I'm in any hurry to get to the ninth floor. But at this point, I just want to get it over with.

"…And he was using his fork to pick food out of his teeth!" the young nurse in front of me exclaims.

"Gross," her friend comments.

I can't help but think that I would trade this night for a date with a guy who picks food out of his teeth with a fork. Hell, I would take a guy who *picks his nose* with a fork.

The elevators finally open, and a mildly British female computerized voice announces, "Ninth floor." I step into the hallway, which is lit by fluorescent lights that show every single crack in the paint on the wall. A giant blue sign has an arrow pointing to the right:

⸰ WARD D

It's not clear to me why the psychiatric unit is called Ward D. I asked Gabby about it when she started the rotation, and she didn't know either. I didn't research it further after that.

After I turn the corner, I see a heavy metal door all the way at the end of the hallway. As I get closer, I can make out the lettering on the sign that is hung on the door. There's a big red stop sign with the warning:

STOP

THIS DOOR IS LOCKED 24/7

There's an intercom mounted next to the door, presumably to contact the nurses' station to gain entrance. And then a keypad below it which can be used by those lucky enough to know the code. And there's one other thing by the door. Something that makes me dread this night even more than I was one minute earlier.

Cameron Berger.

Oh God. What the hell is my ex-boyfriend doing here? Was that what his "hey" was about?

"Amy!" Cameron is waving frantically at me like I'm not five feet away and I might have missed him. "Are you on tonight too?"

Like me, Cam is wearing a short white coat and a pair of light blue scrubs—likely also purchased from the medical student bookstore on the third floor of the hospital—except his are about ten sizes larger than mine because the guy is built like a linebacker. He used to play football in college, but not good enough to go pro, and anyway, he always wanted to be an orthopedic surgeon, not a jock.

"Cameron," I say tightly. "What are you doing here?"

"I'm on tonight." He lifts his chin, which juts out a little more than it should and makes him look a bit like the snooty rich kid in one of those old John Hughes teen romps my mom made me watch when I was a kid. "You too?"

"Where's Stephanie? She's supposed to be the other medical student here tonight." I add accusingly: "It was on the *schedule*."

He lifts a shoulder. "She needed to swap."

Great. This night keeps getting better and better.

Cam's light brown hair is falling slightly in his eyes like it usually does. And like I always used to, I get that urge to brush it out of his face. I better not though, because if I reach up there, I might end up scratching his eyes out. "How have you been, Amy?"

"I'm fine."

"Still living with Gabby this year?"

"Yep."

"Great, great." He scratches at the slight stubble on his square jaw. "Doing anything fun the rest of the weekend? After this, I mean?"

"Not really."

"Yeah." He nods thoughtfully. "Same. I haven't been up to much either, you know?"

I don't know what to say so I just stare at him. I can't *believe* I have to spend the entire night with this guy. The worst part isn't even that he dumped me—I've been dumped before and I can handle it. The worst part is *why*.

At the beginning of the summer, Cam informed me that we couldn't see each other anymore because he wanted to focus all his energy on studying for the board exam, and he was concerned that spending time with me would get in the way of that. That's right—he dumped me for a *test*. Way to strike a blow to my self-esteem.

Amy—test. Amy—test. Well, that's a no-brainer. Never mind that I had to take *the exact same test*, and yet I was miraculously able and willing to juggle studying with a relationship.

I'm glad I didn't know he was on tonight with me. Because then I might have been tempted to break out my little bag of makeup or do something with my dark brown hair besides pulling it into a low ponytail behind my head. And then I wouldn't respect myself anymore.

He's got his eyes on me while I whip out my phone and bring up the number for the psych admin office. I click on it, my fingers crossed, all the while knowing in my heart that everyone has got to be gone for the night. I hold my breath while the phone rings on the other line.

"So this will be an interesting night, huh?" Cam comments.

Still ringing. Five times now. "I guess."

"You have reached Pauline Walter, administrative assistant to the chief of psychiatry. Our office is currently closed. Please leave a message or call back during the hours of…"

Great. I knew they would be closed. And even if I had gotten through to Pauline, what would I have said? I can't do my assigned rotation because the student I'm rotating with dumped me a couple of months ago? That's pretty weak.

"Who are you calling?" Cam asks.

I shove the phone back into my pocket. "Nobody."

"Look, cheer up. Not everyone gets the experience of spending the night in a locked psych unit. It's kind of cool, isn't it?"

I raise my eyebrows—he *would* think so. "So it

doesn't bother you at all that we're going to be locked in there all night?"

"Why would it? It's not like they're going to torture us or do shock therapy. Anyway, we'll have the code to get out."

"What if one of the patients attacks us?"

"That's pretty unlikely."

It doesn't surprise me one bit that Cameron isn't sympathetic. There's clearly something wrong with his empathy gene. Is that a thing? I think I may have learned about that in genetics. I also learned about a disease where your urine tastes like maple syrup. "Fine. Whatever. I guess nothing bothers you."

And then we're just standing there, awkwardly. I wonder if he buzzed to get inside. Well, I'm not going to be the one to do it. I'll stand out here all night if I have to, claiming ignorance. *Nobody let us in—oh well!*

"Look." Cam's cheeks take on the slightest tinge of red—his face always gets splotchy when he's feeling uncomfortable. "Amy, I—"

I don't know what Cam was going to say to me, and I never will, because at that moment, a deafening alarm blasts from the door in front of us. We both leap backward, and a second later, there's a loud click. The door to the psychiatric unit is unlocked.

Cameron steps aside. "Ladies first."

Yeah, the one time he acts like a gentleman…

As the door swings open, my stomach drops. All I can think is that I don't want to be on this unit. I want to turn around and run down the stairs until I'm out of the hospital. It takes every fiber of my self-control to keep from doing it. I really, *really* don't want to be here.

And nobody could possibly understand why except for my former best friend.

5

EIGHT YEARS EARLIER

J ade is late.

That's nothing new. At least, it's nothing new lately. In the last year or two, my best friend has been constantly leaving me hanging. This afternoon, I've been standing in front of our high school for the last twenty minutes and there is no sign of her anywhere. At first, there were kids all over, but it's cleared out enough that I can verify that she is nowhere in sight.

Great.

Jade and I are supposed to be studying together today. I am absolutely *drowning* in Mr. Riordan's trigonometry class, and Jade has always been better at math than me. I need this study session, because we've got our midterm soon, and I'm going to fail if I don't start knowing a lot more trigonometry than I do now.

My phone vibrates in my jeans pocket. I pull it out and a text from my mom is waiting for me.

Home soon?

I peck out a text to her:

On my way. Jade is coming back with me to study.

Okay, see you soon. Love you.

I shove my phone back into my pocket, then I take a swig from my bottle of peach iced tea as I look around for Jade. My eyes wander over to the fence that encloses the schoolyard. But Jade wouldn't be there. That's where all the after-school sports take place, and she's never been an athlete. I can't even imagine Jade Carpenter running laps around the yard. And she's never been into athletic boys. She likes *bad* boys.

As I scan the length of the fence, I realize I've got company. Much to my surprise, a little girl is standing there in the grass. In fact, it's the same little girl with blond curls who I saw over the weekend when we were at Ricardo's. The one who told me to steal that sweater from the store.

Once again, the little girl is all alone. She seems even more out of place here than she did at Ricardo's —standing outside a high school yard, wearing the same exact pink frilly dress she had on the other day with a matching pair of Mary Janes on her little feet. She notices me staring at her, and she flashes me that gap-toothed smile. I raise a hand in greeting, and she waves back.

Maybe she's the sister of one of the students here. That would explain why she would be in Ricardo's, if she were shopping with a big sister who left her alone. And again, they have left her alone here. I should make sure she's okay.

"Amy!"

A sharp nail jabs me in my shoulder, and I whirl around. Jade has finally materialized, again wearing far too much makeup for our study session, as well as a short black skirt paired with ripped fishnet stockings. There's a smell emanating from her that I can't quite identify.

"Geez, what's with you?" Jade rubs her slightly bloodshot eyes. "I was calling out your name, like, ten times!"

"I didn't hear you." I grab my backpack, which I had rested on the ground since it weighs about five metric tons. "I was worried about that little girl over there."

She squints at me. "What little girl?"

I look over my shoulder, back at the yard. The little girl seems to have wandered away. Oh well—I'm sure she's fine. "Never mind. Are you ready to study?"

The plan is to go to my house. We used to go to Jade's house all the time, but for some reason, she's gotten weird about letting me come over. It's too bad, because Jade's mom is way cooler than mine. First of all, she's never home. There are usually no adults around at all. I've never met her dad before. I'm not even sure if Jade knows who he is—in the past, she's told me he's in the military deployed overseas, an astronaut visiting the moon, and once that he died before she was born.

"I don't feel like studying right now," Jade says. "I'm all studied out. Why don't we hang out behind the school?"

It hits me now what that smell is emanating from Jade's clothing. She's been hanging out behind the school *smoking pot* with the stoner kids.

"Jade," I say, "I seriously need to study."

"Ugh, you are *always* studying." Her voice takes on a whiny edge. "For once, why don't we have some fun? You know, Steve Alcott said he thinks you're cute."

"If I don't get a good grade on this test, I'm going to get like a C in math and my mom is going to kill me. And my college applications are going to be screwed."

"So?"

"So you promised me we could study together and you would help me!"

"And I will."

"No. You're not helping me *at all*."

I look at Jade's familiar face and wonder what happened to our friendship. She used to care about the same things I did. She didn't just shrug her shoulders at the idea of getting a bad grade.

"You need to *chill*, Amy." She rests a hand on my shoulder. "This will all work out. Trust me."

"How? How will it all magically work out?"

Jade rolls her eyes. "Fine. Be that way. But I'm going to go hang out with *fun* people."

"Jade…"

Before I can say another word, she's marching away. So much for our study session. I guess I'll have to muddle through it on my own.

I toss my now empty bottle of iced tea into a trash can and take one last look back at the yard, where that little girl was standing. I didn't see any other kids or parents come by to pick her up, but I don't see her anywhere. I crane my neck, searching the area around the school for that pink frilly dress and the blond curls but it's like she vanished into thin air.

She must have left.

6

PRESENT DAY

The person who opens the door to the locked unit is a woman in her forties wearing flower-printed scrubs and a badge pinned to her chest that says "Ramona" in large block letters, with the last name "Dutton" beneath in much smaller letters. Her hair is pulled back into a sensible bun, and she looks like the no-nonsense sort of nurse who has been doing this job for the last twenty years and will be doing it for another twenty years. I can imagine this woman administering shock therapy without blinking an eye.

She narrows her eyes at me and Cameron, sizing the two of us up with one sharp look. "Yes?"

Cameron steps forward first, ever the charmer. "I'm Cameron Berger and this is Amy Brenner. We're the medical students assigned to work here overnight tonight."

Ramona looks us over one more time, then

glances back over her shoulder. She hesitates for a beat, and I'm almost worried she's going to turn us away. Well, maybe *worried* isn't the right word. More like, *hopeful*.

"Yes, fine," she says. "Dr. Beck is at the nurses' station. He'll give you an orientation."

Much like all the other units in the hospital, the psych ward is shaped like a circle. Cameron and I travel in an arc in the direction of the nurses' station. We reach it at about ninety degrees. And sure enough, a man is standing at the nursing station, wearing green scrubs and a long white coat with the name Richard Beck, MD embroidered over the left breast. When he sees us approaching, he raises his right arm enthusiastically.

"Hey there!" he says. "I'm Dr. Beck. You must be…" He reaches into the pocket of his white coat and pulls out a copy of the med student call schedule, which he takes a moment to inspect. "Cameron and Amy. Yes?"

Dr. Richard Beck's appearance surprises me. When Gabby was going on and on about how smart he was, somehow I pictured someone older, with a long white beard that he would stroke while thoughtfully answering questions about the human mind. (Yes, I apparently believed our attending physician tonight would be Dr. Sigmund Freud.) But Dr. Beck is not like that. At *all*. First of all, he's not old. Certainly not old enough to grow a long white beard. He's in his thirties, with slightly sun-kissed brown hair, and a hint of dimples in his cheeks when he smiles at us.

Now I finally get why Gabby likes him so much.

"Welcome to Ward D," Dr. Beck says, his dimples deepening as he smiles wider. "I appreciate your help tonight, and hopefully you can learn a little too."

"I look forward to it," Cameron says.

Kiss-up.

Dr. Beck looks at me as if expecting me to add something. "Thanks," I finally say.

He nods, satisfied with my answer. "Let me show you around."

"Can you show us how the keypad works on the door?" I say, a bit too eagerly. I can't help it though. It's the only way out of here. I'm not going to be able to relax until I've got the code.

"Amy's freaked out about being in a locked unit," Cameron explains. "She thinks she'll be trapped here."

I shoot him a look.

Dr. Beck laughs. "As well you should be! Don't they teach you anytime you're in a movie theater or auditorium to know where the marked emergency exits are? Let me show you how to get out of here if you need to."

The two of us follow Dr. Beck back to the door where we came inside. As we walk past the patient rooms, the door to room 905 cracks open. A pair of blue eyes flecked with yellow peers out at me, and a shiver goes down my spine. Whoever is inside that room is watching us.

And there's also something terribly familiar about those eyes.

It looks so much like…

No. No way. It couldn't be.

When we get to the door to the unit, I see that ominous stop sign pasted on the door, and the keypad to the left of the door is glowing slightly green. Dr. Beck lifts his index finger to the keypad.

"The code is 347244," he tells us.

I whip my phone out of my pocket. Sure enough, there's no service. But I'm able to open a memo note, and I type in the six digits.

"You punch the numbers on the keypad, then hit the pound sign," he explains. Then he demonstrates it himself. After he hits the pound key, a deafening buzzing sound rings out through the entire unit, even louder than it was outside. He laughs at the expressions on our faces. "Loud, right?"

My ears are still ringing. "A bit," I admit.

"We want to know if anyone is entering or leaving the unit," he says. "Now if somebody hits the wrong code, there is a quieter buzzing sound."

He demonstrates this by hitting the number one six times. The sound that results is like somebody getting the wrong answer on a quiz show.

"Nobody is getting out of here if they don't know the code," he says, "but it's helpful to know if somebody is trying to escape."

As I watch him demonstrate the code, I get a prickly feeling on the back of my neck. Like somebody is watching us. I try to ignore the sensation, but then I can't stand it anymore. I rotate my head to take a look, and sure enough, a patient is standing there. Staring at us.

The man is gigantic—way bigger than Cameron and twice as heavy—wearing what looks like a T-shirt on top of another T-shirt, on top of *another* T-shirt, the armpits soaked in sweat, and sweatpants that are hanging down under his massive belly. His eyes have a strange vacant look to them.

"I'm leaving tomorrow," he tells us in a Spanish accent.

Dr. Beck is silent, so I say, "Oh?"

The man turns his attention to Dr. Beck. "My father say I'm leaving tomorrow. So tomorrow, I go."

"Sure," Dr. Beck says agreeably.

"You gotta do it," the man insists. "My father say you have to."

"Don't worry, Miguel," Dr. Beck says.

The man gives us all a long look, then he turns around and walks away, down the hall. His steps are slow and shuffling, like he doesn't quite know where he's going and he's certainly not in a hurry to get there.

"Is he leaving tomorrow?" Cam asks.

"Oh no," Dr. Beck says. "Definitely not. But if I disagree with him, he'll go back to his room and call 911. Easier to avoid that situation."

"Why was he wearing like four T-shirts?" Cam wants to know.

Dr. Beck sighs. "We need to supervise him better when he gets dressed."

I wrap my white coat tighter around my chest. "What was he talking about? With his father?"

"Oh." Dr. Beck shrugs. "He thinks his father is God."

His words sent chills down my spine, but Cam laughs. "So he's a schizophrenic then?"

"*No.*" Dr. Beck frowns. "He's not 'a schizophrenic.' We don't refer to patients that way. Miguel is a human being, and he's more than his psychiatric diagnosis. He is not a schizophrenic—he's a *man* who has schizophrenia. Do you understand that?"

Cam's face turns slightly pink. "Right. Of course. Sorry."

But then when Dr. Beck turns away, Cam flashes me a conspiratorial smile and rolls his eyes in my direction. I don't smile back. I really appreciated what Dr. Beck said—it's similar to what Dr. Sleepy has said. The patients locked in this unit are human beings just like everyone else. A mental health diagnosis is not a death sentence. All the patients in this unit are just trying to get better.

I will make it through the night. Everything will be fine.

7

Next Dr. Beck shows us the staff lounge, which is right next to the entrance, and he wanders off to give us a minute to put our food in the fridge.

The staff lounge is bare-bones. There's one sofa that looks worse than the one Gabby and I rescued from the curb last year, and that is saying a *lot*. There's a single computer in the corner of the room which looks like the kind of computer I used to see in pictures of my parents' house before I was born. Next to the ancient computer is a window. If I had any thoughts in my head about trying to get some fresh air, those thoughts are immediately banished by the set of bars covering the window.

Cameron yanks open the refrigerator door so we can stash our dinners inside. The refrigerator looks like it hasn't been cleaned out since sometime in the last century. There is a brown crusty film all over every surface, and to fit my dinner inside, I have to push away a carton of milk that feels like it's become mostly solid. I don't dare throw anything away though.

Hmm, could this be some sort of psychological experiment? Maybe somebody's watching us with cameras to see if someone will clean out this disgusting refrigerator?

Cameron holds up his phone, jabbing at the screen. "There's no service at all around here."

In spite of the fact that the guy dumped me *for a test*, I try to help him out anyway. "Gabby said there's reception right by the window."

I follow her instructions and walk right up to the window. I press my phone against the cool surface, and sure enough, a single bar appears on the screen. Then a second. Two bars of reception—woo hoo!

Before the bars can disappear on me, I punch in a message to Gabby:

> Arrived on Ward D. You didn't tell me Dr. Beck was so cute!

The message goes through, but a second later, the bars vanish. Just as well, because Dr. Beck is waiting for us.

Dr. Beck is flipping through a chart when we get back to the nurses' station. He looks up and smiles when he sees us.

"So your job for tonight," he says, "is to be available to help out in case of any emergencies on the unit. But other than that, you are here to learn."

"That sounds great!" Cameron says with the enthusiasm of a child who was told he's going to Disneyland.

"But here's the bad news," Dr. Beck says. "The computer system is undergoing maintenance tonight. So tonight we have to rely on paper charts and paper orders only."

That's okay by me. I have a login for the computer system, but I've never even tried it yet. If my recent luck is any indication, an extended conversation with IT will be required before I get it to work.

Dr. Beck gestures at a rack of thick blue binders lined up on a shelf above the nurses' station. "Those are the paper charts. What I would recommend for the night is for you to read up on a couple of patients and interview them. Learn as much as you can about them and follow them overnight."

So much for my plan to hide in the staff lounge all night long.

"I'll teach you what I can tonight," Dr. Beck adds. "This is a unique experience for both of you—a great way to learn about inpatient psychiatry hands-on. Are either of you interested in the field?"

"I am," Cameron says.

Oh my God, that little *liar*.

"How about you, Amy?" Dr. Beck asks.

"Not really," I admit.

Cameron looks at me as if stunned that I wouldn't

at least *pretend* to be interested in specializing in psychiatry. But really, I was kind. If I said what I was really thinking, it would've been something like, *I would rather hang myself by my eyelids.*

Anyway, Dr. Beck laughs. "Your honesty is refreshing," he says. "I get sort of sick of every medical student pretending to be interested in psychiatry."

It makes me feel just a little bit better when the tips of Cameron's ears turn bright red.

Dr. Beck leads us back into the hallway. It's quiet on the unit, except for a strange rhythmic clicking noise. *Click click click.* Like a small person tap dancing in one of the rooms. I do my best to ignore it.

"All the patients in Ward D have their own rooms," he explains. "The rooms don't lock, but we do have two seclusion rooms that lock from the outside using a keypad. But other than that, the patients can wander the unit if they want. There's a patient lounge with couches and a television and even a piano."

"I play the piano," Cameron volunteers. "I actually was offered a chance to study piano in Paris during college."

Dr. Beck ignores his comment. "I encourage you to spend time with the patient you're following, and really dive deep. Most of them will be happy to talk to you, and you can learn a lot. This is the kind of opportunity you won't have later in your training when you're much busier."

Click click click. What is that tapping noise?

"That sounds amazing," Cameron says.

Ugh, he's being such a horrible suck-up. I can't believe I used to go out with him. I can't believe I used to think he was handsome. Or that he was a good kisser. But some of my irritation with him is dampened by the annoying noise that doesn't seem to show any sign of stopping.

Click click click. Like someone is trying to send us a morse code signal.

"What's that noise?" I speak up.

"Oh!" Dr. Beck laughs. "That's Mary. She's always knitting."

He points to the room just in front of us. Room 912. I peek inside, and sure enough, there's a white-haired woman in a long cable knit dress, sitting on a chair, a pair of knitting needles in her gnarled hands. She looks like she's working on a scarf, but the scarf is far too long. Like, ridiculously long. It cascades down her legs, and then across the length of the room three times. It looks like it could be five or six scarves by now.

"What's *she* in here for?" Cameron asks.

It was a little tactless the way he asked, but Mary does look harmless enough.

"You'll see very soon." Dr. Beck winks at us. "She sundowns pretty badly."

"Sundowns?" I ask.

"It happens to a lot of old people with dementia," he explains. "The sun goes down and they get more and more confused and agitated. Keep an eye on her and you'll see."

"She's here because of dementia?"

"Oh no." He shakes his head vigorously. "She's here for a very good reason, believe me."

I sneak a look back into Mary's room. She notices us at the door, and her wrinkled face breaks out into a huge smile that almost makes her lips disappear into her mouth. She waves at us.

I wave back.

"You let her have knitting needles?" I ask in surprise. It was one of the items on the list of things we should never, ever, ever bring onto the psychiatric unit.

Dr. Beck nods. "They're plastic children's safety needles—completely harmless. She's not a high-risk patient, and knitting keeps her happy. So we let her do it—otherwise, she gets too restless."

I imagine a knitting needle sailing through my eyeball at some point during the night. "Oh."

"So as I was saying earlier," Dr. Beck goes on, "we have two seclusion rooms that do lock, but only one of them is currently occupied. Let me show you."

He leads us around the circle to a pair of rooms with keypads next to the doors. One of the doors is open, but the other is closed. I'm disturbed by how close these rooms are to the staff lounge, which is where I'll probably be spending a lot of time tonight. I suppose that's intentional though.

"Seclusion One is occupied right now," he says.

"And I would not recommend visiting with the patient in that room at any point during the night."

"Why not?" Cameron asks.

Dr. Beck hesitates for a moment as his brows knit together. "Mr. Sawyer is… dangerous."

My heart speeds up in my chest. "Dangerous?"

"Not to you though," he says quickly. "As you can see, the door is locked. And within the room, he is also restrained. So he's completely secured. We're planning on transferring him to a more secure facility in the morning."

Oh my God.

"I promise, you're perfectly safe." Dr. Beck flashes a reassuring smile when he sees the look on my face. "There is no chance of Mr. Sawyer getting out of that room." He pauses. "Unless, of course, you let him out."

Dr. Beck is quiet for a moment. It's so quiet that I can hear a sound coming from inside Seclusion One. It's a terrible sound—barely even human. Something between a groan and a growl.

My God, who is in that room? Or should I say, *what?*

"Don't worry," I say. "We'll stay far away."

"Good," Dr. Beck says.

We turn around and walk back the way we came. On the way, we pass room 905 once again. And once again, the door is cracked open. And those blue eyes flecked with yellow are staring out at me.

Watching me.

8

C ameron and I have to choose patients to follow for the night.

The charts are all located at the nurses' station, so we head over there to look through them and take our pick. Dr. Beck disappears into his office, while Ramona mans the floor, although what she's actually doing at the moment is flipping through a home living magazine.

The charts are arranged on a shelf above the nurses' station, in order of room number. There's only one chart that isn't on the rack and is instead lying on the table below. The name SAWYER is printed on the label on the spine of the chart. That was the name of the patient in Seclusion One. Dr. Beck must have been looking through the chart.

I stare at the chart for a moment, seized by curiosity. Who is in that room? What kind of person needs to be locked up that way? Like an *animal*. It seems cruel and inhumane but it's not my place to say it.

I don't dare touch the chart. It feels like even doing that would be a betrayal of Dr. Beck's trust. Or that if I opened it, the monster inside that room might come leaping out of the pages.

"Anyone you've got your eye on?" Cameron asks me.

"Why?" I shoot back. "Would you steal them from me?"

He clutches his chest. "Why would you say that? If there was a patient you were interested in seeing, I would give you priority. I'm a gentleman."

"Oh right. Of course."

He juts out his lower lip. "Come on. When have I ever been a jerk to you?"

"How about when you *dumped* me?"

"I mean, except for that one time."

I roll my eyes. "Whatever. I don't care. Pick whatever patient you want. You always get what you want anyway."

"What is that supposed to mean?"

"I mean…" I drop my voice a notch so that Ramona doesn't hear us. She doesn't need to know all about the drama between me and Cam. "You weren't on the call schedule for tonight. I don't even understand why you're here. Did Stephanie really ask you to switch?"

Cameron is quiet, for once at a loss for words. I had been hoping he would confirm his story that

Stephanie had some terrible emergency and begged him to switch shifts at the last moment. But I've got a bad feeling that the switch was his idea.

I was legitimately shocked when Cam broke up with me. I didn't think we were going to be together forever—I saw the writing on the wall for the two of us. There were couples in our class that were considering going into the residency match together to ensure they would end up in locations near each other after medical school, but that notion never once entered Cam's thoughts. After all, orthopedic surgery is really competitive. Going into the residency match with another person would only drag him down and reduce his chances of getting a slot.

Even so, I figured we would at least date for a few more months. Maybe once our schedules got busy, we would start to drift apart. Or maybe we wouldn't. Maybe we wouldn't go into the residency match together, but we would end up both getting a residency slot in the city, and maybe we'd even keep dating. Maybe.

I didn't expect him to just… end it.

I wonder what Cameron ended up getting on that board exam. I wonder how many points our breakup was worth to him.

"It doesn't matter to me which patient you see," I say as I push the thoughts of our miserable breakup conversation out of my head. "Take your pick."

"If you're sure…"

"Of course I am. Why would I care about *that*?"

He flinches slightly. "Look, I've been wanting to talk to you. And you won't take my calls."

"Hmm. Wonder why."

"Can we just…" Cam glances over at Ramona, who is within earshot. "Could we talk sometime tonight? I feel like you got it all wrong."

"I'd rather not, Cam."

"Please?"

His face is slightly scrunched up, and for a moment, I feel a stab of guilt for being so cold to him. Then I remember what he did to me. "I can't talk about this right now. Let's just figure out who we're seeing tonight."

Cam looks like he's going to protest, but then he changes his mind. "Fine."

I try not to think about Cameron as I study the line of charts up above the nursing station. My eyes dart between the labels and come to rest on the chart of the patient in 905. The one with the blue eyes flecked with yellow. My whole body turns cold when I see the name written on the chart:

CARPENTER

Oh no.

9

EIGHT YEARS EARLIER

Jade's house is a lot different from mine.

I barely noticed the differences when I was a kid. In fact, I used to think of Jade's house as the "fun house." Because in my house, there were so many rules. You had to put away your toys after playing with them. Dishes had to go right in the dishwasher after use. You had to brush your teeth before bed.

Jade's house didn't have those rules. As far as I could tell, she didn't have *any* rules.

I haven't been to Jade's house in a few months, but today she has invited me over to study together. Well, I'm hoping we'll study. Jade will undoubtedly try to distract me by talking about cute boys in our class or how she could get us fake IDs. But I'm determined to keep her on track, even though it's gotten a lot harder lately.

As I follow Jade down the walkway to her ranch-style house, I can't help but notice how desperately in need of repairs it is. The house was a mess back when we were kids, but now it looks like a wolf could easily huff and puff and blow it all down. The four steps to get to the front door have nearly disintegrated after several years of snow storms chipping away at them, and when I grab onto the railing so I don't fall, a large splinter lodges itself in my index finger.

"Ouch!" I cry.

Jade whips her head around to look at me. "What now?"

She's already in a bad mood. Maybe the study session isn't a great idea. But I need help for the midterm, and Jade has always been my saving grace. "I have a splinter."

"Well, who told you to touch the railing?"

Apparently, there *is* a rule for Jade's house now. Do not touch the railing, because you will be impaled by a giant splinter.

"Let me see." Jade grabs my injured left hand. She squints down at the shard of wood. She plucks it out with her long fingernails as I let out another cry. "Got it! God, you're such a baby, Amy."

A drop of blood oozes out of my fingertip, and I suck on it. I wonder if Jade has any Band-Aids at her house.

The screen door is barely hanging on by its hinges, but it doesn't matter since the screen has been ripped in half. Jade unlocks her front door and the two of us stumble into her living room.

What hits me first is the smell.

Not that Jade's house ever smelled good exactly. It's always stunk of a combination of cigarette smoke and Mrs. Carpenter's perfume. And it definitely smells like those two things today, but there's something else. Like something rotting, but there's also a sickeningly sweet undertone to the odor. I don't know what it is, but I'm not sure how I'm going to be able to focus on math with that stench in the air. I'll have to breathe through my mouth the whole time.

"What?" Jade says.

"Nothing."

"You're making a face."

It's hard to hide my reaction. But I can't very well tell my best friend that her house smells like a big old pile of garbage. "No, I'm not."

Jade tosses her backpack onto the floor, but I'm hesitant to put my own down. Every spot on the floor is occupied by clothes or books or other junk. I start to put it next to the sofa, but a little pile of dishes is already there. And the top dish still has some old food caked on it. I wonder if Jade will want to bring the dishes to the sink, but she doesn't seem at all concerned.

Finally, I bring my backpack with me to the sofa, which is the same one that they have had ever since I have known her, and I rest it protectively on my lap. Of course, to sit down, I have to push away a bunch of jackets that are stacked on the sofa. I glance over at the coffee table, which has five ashtrays on it, all of which are stuffed with multiple cigarette butts.

Jade's house was never exactly *clean*, but this is another level. It almost feels like I'm sitting in the middle of a garbage dump. In the back of my head, I wonder if I should say something to my mother. Jade would kill me, but it can't be okay to live like this.

Can it?

"Let's get started." Jade tugs the backpack out of my hands. "You have your notes from today?"

She puts my backpack on the coffee table, and I cringe when it lands in a circle of what looks like some old juice or soda that never got cleaned up. I inhale sharply, and Jade turns to frown at me.

"*What?*" she says.

"Nothing."

"Why are you being so weird, Amy?"

"It's just…" I point at the mystery sticky spot on the coffee table. "I don't want my bag to get all dirty, you know?"

"Oh my *God*." She rolls her eyes dramatically. "I'm so sorry, your *majesty*. I didn't realize I had to *clean* for your arrival. Would you like to grab some cleaning fluid and a rag and give the table a once over?"

She's being sarcastic, but the truth is, I would. I've never been a huge sucker for cleanliness, but there's something about this house that makes me want to grab a vacuum and a mop and just go to town. Just sitting here makes a creeping crawling sensation go up the back of my neck.

And then a fruit fly buzzes past my ear. Then a second one. I wonder if the creeping crawling sensation in my neck is not entirely my imagination.

Before this conversation can escalate into something worse, the front door creaks open and then slams shut, hard enough that the entire foundation of the house seems to shake. I glance up at the ceiling, wondering what the chances are that the roof could collapse on me. Probably not too likely.

"Jade!" It's Mrs. Carpenter's raspy voice. "Jade! Where are you?"

Jade swears under her breath. "I'm in here, Mom!"

Mrs. Carpenter stumbles into the living room. Much like the house, she looks worse for wear from the last time I saw her. She has always kept her hair platinum blond, but now she's got about two inches of dark roots showing. She's always worn a lot of makeup, especially compared to my own mother, but what she's wearing now is next level. The mascara is caked on her eyelashes, and her eyelids are shaded with dark blue. The lipstick she's wearing is meant to make her lips seem fuller, but really, it looks like her lips got painted by a kindergartener who didn't know how to stay within the lines.

Mrs. Carpenter does a quick double take when she sees me sitting on the couch, and her painted lips set into an angry line. "Jade, who told you you were allowed to invite your friends over to steal my stuff?"

Jade folds her skinny arms across her chest. "Nobody wants your crappy stuff, Mom."

"Oh yeah?" She comes around the couch and stands over us, teetering on her startlingly high heels. "So where are my pills, huh?"

"I don't know," Jade says, although she is not looking at her mother. "You keep everything locked up anyway."

"I know you know how to get into all my stuff. Don't lie to my face, Jade."

"I'm not lying."

"Yeah, right. Give me my pills *right now*."

"I don't have them!"

"Bullshit!" Mrs. Carpenter grabs one of the ashtrays off the coffee table, and before I even know what's happening, she has hurled it at the wall, where it shatters into a hundred little pieces, scattering ceramic shards and cigarette butts all over the floor. "You're a lying little thief!"

Jade's eyes widen a couple of millimeters, but she doesn't react. I, on the other hand, feel like my heart is about to explode out of my chest. I grab the strap of my backpack and snatch it off the coffee table. "I better go," I mumble.

I hurry out the front door as quickly as I can. I don't know what to do at this point. I feel like I should tell my mom what is going on at the Carpenter house- hold. Mrs. Carpenter has always seemed different from other mothers but in a fun kind of way. She was the kind of mom that let you eat cake batter, even though it has raw eggs in it. Or she let you stay up as long as you wanted at sleepovers. And when she drove us around, she used to try to hit potholes on purpose, because it was fun when the car bounced. And she had this really loud, infectious laugh that made you want to laugh too.

I barely get to the end of the driveway when I hear footsteps behind me. I turn around just in time to see Jade standing behind me, breathing rapidly, her face slightly pink.

"Hey," she says. "Sorry about my mom acting weird."

"Yeah," I mumble. "It's okay. I should go."

"Okay, but…" She scratches the back of her neck. "You're not going to tell anyone about all this, right? I mean, it sounds worse than it was. She's just cranky because she was working late last night at the diner."

"Uh-huh."

Jade's gaze crawls over my face. "Amy. You can't go telling everyone that my mom is a crazy person. Our neighbor called child protective services, so we've already got one strike against us. I'm going to, like, end up in foster care. And it will be all your fault."

I dig the fingernails of my left hand into my palm, and my index finger smarts where the splinter had been lodged. I don't *want* to tell on Jade's mother. I don't want my best friend to end up in foster care— she doesn't have anyone else to live with.

She reaches for my arm. "Promise you won't say anything?"

"What pills was she talking about?"

She lifts a shoulder. "Who knows? She takes some medicine for her blood pressure or something. She probably just lost them."

Except why would Mrs. Carpenter accuse Jade of stealing blood pressure medication? That doesn't make any sense.

"Please, Amy?" She squeezes my arm. "That wasn't a big deal *at all*. Like, she's already probably asleep in the bedroom by now. Like I said, she was working super late last night. Anyone would get crabby."

My gut is telling me that I should at least tell my mom what happened. My mom always knows what to do. But Jade is my best friend, and I don't want anything bad to happen to her. And she's asking me to promise. How can I say no?

"Okay," I say, "I won't tell."

10

PRESENT DAY

No. *No.*

I take a step back from the chart rack, my stomach sinking. I wanted it to be some kind of mistake, but it isn't. There's a reason the person in 905 looked familiar.

She was my best friend. Jade Carpenter.

It's a coincidence, but it's also not. This hospital contains the largest psych ward in the area, and we're a stone's throw from the house where Jade grew up and possibly still lives. And let's face it, Jade had serious problems. She's surely been bouncing in and out of Ward D since we were sixteen. So really, I shouldn't be surprised to see her name on the census.

I wonder why she's here. I know what she did to earn her first admission to a psych unit, but I don't know why she's here right now. What did she do this time? It couldn't be worse than what she did when we were kids.

I could look. Nothing would be stopping me from grabbing her chart and flipping through it to find the answer. Well, it would be morally wrong to do it. And there are probably some legal issues as well, since we were told we're not supposed to be looking at charts of friends or family members. But it's not like anyone would ever find out.

I don't even have to read the whole chart. I could just read the first few pages. Nobody would know.

"Go web!" a voice calls out from behind the nurses' station.

I jump away from the charts, my face on fire. I feel like I've been caught doing something naughty, although it's not like anyone knew the thoughts going through my head. And certainly not the man in a slightly crusty Spider-Man T-shirt and sweatpants, standing in front of the nurses' station, with a white band around his wrist that signifies that he's a patient and not one of us. As if there was any doubt.

The man is staring down at his wrists, his lips pressed together in concentration. "Go web," he says again, enunciating each of the two words.

Cameron lays down the chart he had plucked from the rack. "Who's *that*?"

"Him?" Ramona lifts her eyes from a glossy photograph of the do's and don'ts of fashion. "Oh, that's Daniel Ludwig. But we all call him Spider-Dan." Her lips twitch slightly. "Because he thinks he's Spider-Man."

Dan Ludwig stares down at his wrists. "Go web,"

he says one more time in a voice that is almost a monotone.

Cameron's mouth drops open. He turns back to the rack of charts and grabs the one labeled LUDWIG. "Dibs!"

So much for him being a gentleman.

I turn back to the rack to make another selection. I am not going to look at Jade's chart. That would be really, really wrong. I can't believe I was even contemplating it. I'll find another patient to see.

I look at the next chart in the line. Room 906. The name on the chart is SCHOENFELD. I pull it off the rack and read the patient's full name off of the demographics sheet: William Schoenfeld. Well, I definitely did not go to high school with the guy. And he doesn't seem to be locked up in seclusion, tied to his bed with restraints. That might be as good as it gets.

I turn the chart to the first page. Most of the information is probably in the electronic medical record that is inaccessible right now, but the chart at least has printed information from the emergency room visit that brought him here a few nights ago. William Schoenfeld is a twenty-nine-year-old man with no past medical history who presented to the emergency room after several months of hearing voices telling him to kill people.

The emergency room note goes on to describe Mr. Schoenfeld as unkempt and confused, frequently mumbling to himself. He was diagnosed with schizophrenia and prescribed a course of antipsychotics. He was then voluntarily transferred to the psychiatric unit for further evaluation and treatment.

That's when the notes stop.

I stare at the last page of the chart, not sure what to do. Presumably, Mr. Schoenfeld is not dangerous— if he were, he would be locked up like Mr. Sawyer. But on the other hand, this is a man who has been hearing voices telling him to *murder* people. Maybe this isn't the patient I want to see.

But in some ways, that's exactly why I want to see him.

After all, if you meet someone who is truly mentally ill, that's the only way to know that you're sane.

11

Room 906 is around the corner from the nurses' station. Cameron has already disappeared to interview Spider-Dan, so it's just me alone walking around the circle of the psychiatric unit. And as I walk, I hear a sound:

Click click click.

It unnerves me for a moment, until I remember Mary and her knitting needles. As I pass by Room 912, she is still sitting in her chair, knitting away. She sees me and flaps her hand. "Hello!" she calls out.

I wave back. "Hello, Mary."

She beams at me, excited that I know her name. "What's your name, dear?"

I hesitate for a moment. "Amy," I finally say.

"What a pretty name." Her wrinkles deepen as she smiles. She's got to be at least eighty years old. Maybe ninety. "You be careful tonight, Amy honey."

"Uh, okay," I say.

After that slightly ominous warning, I continue to room 906. The next room over is Jade's room, but thankfully, she doesn't peek her head out again. It occurs to me that I could have picked a patient in a room that wasn't immediately next to hers. But I chose not to.

Maybe part of me is hoping to run into her. I can't deny that Jade and I have a lot of unfinished business.

When I look inside room 906, I don't know what I was expecting to see. The description in the emergency room note made it sound like William Schoenfeld was a raving lunatic. So I'm surprised to find a man in his late twenties, wearing a clean T-shirt and jeans, his dark short hair neatly trimmed, his face with a couple of days' growth of a dark beard, and a pair of wire-rimmed glasses perched on his nose. And he's not pacing the room, ranting and raving. He's sitting in his bed, quietly reading a book.

I rap gently on his open door. "Hello? Mr. Schoenfeld?"

The man looks up. He picks up a bookmark that was lying on the bed and places it inside the book. He then rests the book on top of a stack of other books on the dresser next to his bed. "Yes?"

I wring my hands together. "My name is Amy. I'm a medical student."

He has a disarmingly ordinary appearance, which is not at all what I expected. I expected him to look more like Spider-Dan, or that guy who thought his father was God. This guy looks… normal.

Except for the fact that he's hearing voices telling him to kill people.

"Can I help you, Amy?" he asks. He sounds pleasant enough, but there is a wariness in his tone. He's put up his guard and doesn't trust me.

"Yes, I…" God, this is really awkward. But then I remind myself that Mrs. Pritchett said I was a good listener—I can do this. "I'm on-call here for the night, and I'm trying to get to know some of the patients."

His thick dark eyebrows shoot up, and I quickly add, "Medically, that is. Or, you know, *psychiatrically*. Like, why you're here in the hospital and all that. I'd like to hear your story."

He looks at me for a very long minute, then finally says, "Sure. Have a seat."

I grab the chair on the other side of the room and pull it closer to him. But not *too* close. I leave enough distance so that I could make a quick exit before he grabs me. "Thank you so much, Mr. Schoenfeld."

His hazel eyes skim over my face. "Will. Please call me Will."

"Sure. If you'd like." I clear my throat, folding one leg over the other. "So I guess I was just wondering how it all got started. I mean, I heard that you were… you know…"

"Hearing voices?"

"Well. Yes."

"That's right." His eyes make contact with mine. "For a few months now."

"And the voices were… saying things?"

One corner of his lips turns up. "Yes. As voices often do."

"What were they saying?"

A muscle in Will Schoenfeld's jaw twitches slightly. "They told me to kill people. Like, I would be standing with a friend, and a voice would whisper in my ear, 'Push him into traffic.'"

"That must have been upsetting to you."

A flash of irritation passes over his features. "You think?"

I cross and uncross my legs. I was proud of how good I'd become at talking to Dr. Sleepy's insomniac patients—most of them were eager to open up and tell me all about their lives (and their pets). But Will is different. He doesn't want to make this easy for me. "But you never… I mean, just because the voices were telling you to do that, you never…"

He arches an eyebrow. "If a voice were telling you to kill somebody, would you do it?"

I get a sick feeling in the pit of my stomach. I had hoped to come in here and see a raving lunatic. But Will Schoenfeld looks completely benign. He could be absolutely anyone. Some guy you passed on the street. A friend. A neighbor.

He could be a medical student.

"Do you still hear the voices?" I ask.

"Like, right now? Sitting here?"

"Well…"

He pushes his glasses up his nose. "Are you asking me if there's a voice in my head telling me that I should kill you right now?"

I bite down on the inside of my cheek, unsure how to respond to that.

"No," Will says. "I don't hear the voices anymore. The medications got rid of them."

According to the printed medication list Ramona showed me, Will Schoenfeld is on a cocktail of two antipsychotic medications. He's only been on them for a short time, but they seem to be working.

Or so he says.

"Do you live with anyone?" I ask.

"No. I live alone."

"So you're not married?"

"No. Never."

"Do you have a significant other?"

He squirms. "This isn't exactly an ideal time in my life to be getting involved with a woman. I need to get myself together first."

That's the most logical thing I've heard anyone say since I've been here.

I glance at the stack of books on his dresser. I hadn't noticed it before but he was reading *A Prayer for Owen Meany*, which is one of my favorite books of all time. I don't know if I've ever seen anyone approximately my age reading that book before, and I'm not sure how to feel that the first person I've seen reading it is in a psychiatric ward.

"What?" Will says.

"That's my favorite book," I say. "*Owen Meany*."

For the first time since I came into the room, I get what looks like a genuine smile out of him. "I love John Irving," he says. "He's been my favorite since I was ten years old."

"Oh my God, me too!" I cry. "I've read everything by him."

"So have I." He gestures at the stack of books, which I now realize is all John Irving books. "I brought them with me to keep me company. I've been rereading them since I got here." He picks up the thick paperback copy of *Owen Meany*. "This one, I've read about fifty times."

"I've read it a hundred times."

He laughs. "Competitive, are you?"

"Well, like I said, it's my favorite."

"I love to read," he says. "I try to read at least one or two books a week, and I try to *re*-read at least one Irving book a month."

"That's impressive," I comment. "I don't have time to read more than a few books a year. What do you do for work?"

In an instant, the walls go up again. When he answers, his tone is flat again. "I drive for Uber."

Well, that does it—I'm never taking an Uber again. My mother will be thrilled. But the truth is, I'm surprised by this choice of occupation. He looks more like he would be a teacher or a writer. He doesn't look like someone who would drive for a living. Then

again, I'm sure it's steady, flexible work if that's what
he's looking for.

"So I guess you see a lot of people in the course of
your job," I say.

He pushes his glasses up his nose again. "That's
right."

"And did the voices ever tell you to…"

Will Schoenfeld tilts his head to the side. He's
quiet for a long time, then he finally says, "I already
told you. I would never hurt anybody."

He holds eye contact while he answers my question. Why wouldn't he tell me the truth? What does
he have to gain? We're here to help him, and as far as
I can tell, he's here voluntarily. Doesn't he *want* to get
better and stop hearing voices? Still, something in my
gut is screaming one thing:

This man is lying to me.

12

HOURS UNTIL MORNING: 12

E ven though we talk for another twenty minutes, Will never opens up to me again— not the way he did when I brought up John Irving. I even try talking about books again later in our conversation, but the walls are already up. He doesn't trust me.

I guess that's what you call *paranoia*. The antipsychotics might have gotten rid of the voices in his head, but some of the symptoms of his schizophrenia remain.

When I get out of room 906, I can't help but look over at the seclusion rooms down the hall. The first room is still locked tight, the keypad glowing faintly green. I wonder what it must feel like to be locked inside a tiny room with no way out.

I have to pass by the seclusion room on the way back to the nursing station. I walk quietly, scared that the man inside is somehow watching me. That he will lure me over and get me to release him. After all, Gabby says I am very impressionable. She tells me I'm not allowed to watch commercials anymore because I buy everything I see an ad for.

I almost get past the room. I have just cleared the doorway when a horrible loud noise sounds from behind the door. A dull, sickening thud. It almost sounds like somebody has hurled himself at the door.

I jump back about three feet, pressing myself against the other wall. I hear the noise again, and this time the door to Seclusion One vibrates. And as I stare at the door, it happens again. That loud thud, followed by the door vibrating. And an anguished growl from inside.

Someone or some*thing* is trying to break down the door. But how can that be? Dr. Beck told me the man in that room is restrained.

Unless he got free from the restraints.

I gulp in air, trying to calm my racing heart. That's when I hear another sound, one a lot less ominous. It's the sound of a woman laughing.

I swivel my head to the right, and sure enough, a young woman is standing in one of the doorways. She's got her hair gathered into a ponytail high atop her head, and while I guess you would call her a blonde, she's got at least an inch of darker roots. She's wearing a tank top with no bra, and a pair of pink sweatpants. And her eyes are blue, flecked with yellow.

"You," she says, "are still pathetic."

"Jade," I gasp.

I can't believe I'm seeing her again after all these years. Nearly a decade since that day in high school when… Well, I don't want to think about what happened that day. I've spent a long time trying not to.

"It's been a while," she acknowledges.

I scratch at a little dry patch on the back of my elbow. "You look great," I say, almost automatically.

"Oh, shut *up*, Amy." She crinkles the bridge of her nose. "I'm fat like a house. It's from the medications. They make you want to eat until you explode."

Jade isn't "fat like a house," as she's so colorfully put it. She used to be way too skinny in high school—painfully thin—and now she looks like a healthier weight. But admittedly, she has purple circles under her eyes, and the hair coming out of her ponytail looks matted. I haven't caught her on her best day. Then again, I'm wearing scrubs and sneakers without even a scrap of makeup. At least she's got on some eyeliner and a slash of red lipstick.

"How are you doing?" I ask carefully.

"Not as good as you." She looks me up and down, an appraising look in her eyes. "I guess you went to medical school, just like you always wanted."

"Um. Yeah."

"Too bad you had to destroy my life to get there."

I suck in a breath. I thought maybe after all these years, Jade would have forgotten what happened. Well, not *forgotten*. But maybe look at it with a little more perspective. Maybe realized that I didn't do what I did to ruin her life. That I didn't have a *choice*.

"I'm sorry," I mumble. "I didn't mean it to happen the way it did. You know that."

Jade doesn't respond to my apology. She folds her arms across her chest, and I notice a long red scratch running down the skin of her left forearm.

"I'm sorry about your mom," I blurt out.

She shoots me a seething look. "Yeah, so sorry you couldn't even be bothered to come to the funeral."

"It… it was a busy time for me."

"Yes, I'm sure. Busy, important Amy. She's got better things to do than pay her last respects to her best friend's mother."

I don't bother to point out that when Mrs. Carpenter died, Jade and I hadn't been friends in a long time. It wouldn't make things better to say that.

"So you read my chart, I guess," she says.

"No, I didn't."

"Liar."

"I didn't." I lift my chin. "I wouldn't do that. That would be wrong."

She laughs bitterly. "Yes, you're just the queen of moral behavior, aren't you?"

"I didn't," I insist. "I was just interviewing the guy in 906. That's the only chart I've looked at tonight."

Jade looks over at Room 906. The door is still cracked open, and presumably, Will is inside reading again. "Oh, him. He's cute, isn't he? Kind of your type. Lanky, nerdy."

"Jade…" My cheeks burn. "He has schizophrenia."

"Oh, so you've got something in *common* then, don't you?"

There have been a few times in my life when I have wanted to smack Jade in the face, and this is one of them. Thankfully, I know enough to restrain myself. But I need to avoid her come three in the morning, because I won't be thinking nearly as clearly by then.

"Anyway," she says, "he's more your type than that other dopey medical student. The big guy who keeps giving you the moon-faced looks. What—is he in love with you?"

"*No.*" Jade doesn't need to hear the story about how I got dumped for the board exam. "I hardly know him."

"If you say so," Jade says in her singsong voice.

I hadn't expected Jade to greet me with open arms, but I also hadn't expected her to be this obnoxious and angry at me. I've got to make an effort to avoid her the rest of the night. I'm not in the mood for her mind games.

"I don't have time to talk right now," I tell her. "I have to get back to work."

"Oh, that's a shame." She pulls a frown. "Because

I've got the entire night free with absolutely nothing to do."

And then she winks at me.

13

EIGHT YEARS EARLIER

I don't understand the point of trigonometry.

I've been sitting at my desk in my bedroom, attempting to do problems for the last two hours, and I am no closer to having a good understanding of the material. More importantly, I don't understand *why* I need to know this. Will I ever be at a grocery store and need to know the sine of thirty in order to calculate how much change I'm getting? This is like the most stupid and pointless thing ever. And because of it, I might get my first C of high school.

This is hopeless.

I wish Jade had agreed to study with me. Instead, she is currently getting high with a bunch of losers behind the school. We have always studied math together—it's what has gotten me through all my high school math classes so far. I need an alternate plan.

I grab the snow globe on my desk and give it a good shake. Little fake snowflakes scatter over a green

Statue of Liberty. The globe was a gift from Jade last year. Our high school class went on a class trip into the city for a Broadway show, and she snuck away from the group to get it for me from a souvenir stand. She could have been barred from seeing the show at all for pulling a stunt like that, but she did it anyway. That's Jade—always willing to take risks.

I slam my trigonometry textbook shut. I lean back in my desk chair, shut my eyes, and rub my fingertips against my temples. Okay, the important thing is not to panic.

Don't panic, Amy!

I just need to buckle down and study. I can do this. This is going to be fine. Good thing my peach iced tea has a lot of caffeine in it.

I open my eyes, ready to tackle more trigonometry problems. But when I open them, I receive a terrible surprise:

It's that little girl with the blond curls and frilly pink dress.

And she's standing in the corner of my room.

I blink a few times. It was strange to see that little girl all alone in Ricardo's. And it was stranger still to see her at the high school. But it is really, *really* strange to see her in my room.

In fact, it's impossible.

I stare at the little girl. My lips part, trying to form a question. *What are you doing here?* But I can't make myself say it. Because there's no way a little girl is standing in my room. It's crazy to even think it. And it's far more crazy to be talking to her.

"You're going to fail this test," she informs me in her sweet little girl voice.

My mouth feels almost too dry to speak. "No…"

Okay, I have done it. I have spoken to the girl who isn't actually there.

"And then you won't get into any colleges," she continues. "You will never go to medical school. Your whole life will be ruined."

I open my mouth again to respond. Even though this girl isn't real, I want to tell her she's wrong. I'm going to pass this test somehow. I'll get into college, and I'm going to become a doctor like I've always wanted. She's *wrong*.

Although the fact that she's here at all makes me seriously worry about my future.

There's a loud knock at my bedroom door. I jerk my head in the direction of the door just seconds before my mother's voice rings out: "Amy! Dinner time!"

I look back at the little girl, but she's gone. I rub my eyes, my head suddenly throbbing. I scan the room, from my Jonas Brothers and Taylor Swift posters on the walls to my pink and green bedspread to my bookcase and the trophy I won last year for my performance on the debate team. But the little girl is nowhere to be seen.

The door to my room cracks open and my mother

peeks her head in. "Amy? I told you dinner is ready. Come down."

"Uh-huh," I manage.

My mother squints at me. Her graying hair is gathered into a messy bun behind her head. It's not stylishly messy—just messy. She used to be one of the prettiest of all my friends' mothers, but it feels like the last two or three years, she suddenly got older all at once. "Are you okay, sweetie?"

"Yeah." I squeeze my hands into fists, digging my fingernails into the palms of my hands. "I just… I'm having trouble with trigonometry."

She doesn't look as concerned as I feel. "Well, I'm sure you'll figure it out. You always worry about your math test, but you always do well in the end."

"That's because of Jade."

My mother's lips tighten the way they always do whenever I bring up Jade recently. When we were little, she liked Jade. In fact, she was always encouraging me to invite her over. She was always insisting Jade stay for dinner, then afterward, she would drive the two of us to Jade's house to make sure she got home okay, even though it was only a ten-minute walk. One time, she came in and said we were going to play a game where we cleaned Jade's house, which we proceeded to do for the next two hours until Jade's mom came home.

But something has changed. Lately, Mom has been telling me that I shouldn't hang out with Jade anymore. I don't know what she would've said if I told her about how messy Jade's house was, or the way her mom had broken that ashtray, but I kept my word and didn't tell her.

"Maybe we should get you a tutor," she says. Even though we can't afford it. Dad got his hours cut back at work, and money has been tight.

"Um," I say. "It will be fine."

"Are you sure?"

If I asked for a tutor, my mother would get me one in a heartbeat. She always says that nothing is more important than my education. But I don't want the whole family to be making sacrifices just so I can get a better grade in trigonometry.

"No, don't worry about it," I say. "I'm good."

"I'll tell you what." She smiles at me. "Let's have dinner, and after we eat, I'll help you with some of the problems."

"Okay," I agree, even though the only person in the world worse at math than I am is my mother.

"Don't worry, Amy. I'm sure you'll do fine. You always do."

I'm not so sure I'm going to do fine on this test. But right now, I'm a little less worried about the test than I am about the little girl I keep seeing everywhere I look.

14

PRESENT DAY

Cameron is sitting back at the nursing station, working on a handwritten note about Spider-Dan.

Even though Dr. Beck didn't tell us we needed to write a note, Cameron always goes above and beyond. That's how he is. Whenever we had a test, he would read and re-read the material over and over, highlighting every sentence in the textbook in a different color, and then he would do every single practice question he could get his hands on. Twice.

Cameron claims it's because orthopedic surgery is extremely competitive, so his grades need to be stellar to get into a residency program. I don't need to be as competitive, because I don't want to be an orthopedic surgeon. I want to be… Well, I don't know what I want to do in terms of a specialty. I know I want to be a doctor, and so far, that's good enough. I figure by the end of third year, I'll get it sorted out.

The only thing I know for sure is that I don't want to be a psychiatrist. (Or an orthopedic surgeon.)

I used to think it was sexy that Cameron worked so hard. I liked how driven he was. I mean, every time I studied with him, I felt stupid, but I always ended up acing the exam because he would push me to go above and beyond. I don't know when it stopped being sexy and started being annoying.

Maybe around the time he dumped me to study for the board exam.

Dr. Beck wanders over to join us at the nurses' station, his hands pushed deep into his white coat pockets. My heart leaps when I see him. "Dr. Beck," I say. "I need to talk to you."

"Of course." He smiles at me and those dimples poke out. Or in. Or whatever dimples do. "What's up, Amy?"

I toy with the drawstring of my scrub pants. "So you know that patient in the seclusion room? Sawyer?"

"Yes…"

"I heard a strange noise coming from the room." I crane my neck to look down the hall. "You said he was restrained, but it almost sounded like… like he was throwing himself at the door."

Dr. Beck frowns. "I don't see how he possibly could have gotten out of the restraints. We put them on both arms after he had dinner." He looks over at Ramona, who is standing by a med cart in the hall-way, emptying multicolored pills into a tiny plastic cup. "You secured both of Sawyer's restraints, didn't you?"

"Yes, of course, Doctor," Ramona says.

"I just…" I shift between my sneakers. "That's what it sounded like. Like somebody was trying to get out."

Dr. Beck stands there for a moment, a troubled expression on his face. "I appreciate you letting me know, Amy. We'll proceed with caution when we enter the room in the morning."

Hopefully, that won't occur until *after* I've left in the morning. Dr. Beck was emphatic that Cameron and I would not be in any danger from the patient in seclusion, so I hope he waits until after we're done and there's more staff on the unit.

Dr. Beck looks down at Cameron, who now seems to be on page five of what promises to be an epic note. His tongue is sticking out of the corner of his mouth like it always does when he's deep in concentration. I used to think it was cute.

"I didn't say you had to write a note on your patient," Dr. Beck says.

"I like to write them," Cameron lies through his teeth. "It helps me organize my thoughts."

Dr. Beck shoots me a look, and I could swear he rolls his eyes a bit. Gabby was right—I *do* like him. "Sure. Knock yourself out. Who did you see?"

"Daniel Ludwig."

"Spider-Dan!" Dr. Beck claps his hands together.

"My favorite patient! A textbook case of schizophrenia. Isn't the brain absolutely fascinating?"

"I completely agree," Cameron—who has never disagreed with a professor once in the entire time I have known him—says.

"I've always been intrigued by what causes a normal brain to create such powerful delusions." Dr. Beck's face lights up as he talks. You can tell he's one of those people who is extremely passionate about his career, and it makes me respect him more. "The basis of schizophrenia is thought to be an imbalance of neurotransmitters in the brain that occurs in just the right way to create the classic constellation of symptoms."

Cameron nods vigorously. "It's *so* fascinating."

Dr. Beck smiles at him. "Cameron, can you please elaborate on the classical symptoms of schizophrenia?"

For a moment, Cam is caught off guard. But he quickly regains his composure. "Well," he says, "he's got both positive and negative symptoms."

"Such as?"

Cameron looks down at the stack of handwritten papers in front of him, detailing everything about the patient from the moment he was born to five minutes ago. "He's got positive symptoms like delusions of being Spider-Man, he hears voices, and he's got disorganized speech. But he's also got negative symptoms, like he won't look you in the eye, he doesn't have any friends, and he talks in a monotone."

Dr. Beck nods, impressed. "Someone came prepared tonight."

Cameron beams. Oh great, now that he got some positive feedback, he'll be completely intolerable.

"He thinks that the webs in his hands are linked to urination," Dr. Beck explains to me. "So he just stands over the toilet, trying to shoot out webs. And of course, it's all made much worse by the fact that the medications he's taking cause urinary retention."

"Poor guy," I murmur.

"You should go see him, Amy," Dr. Beck says. "He's got a classic case of schizophrenia, as I said. It will be a good learning experience."

"I already saw a patient with schizophrenia." It's better than saying that the idea of interviewing a man who thinks he's Spider-Man makes me uneasy. "William Schoenfeld."

Dr. Beck considers this. "He's interesting in a different way. His presentation is atypical for paranoid schizophrenia."

"It is?"

"I'd say so," Dr. Beck says. "He has the positive symptoms Cameron mentioned, such as hallucinations. And definitely paranoia. But not many negative symptoms. Also, he says he only started hearing the voices a few months ago, and it's pretty rare for a man in his late twenties to have a first schizophrenic break. Usually, males present in their late teens or early twenties."

I frown. "So what does that mean?"

"Could be an atypical presentation of schizophrenia, like I said." He lifts a shoulder. "But there's also a chance that his symptoms started a long time ago. Way before a few months ago. After all, many people with schizophrenia aren't aware that they're experiencing symptoms." He drums his fingers on the table. "He could have been hearing those voices for *years*."

I try to imagine what it must be like to spend years of your life hearing voices telling you to kill people.

"Anyway." Dr. Beck waves a hand. "The medications are currently suppressing Schoenfeld's symptoms. Go see Daniel Ludwig. I think you'll find it very interesting."

"I'd be happy to introduce you, Amy," Cameron speaks up.

Great. They're both looking at me. I'm going to have to do this.

"Sure," I say. "Let's go."

15

S ince the patient rooms are so small and there are two of us, we decide to interview Spider-Dan in the patient lounge.

The patient lounge is larger than the staff lounge, but it's not any nicer. Also, it must have been painted recently because there's a faint fresh paint smell hanging in the air. I wait there, sitting on a sofa that has a pattern of cherries on it. I can't stop tapping my feet. *Tap tap tap.* Between me and Mary with her knitting needles, we could be a band together. *Tap tap tap. Click click click.*

I try not to think about Jade. I get to leave here after tonight, but Jade is stuck here indefinitely. I don't know what she did to land herself in this place, but I don't doubt she deserves to be here.

What I know for sure about Jade is that she's bipolar. That was the diagnosis she got when she was hospitalized when we were sixteen years old. I found out after that her mother had the exact same diagnosis —these things tend to run in families. They put her on a medication to control it, then a second medication. She seemed so different once she was on a bunch of medications—like a zombie. She wasn't my best friend anymore. It was like she had a frontal lobotomy.

Well, the best I can say is that she seems like her old self right now.

God, I hope she doesn't tell Dr. Beck that she knows me. That would be beyond mortifying. Especially if she tells him that—

"I'm not supposed to have these crackers!"

An elderly man is standing in front of me, gripping a crumpled paper bag. I don't know who he is, but he's got a white wristband on his left wrist, which means he's a patient. He looks like that actor who used to be in the westerns a long time ago—my grandmother used to love him. Clint Eastwood, I think his name was.

"Excuse me?" I say to the old man.

"These crackers." The Clint Eastwood look-alike shakes the bag in my face, which I can now see contains about a dozen packets of saltines. "I'm diabetic! Who gave me all these crackers?"

"Um," I say. "I'm not sure."

"I'm not supposed to have them," Clint informs me. "This is a mistake. These crackers could kill me!"

"I don't think they're going to kill you."

"How do you know? Are you a doctor?"

"I'm a medical student."

Clint shakes the bag of saltines at me again. "This should be part of your training. You don't give crackers to a diabetic."

"Well," I say, nodding at the garbage in the corner of the room, "you could just throw them out then?"

"I'm not wasting food! What the hell is wrong with you?"

"Um." I would be happy to take the crackers, except I'm not sure what to do with them aside from throwing them in the trash, which is apparently unacceptable. "Why don't you bring the crackers back to your room and we'll have someone get rid of them for you?"

He looks at me for a long time, considering my proposal. Then he shakes his head. He walks off, grumbling, "Useless. All of them—useless."

Okay, that was strange.

Before I have time to look up in UpToDate whether crackers could actually kill a diabetic, Cameron's voice rings out through the hallway. "Here we are!" he booms. A second later, he and the man in the Spider-Man T-shirt show up at the door to the lounge. "That's Amy. The other student. The one I was telling you about."

What did he tell Spider-Dan about me? I can't even imagine. *Amy is another medical student who is working here tonight. She's smart, but not as smart as I am. And she's always dragging me out to get Indian food, and I go, even though it always gives me heartburn.*

Spider-Dan looks me up and down, and nods without expression. He doesn't seem upset that I'm there, and he doesn't seem happy either. It's like talking to a robot. It reminds me a bit of how Jade was on her medications. And it's very different from how *my* patient, Will Schoenfeld, acted.

I scoot down the sofa so that Spider-Dan can sit, while Cameron pulls over a chair. Cameron is quite a bit bigger than Spider-Dan—between the two of them, Cameron looks far more like a superhero in disguise. Spider-Dan looks to be in his mid-forties, with thinning brown hair and a double chin. While he sits, he holds out his hands with the wrists pointed up, and he looks down at them.

"Hi," I say. "I'm Amy."

"Hi," Spider-Dan says, still not looking up at me.

"So I was telling Amy a little bit about you," Cameron says. "About your webs."

Spider-Dan nods with a tiny bit more enthusiasm. He points down at the tendon on his left wrist. "You see these? I think these are kind of like webs. The webs are underneath my skin. And I need to get them out. I think I could get them out, but I can't do it. I don't know how to do it. But I think if I could get them out, they would be webs."

"He's web-challenged," Cam tells me.

"I see," I murmur.

"You know," Cam says to Spider-Dan, "a lot of the Spider-Man superheroes actually don't shoot webs out of their bodies. They make them themselves. So technically, you *could* make your own webs."

Spider-Dan stares at him.

"Like out of dental floss or something," Cam adds.

"Dental floss," Spider-Dan repeats.

I shoot Cameron a look. He shrugs. "What?" he says. "Just making a suggestion."

"Mr. Ludwig," I say. "I was just wondering, do you have superpowers?"

He nods again. "I have Spidey sense. Like if something is wrong, then I know about it. Because the sense is in the spider. That's how you know. That's how everybody knows."

I look over at Cam to see if this is making any sense to him. He shakes his head.

"And I've got a ring," Spider-Dan goes on. "The ring gives me power. If I wear the ring, then I have more power."

"No," Cam says patiently. "You're thinking of the Green Lantern. He's the one with the ring."

Spider-Dan looks at Cameron, a slightly put-out expression on his face. "No, I have the ring. Not Green Lantern. I need it if I'm going to fight Dr. Octopus and the Green Goblin. So that's why I have to have the ring. The ring is in the thing. It's the bling.

It's the sting. And if I get the thing, then I'll have the ring. So that's why I need it."

Spider-Dan looks between the two of us. He has no idea that what he just said was complete nonsense. How does somebody get to the point where their brain stops functioning like a normal brain? That their reality completely breaks from the reality that every other person in the world lives in?

And what's to stop it from happening to anyone else?

"Dan," Cam says, "do you think that the Green Goblin is around here somewhere and is trying to hurt you? "

Spider-Dan considers this question for several seconds. Like it's really important for him to let us know whether the Green Goblin is out to get him or not. "No, I don't think that," he says thoughtfully. "But my sense tells me that *somebody* here is trying to hurt me…"

"Who?" Cam asks.

Spider-Dan takes a shaky breath. "Damon Sawyer."

Cameron blinks a few times, surprised by this response. Obviously, this isn't something Spider-Dan told him the first time. *Sawyer*. That's the name of the patient in the Seclusion One room. The one who somehow got out of his restraints and has been throwing himself at the door, trying to break it down.

"You think Damon Sawyer wants to hurt you?" Cam presses him.

Spider-Dan is quiet for nearly a full minute. Finally, he says, "Not just me."

"Then who?" I blurt out.

"All of us," Spider-Dan says in his monotone. "Damon Sawyer wants to kill every single one of us tonight."

"Why…" My voice is a hoarse croak. "Why do you think that?"

"Because that's what he told me he's going to do."

16

"You don't really think we're in any danger, do you, Amy?"

Even though Spider-Dan is safely back in his room, I can't seem to stop shaking. I've been sitting on the couch in the patient lounge for the last five minutes, unable to get myself to leave. I can't stop hearing the words echoing in my ears:

Damon Sawyer wants to kill every single one of us tonight.

"Sawyer's locked up in that seclusion room," Cameron points out. "He's in restraints."

Is he though? I heard him slamming his body against the door, which I'm not sure he could have done if he was restrained.

"And even if he weren't," Cam adds, "there's no way out of the room. Not without the code."

"You don't know that."

"Dr. Beck didn't look worried."

That's not entirely true. When I suggested that

Sawyer might have gotten out of his restraints, Dr. Beck looked decidedly concerned, although he seemed to be trying to hide it for our sakes. After all, one of the first things he told us when we got here was that the patient in the seclusion room was dangerous. He made a point of telling us to avoid the room for our own safety.

"Look," Cam says. "You have nothing to worry about. I'm not going to let anything happen to you, okay?"

"Well, that's a comfort," I mutter.

"Amy…"

"I don't know why you keep acting like we're great friends," I say. "We weren't friends before, and we're not friends now."

He considers my statement for a moment. "Listen," he says. "I brought you something."

He digs into the pocket of his scrub shirt, and to my total surprise, he comes up with a packet of Ring Dings. I can't even believe it when I see them. Ring Dings are like my favorite sweet treat in the entire world. I have a rule that I can't buy them for myself, since I would just gorge myself. I like them better than a chocolate soufflé or any kind of other fancy desserts. They're like the perfect food—you've got the creamy center, the chocolate cake, and then the chocolate coating. What more do you need out of life?

I have to admit, the sight of those snack cakes does make me feel better.

"You brought that for me?" I ask.

"Well, I saw you were going to be here with me tonight, and I know they're your favorite..."

Cameron's hair is falling slightly in his eyes again, and once again, I get the urge to push it away. That's the sort of thing I used to do before he broke up with me for a test. It's one of the first things I did before he kissed me for the first time.

It was at a party. Where else? One of those medical school parties, celebrating the end of yet another exam, with far too much alcohol. As opposed to college parties, by now we were all old enough to buy alcohol without a fake ID, so we always went a little nuts.

It took place the night of our big pathology exam. I had studied so hard for that exam, but this was one of the times it didn't pay off. The exam was just so random. Our professor, Dr. Miller, asked questions along the lines of, "In the textbook, what did it say on page 121 paragraph three about the etiology of lung cancer?" That was an *actual question* on the test. How do you answer something like that? The only way is to look at the four choices, close your eyes, and point randomly to one of them.

So that night, I was utterly convinced I was going to fail and determined to get drunk enough to forget it.

I was only on my second beer of the night when I literally bumped into Cameron Berger while I was on my way to the bathroom. It was easy to bump into him, because he took up about ninety percent of the hallway.

I had never been friendly with Cameron. He hung out in a different crowd than I did. Weirdly, medical school reverted to high school social patterns: there were the popular kids, the geeks, the stoners—you get the idea. Cam was one of the more popular kids in our class—very good-looking and had top grades and an easy kind of charm. He even had these white, perfectly straight teeth. It was almost maddening. Mostly, my friends and I made fun of him for being just a little too perfect. For trying just a little too hard.

But this time Cam had that same haunted look as a lot of the other kids at the party. The look of somebody who was pretty sure he had failed pathology. And he was somebody who really wanted that top grade. After all, how else was he going to match in an orthopedic surgery residency?

I raised my beer bottle. *Screw Dr. Miller*, I said, which was the official toast of the night.

He stared at me for a moment, then his face broke into a smile. And I realized for the first time that his teeth weren't quite as perfect as I had thought. His second incisor on the left had a tiny chip on it, which he later told me was from a football tackle. *Screw Dr. Miller*, he said.

And thank God for grading on a curve, I added.

We hope, he said.

We hope, I agreed soberly.

For a moment, I almost felt like I needed to introduce myself, even though we had been classmates for an entire year in a class of only a hundred students. I hardly knew him, yet I knew him really well. I already knew he wanted to do ortho, he played college football, and he asked *way* too many questions in class about the professors' research. I also knew he had a girlfriend in our class named Jess, although rumor had it, the two of them were on the rocks—and she had left the party half an hour earlier, claiming to be sick to her stomach.

But one thing I didn't know about Cam and learned later that night was that he was a *very* good kisser. And also, after that last beer, he stopped drinking so that he would be sober enough to drive me home safely.

I didn't expect to fall in love with him though. I thought after we made out that night, he would wake up in the morning, thinking to himself, *Oh God, what did I do last night?* I didn't expect him to call me the next morning to see if I was feeling okay and ask if I felt up for having some dinner. When I asked him about Jess, he told me he had just officially broken up with her.

Because of me, apparently.

I definitely didn't expect to date him for an entire year. And when he dumped me, I didn't expect it to hurt as much as it did.

Even though it pains me, I put the Ring Dings down on the couch. "I don't want this," I say.

"Of course you do."

"No, I don't," I snip at him. "I don't want your Ring Dings. I don't want your protection." I grit my teeth. "Frankly, it would be perfectly fine with me if I didn't see you ever again."

Cam's shoulders sag. "I know you're mad…"

"I'm not mad," I say. "You did the right thing. I mean, it's not like we were going to get *married* someday. It's good you ended it. Now you can have lots of hot sex this year with nurses."

"Amy!" Cameron's broad face turns pink. "That's not what I want."

"Liar."

He brushes the hair out of his own eyes. "What if I made a mistake?"

Is he serious about this? Because if he is, I really might lose it tonight. Yes, it sucked when he broke up with me. But it's over. It's *done*. I can't start this up again. If for no other reason, because Gabby will legit kill me if she has to comfort me through another breakup with Cameron Berger.

"Cam, don't do this," I say.

"Why not?" He offers a lopsided smile. "You can't say we weren't good together."

I am about to tell him exactly why getting back together would be a terrible mistake when I realize we're no longer alone in the patient lounge. Unsurprisingly, a patient has wandered into the room. I look up and recognize Will Schoenfeld. The guy who hears voices telling him to kill people. Well, *used to* hear voices telling him to kill people.

Or so he says.

"Hey." Will stares down at the two of us huddled together on the couch. "Is this room free? I was going to play the piano."

"Uh…" Cam looks up at Will, who is already walking over to the piano in the corner of the room. "We should go back to the staff lounge. We can grab dinner."

"I'm not hungry," I say, hoping Cam can't hear my stomach growl as I say the words.

"You're welcome to listen to me play," Will says as he sits down at the piano bench. He cracks his knuckles, then he rests his fingers on the keys. A second later, the sound of Mozart fills the room.

Cam gives me a look like he wants me to come with him, but I don't budge from the couch. Thankfully, he doesn't push me. I watch him stalk out of the room, his heavy footsteps accompanying the sound of music drifting from the piano.

"Any requests?" Will asks me.

"What you're playing is fine." I close my eyes for a moment, letting the music wash over me. He's really good. Almost professional level, but what do I know? "Are you practicing for anything in particular?"

Will grins at me. "Actually, I just came in because it sounded like you were trying to end that conversation."

I can't help it—I laugh. My first laugh the whole damn night.

"So… what is he? Your ex-boyfriend?" he asks.

"That's kind of a personal question…"

"Hmm. It feels like you asked *me* a lot of personal questions."

I close my eyes again. "That's different."

"Fine, you want me to shut up," Will acknowledges good-naturedly. "Okay, I get it."

He goes back to playing the piano, and it's nice to zone out to the music. It's sad that somebody with so much talent had their brain crap out on them like that. But isn't that what they say? That people with incredible talent are more susceptible to mental illness? Or maybe I just made that up.

Whatever is going on in his brain, Will seems like a nice guy. He did rescue me from an uncomfortable conversation with Cameron. Maybe he could help me out with some of my other questions.

"Hey," I say. "Can I ask you something?"

"Sure. Shoot."

"How dangerous is that patient in the seclusion room?"

Will's fingers freeze on the keys. "You heard about that guy?"

"A little. His name is Damon Sawyer, right?" I study his face. "Did you know him?"

"No," he says, a little too quickly. "I've only been here a couple of days, and he mostly stayed in his own room."

"But you knew he was in seclusion…"

He isn't playing the piano anymore. He turns on the bench to look at me. "They stuck him in there last night. They told us all to stay in our rooms so I didn't see the commotion, but I could *hear* it. We all could."

"Hear what?"

Will's Adam's apple bobs. "He was screaming. Screaming that he was going to kill everyone here. It was pretty disturbing, to be honest."

I would definitely agree with that assessment. "But he's locked in seclusion now."

"Right. They tied him up in restraints and everything."

I frown. "How do you know about that?"

"I could hear him screaming about it." Will shakes his head. "I don't know what he was doing that made them stick him in there, but the guy is obviously disturbed. *Really* disturbed."

"So if he heard voices telling him to kill people, he would do it?"

Will drops his eyes. "Yeah. I'd imagine so."

A chill goes through me, and I hug myself, rubbing my upper arms with my hands. "Dr. Beck said he's leaving tomorrow. They're putting him somewhere more secure."

"Good."

Will stands up from the piano bench. All the humor seems to have disappeared from his face, and he is still avoiding my eyes. "I'm going to head back to my room. The meds... They really make me tired."

"It's worth it though, right?"

He hesitates. "Yes. Of course."

"Okay. Well, thanks for the music."

"No problem." He lingers for a moment at the piano, and he looks like he wants to tell me something. But then he shakes his head. "Good night, Amy."

"Good night," I say.

Although really, the night has just begun.

17

HOURS UNTIL MORNING: 10

I return to the staff break room to retrieve my cheese sandwich and attempt to eat it. I still don't have much of an appetite, but I've got to have some sustenance to get through the night. Also, I want to send Gabby an update text.

When I open up the fridge, my dinner is now *touching* the milk that has gone solid, but I try not to think about it. The sandwich is wrapped and inside a bag—it will be fine. The whole refrigerator has a sour milk smell to it. Maybe I really will clean out the refrigerator tonight. It will give me something to think about besides the guy in seclusion who apparently wants to kill us all.

But first, I need to send a text to Gabby.

I follow her instructions the same as before. I get right up close to the window, pressing my phone against the glass. But while the last time I got a couple of bars, this time my phone still says "No Service." So I can't receive any of the messages that have come through since I got here, and I can't send any either.

Great.

I drop my phone back in my scrub pocket and return to my gross sandwich. It's bread, mustard, and two-year-old American cheese. It might be the worst sandwich I've ever had. But it's the only food I brought tonight.

As I take a bite of my sandwich, footsteps grow louder outside the door. I lay down my sandwich on the table. "Cam?" I call out.

There's no answer.

This time I carefully push back my seat and stand up. I squint at the open doorway to the staff lounge. "Cameron?" I say. When there's no answer, I try again: "Dr. Beck?"

There's no answer. But the footsteps grow louder.

"Jade?" I say in a choked voice.

There's no reason to panic. Just because somebody is walking around right outside the door, it doesn't mean someone is trying to attack me. I'm sure I'm perfectly safe. There's only one dangerous patient on this unit, and he's locked in seclusion.

Isn't he?

I step tentatively in the direction of the door to the lounge. Just before I reach it, a figure appears in the doorway, completely filling the open space. It takes me a second to recognize Miguel, the man who greeted us when we first came in. The guy who thought he was the son of God.

He's still wearing four T-shirts all on top of each other, adding even more width to his already bulky frame. Except he's got something on his face now. He has white streaks across his cheeks that look like warpaint. Although when he gets closer, I think it might be cream cheese.

"You," he says.

I stare at him. "Are… are you okay?"

"No, I not okay," he says in his accented English. "I told you, my father say I need to get outta here. *Quiero ir.*"

"I'm sorry." I look over his shoulder, hoping somebody else is watching this exchange. That it's not just the two of us alone out here. "I don't have the authority to let you leave."

His bloodshot eyes make contact with mine. "You got the code?"

347244. I've got it written down in my phone, but I memorized it too. "No. I'm afraid not."

"Damn." His face falls. "We gotta get the code. My father say we gotta get out of here."

"How about in the morning?" I suggest gently.

"No, you don't understand." Miguel grits his teeth. "The morning is too late."

"But why?" I press him.

"Because my father say Damon Sawyer is gonna kill us all by the morning. Kill us all. *Muerto*."

As he utters the words, a sickening thump echoes from deep in the hallway. The whole wall seems to vibrate this time. I'm not certain, but I think it's coming from Seclusion One.

The man inside is trying desperately to get out.

But he can't. He *can't*.

"Excuse me," I manage. I push past Miguel and race into the hallway, breathing hard. Whatever else, I don't want to be alone anymore. I've got to find Cameron or Dr. Beck or Ramona or *somebody*. I can't be the only staff member here. It's not safe. That much is obvious.

Except the hallway is completely silent. Where *is* everyone?

I check behind me. Miguel hasn't followed me. I hear a soft buzzing sound, which means he's trying to get out but he doesn't know the code. I hear it a second time. He's trying numbers, attempting to escape.

I walk briskly through the silent hallways, the fluorescent lights flickering overhead. Granted, it's late. But it shouldn't be this quiet on a psych ward. Should it?

I finally run the full loop around the circle, and I come across the door labeled Attending Physician. I don't want to bother Dr. Beck, but it feels like he ought to know that one of his patients is trying to escape the unit. So after a few seconds of contemplation, I knock on the door.

After a moment of shuffling, the door cracks open. Dr. Beck is standing in the doorway, wearing only his scrubs, his white coat tossed haphazardly on a sofa in the corner of the office that I suspect doubles as a bed on overnight shifts.

"Hi, Amy." He squints at my face. "You okay?"

"Fine," I lie.

"What's up?"

For a moment, I stand there, frozen, having forgotten my reason for coming here in the first place. Then it hits me. "That guy Miguel is trying to get out. He's typing codes in the door, trying to get it to open."

"Oh." Dr. Beck shrugs. "Well, that's okay. He doesn't know the code, so he's not going anywhere."

I feel slightly deflated by his response. I had hoped he'd march over to the door and take care of the situation. But I suppose he's right. As long as none of the patients on the unit know the code to the door, nobody is going anywhere. The only people who can leave are me, Cameron, Ramona, and Dr. Beck.

"Are you sure you're okay, Amy?" he asks gently.

"Yes," I say, although with a little bit less certainty than before. "It's just hard being here all night. That's all."

He nods sympathetically. Unlike Cameron, he's got the empathy thing down pat. I bet he's incredible with patients. He's young, but he's got the air of somebody who has been doing this for many years. "I get it. I forget how scary it can be the first time."

I manage a smile. "You were scared on your first night in a psych ward?"

"You have no idea." He grins at me. "One of the patients—this guy built like a linebacker—followed me around the unit the entire night. He didn't try to hurt me, but wherever I went, he was there. Like my shadow." He cocks his head. "In retrospect, he just wanted to talk to me. But I was too scared to realize it."

"Has… has a patient ever tried to hurt you? Like, physically?"

"Yes." His brown eyes darken slightly, but he decides not to elaborate. "But that was a completely different situation. Nothing bad is going to happen here tonight. Nobody here wants to hurt you."

"Except Damon Sawyer," I blurt out.

Dr. Beck's eyes widen. "He… you didn't open the door to the seclusion room, did you?"

"No! Of course not!"

"Good." His shoulders relax. "Look, it's unusual to get patients like him here. But he'll be gone in the morning. And he's not going to hurt anyone as long as he's locked in that room. He can't get out—trust me."

Except he already got out of the restraints.

Dr. Beck looks down at his watch and back up at me. "Soon everyone will be going to sleep. Try to get some reading done, and if it's quiet, you're welcome to sleep in one of the empty patient rooms."

There is no chance in hell I'm going into one of those patient rooms and sleeping in the bed. No *way*. I'll tough it out on the sofa in the lounge. Cameron is still trying to make nice after what he did to me, so he'll definitely let me have it.

Dr. Beck goes back into his office, leaving me all alone in the hallway. He's right. I should try to do some reading and then get some sleep. Soon enough, it will be morning.

I turn around to go back to the staff lounge, hoping to finish my sandwich. But the second I turn around, I realize somebody has been standing behind me.

It's Jade.

18

EIGHT YEARS EARLIER

J ade and I are supposed to be meeting at the library in the school, and of course, once again she's late.

I stand by the entrance to the library, sipping on the remainder of my peach iced tea. When we were in trigonometry last period, Jade promised we would meet after school to study. The school library is open until five, so I thought that would be a good place to do it. No excuses.

And apparently, no Jade.

I finish the last of my drink and toss it in the garbage by the entrance to the library. I check my watch. It's three-thirty, which means most kids and teachers are already gone except for a few afterschool clubs running. Jade is probably gone too. Or out back, smoking pot. I was stupid to think she might actually show up this time.

I should just go home.

Except I need her help. My mom tried to help me last night, and that was a joke. She was even worse at understanding the material than I was. The two of us both ended up frustrated and shouting at each other. She promised that we would get a tutor, and I finally cracked and agreed to it. Still, the midterm is a lost cause.

But on the plus side, I haven't seen that little girl anywhere today.

"Amy!"

Oh my God, it's a miracle—Jade is dashing down the hallway in the direction of the library, her backpack slung over one shoulder. She's waving frantically at me. "So sorry I'm late, Amy!"

"That's okay," I say.

When she gets close, I do detect a whiff of marijuana, but it's not as strong as yesterday. Hopefully, she can still do math while slightly baked. Jade is somewhat of a math prodigy, so I'm sure it will be fine.

"You ready?" I ask.

She bobs her head. "Yes! Oh my God, we are going to do *so* much math today. Like, you have no idea how much we're going to do. We're going to study for the next eight hours. I'm telling you, eight straight hours of doing math. You are going to be vomiting up sines and cosines by the end of this!"

I laugh. She doesn't seem like she's on pot right now—she's like a ball of energy. "Okay… so let's get started."

"Yes! We need to get started right away." She starts to walk into the library but then stops herself. "Oh, wait! Stupid me, I forgot my textbook in the classroom. Let me just go grab it, okay?"

I make a face. "Jade, you know all the classrooms are going to be locked up by now. We can just use my book."

"Use your book? No, that's silly!" She laces her arm into mine. "We'll just get the janitor to open up the room. Come on. It will just take a second."

Before I can protest, Jade is dragging me down the hallway toward the stairwell. Her hand gripping my arm has an angry circular red mark in the fleshy part between her thumb and forefinger. It almost looks like a burn. I wonder how she got *that*. But if I ask her, she'll just make up some wild story.

When we get to the stairs, Jade is sprinting up them two at a time, and I have to race to catch up. Mr. Riordan's classroom is all the way up on the fourth floor, which is usually deserted by now except for the cleaning staff. Sure enough, when we get there, there are no traces of any students or teachers—just a middle-aged man pushing a mop across the floor in front of the lockers.

Jade goes right up to the janitor, smiling with her bright red lips. "Hi there!"

The janitor slowly lifts his eyes from the bucket on the floor. "Yes?" he says in an accent I can't quite identify.

"I forgot my textbook in room 428," Jade says cheerfully. "Do you think you could let me in?"

I can't help but notice that as she makes the request, Jade sticks her chest out. The janitor's eyes flicker down to her breasts briefly.

"It'll just take a second," she adds. "I *really* need the book to study for my test tomorrow. I would be *so* grateful."

After another hesitation, the man nods. He reaches into his pocket for a keychain that contains an impossible number of keys. We follow him down the hall to room 428, and for some reason, my heart skips slightly as the lock turns.

"Thank you so much!" Jade gushes. "We'll just be a minute."

The janitor nods and goes back to his mop and bucket. I step into the classroom with Jade, holding the door open while she goes to grab her book. But to my surprise, she pushes me out of the way and shuts the door behind me. She presses her index finger to her lips.

"You keep watch," she tells me. "Let me know if anyone is coming."

"What?" I say. "Watch for what? What are you talking about?"

To my horror, Jade walks over to Mr. Riordan's desk and yanks open the bottom drawer. Her eyes light up. "Score!"

"Jade…"

"It's all the copies of the test for tomorrow!" She

pulls a small stapled document out of the drawer and holds it up. "This way we don't even have to study for eight hours! All we need to do is solve these problems, and then we'll both get a hundred. Aren't I smart? You are *so* lucky I'm your best friend."

"I'm not doing that!" I glance out the window of the classroom to make sure nobody is looking in. "Jade, you have to put that back. This is cheating. We could get in a lot of trouble."

"Oh my God." She rolls her eyes. "You are so freaking dramatic, Amy. It's just one test! It's not even a big deal. When are you ever going to use sines or cosines in your life ever again?"

I had no idea this was what she was planning. This is so stupid. I don't know what is worse—the idea of cheating or the possibility of getting *caught* for cheating. Yes, the fourth floor is mostly empty now, but that doesn't mean someone won't see us. I look out the window of the classroom one more time, searching for someone who might rat us out.

And that's when I see her.

The little girl.

She is standing right outside the classroom, her blond hair curling around her face. Staring at me.

"Jade!" I rip my gaze away from the window. "We've got to get out of here. Right now."

Jade stuffs the copy of the exam into her backpack, then she joins me at the door. When we get back in the hallway, the only person there is the janitor. No teachers, no students. No little girls.

Jade wiggles her fingers at the janitor. "Got my book! Thanks again!"

She grabs my arm again and starts pulling me toward the staircase while I'm internally freaking out. I thought we were going to have a study session. I had no idea that this was what she had in mind.

"Jade," I hiss at her, "I'm *not* looking at that test."

She pulls me into the stairwell and then stops, folding her skinny arms across her chest. "Why not? You want to do well on the midterm, don't you?"

"Yes, but not like that!"

She lets out an exasperated huff. "Don't be stupid, Amy. You have zero idea what's going on in this class. We can't fix that by tomorrow morning. The only way you're going to pass this midterm is with a copy of the exam. Otherwise, you're totally screwed!"

She's right, of course. Without help, I'm going to fail this exam. Even an eight-hour study session wouldn't be enough to save me, and I doubt Jade is willing to do that with me.

But I don't care. I'm not cheating. I would never do something like that.

Never.

19

PRESENT DAY

HOURS UNTIL MORNING: 9

"You look terrible, Amy," Jade says.

"Thanks," I mutter.

"You look like you've been popping Lithium."

Whatever that means. "I'm fine. Really."

Her features soften, and for a second, the years melt away. And she is the old Jade, the one I used to walk home with every day from school. The first person I told when anything good happened to me. My best friend. "Hey," she says. "Can we talk?"

I don't agree right away. As much as she sometimes looks like the old Jade, I have to remember that a lot of years have passed. I don't know what kind of person she is anymore, except that she's here.

Granted, I would have a better idea if I looked through her chart. But I'm not going to do that.

"I'm kind of busy," I say.

Jade sticks out her little pink tongue. "Liar. You have absolutely nothing to do. You're just sitting around and making sure none of us hang ourselves or something."

"Fine," I say. "Let's talk."

"Not here."

Before I can stop her, Jade has grabbed me by the arm and she's pulling me down the hallway. We pass by room 912, where Mary is still clicking away with her knitting needles, then room 906, where the light is on and presumably Will is reading *Owen Meany*. Then we come to a stop at room 905.

Jade shoves open the door and raises her eyebrows at me. I take a deep breath and step inside her room. Jade won't hurt me. At least, she won't hurt me *physically*.

Once we are inside the room, Jade sits on the one chair in the room, leaving me with two options: sit on her bed or stand. I choose to stand.

"Look, Amy," she says. "I'm sorry I was such a bitch to you before."

I blink at her in surprise. I'm so surprised that I actually do sit down on her bed, which creaks threateningly under my weight. The mattress is not exactly high quality.

"You've got to understand." She plays with the white laminated band around her left wrist, which gives her name, date of birth, and hospital ID number. "When I saw you, I just felt like such a loser. Here you are, basically living the life you always wanted. I mean, you're going to be a *doctor*. And here *I* am. I'm nothing. I'm nowhere. And honestly…" She takes a shaky breath. "I don't know if I'm ever going to do anything with my life. I couldn't even hold down a freaking waitress job. Even my *mom* was able to do that."

"I'm sure you'll be okay."

Jade shoots me a look. "What exactly are you basing that on? I'm hospitalized in a psychiatric unit right now. What makes you think I'm going to be okay?"

"Because you're getting help," I point out. "The doctors are adjusting your medications, and they're going to fix your problems. And then you can do… whatever you want to do. You can be a fashion designer if that's what you want."

That's what Jade wanted to do through most of grade school and middle school. Then when we got to high school, she had a different career aspiration what seemed like every single week, and it always seemed like she was super excited about this new future career. In retrospect, it was just her mania.

"They're never going to get my medications right," Jade grumbles. "They've been trying for the last eight years."

"It just takes time…"

She tugs on her wristband. "There's optimistic

and there's just plain stupid. I'd love to live in your magical happy land where this is the time they finally get it right. But after eight years, you give up hope. I don't know if there's any hope for me anymore. I mean, they never figured it out for my mother."

I frown, remembering the woman who had Jade's nose and chin, but darker eyes and bigger boobs. I never heard the details of her overdose. I wonder if Jade was the one who found her. I can't even imagine. Jade wasn't super close with her mother, but the two of them were very protective of each other.

Jade is only twenty-four, like me. I can't imagine losing my mother so young. Even though she can be annoying sometimes, I don't know what I would do without her. A girl needs her mother.

I wish I had told her I loved her before I hung up with her.

I get the sudden urge to wrap my arms around Jade in a hug. She's been through so much, and the two of us used to be so close. But given she's a patient here, it would be wildly inappropriate.

"So." She lifts her blue eyes flecked with yellow. "Enough about my pathetic life. Tell me about you."

I lift a shoulder. "Nothing to tell. I'm a medical student. That consumes every moment of my existence, from morning through night."

"So you say." She gives me a sly smile. "But what about that other medical student? Cameron, right? Do not even try to tell me there isn't anything going on there. I could see the way he was looking at you."

Jade was always insanely good at figuring these things out. "There used to be. Not anymore."

"Why not? He's so handsome!"

"He broke up with me. He told me he needed more time to study."

"No!" Jade cackles with laughter. "Oh, Amy, I'm so sorry! But like I said, he isn't even your type."

She's right. Cameron isn't my type. But stupid me —I had been starting to really like him. Even though he's a kiss-ass and he studies far too much, he can also be very sweet. Like, if we went to a restaurant, he would always hold out my chair for me. And he liked to open the car door for me too. You don't meet many guys who are twenty-four years old and try so hard to be a gentleman.

Even if he hadn't ended it though, it was never going to go anywhere. I never felt like Cameron was the guy I was going to end up with. Still, I didn't want it to *end*.

"You should hook up with Will," Jade says.

It takes me a second to even figure out what she's talking about. "You mean the guy in 906?"

"Sure," she says. "He's your type, right? I heard the two of you bonding over the same dorky books you always liked in high school. And it's not like either of you has anything better to do tonight. So why not?"

I stare at her. "Because he's my *patient*. And he's on a *psych ward*."

"Ugh, you always were such a square."

I don't even know what to say to that. But I can say with a hundred percent certainty, I am not hooking up with anyone tonight. Not Cam, not Will —all I want is to get out of here in one piece.

"And how are you… otherwise?" Jade asks.

There's a subtext to her question that makes me very uneasy. "Fine," I answer.

"Are you still…" Jade drops her voice a notch. "Seeing things?"

I stare at her. "*No.*"

"Because you used to sometimes—"

"No, I didn't." I get up off the bed, my legs wobbling beneath me. I'm just about done with this conversation. "You're mistaken."

She raises her eyebrows. "Oh, is that how you want to play it, Amy Brenner?" She stands up too, so she can look me in the eyes. "You don't want anyone here to know that you're more like us than they think."

I grit my teeth. "I don't want anyone to know, because *it's not true.*"

Jade's lips curl. "Now, we both know that's a bald-faced lie."

I almost jump out of my skin at the sound of a knock on the door to Jade's room. A second later, Ramona peeks her head into the room. "I've got some pills for you, Jade," she sings out.

How long was Ramona standing outside the door to room 905? How much did she hear of our conversation? I study Ramona's face, but it's blank. She doesn't seem like she had heard any part of what Jade had been accusing me of. She blinks when she notices me standing in the middle of the room.

"Amy." Ramona scratches her chin. "Weren't you seeing Schoenfeld in 906?"

Jade is smirking at me. "I decided to see a second patient," I mumble. "May as well. I've got the whole night."

"Good for you," Ramona says. "Most of the students who rotate through here just want to do the bare minimum. They all think of psych as the easy rotation."

"No," I say. "I definitely don't think it's easy."

20

I have no appetite at all.

I return to the staff lounge after talking to Jade, and my cheese sandwich is waiting for me. But it's utterly unappetizing. I know American cheese never expires, and it will probably be safe to eat long after I have graduated from medical school, gone through residency, and retired and moved to Florida, but I still don't want it. I don't even want to look at it. I stuff it back into the paper bag and toss it in the trash.

I dig out my phone and try once again to get some service on it. For a split second, I have a bar. But then it vanishes.

I suppose I could call Gabby from one of the landlines. Of course, it's getting very late. And I'm not sure if I've ever actually called her. In our entire two years of being roommates and best friends, I'm not sure we've ever spoken on the phone. We've only exchanged text messages. Besides, if she sees a call coming from the hospital, she'll almost certainly send it to voicemail.

I almost wish Cameron were here. I don't know where he went. His dinner is missing from the refrigerator, so he obviously came back here to eat it after we interviewed Spider-Dan, but I haven't seen him since. He's probably interviewing another patient. I know he wants to impress Dr. Beck, because he wants to impress everyone.

After I toss my dinner in the trash, I decide to make good on my statement to Ramona about seeing a second patient. After all, I've got plenty of time. So I head back to the nurses' station to find another chart.

I notice this time the chart labeled SAWYER has disappeared. It's a shame, because I was very curious to see exactly what sent him here. And it would be comforting to look through it and reassure myself that he's not some sort of murderer. Of course, I can't guarantee anything in the chart would be comforting. So maybe it's better that I'm not looking.

Jade's chart is still up on the rack. She thinks I would look at it without her permission, but I'm going to show her that I'm better than that. I'm not looking at that chart. Whatever sent Jade to the psych ward, that's her business. Instead, I reach for the chart for room 912.

Mary Cummings.

After all the excitement tonight, it will be a nice change of pace to interview a sweet old woman sitting in a chair knitting a scarf. There isn't much scary about Mary.

I flip through Mary's chart to find out exactly what brought her to Ward D. I learn that Mary is seventy-eight years old, and one day while she was out in her backyard, she heard the sound of a child in the house next door swinging back and forth on the swing set. She found the sound of this so grating, she marched over to the house, threw the child off the swing, and refused to let anyone near the swing set again. Until Mary herself had to be forcibly removed by the police.

In Mary's defense, swings can be *really* annoying. Like, when they squeak a lot. I can't entirely blame her.

I have to go past Seclusion One in order to get to Mary's room. Thankfully, no pounding noises are coming from within the room. The man inside the room has gone quiet, at least for now. I stand there a moment, looking at the metal door, which dents outward in the center, just like it would if somebody were throwing himself against it. The keypad next to the door glows green.

"Let... out..."

The sound is like a hiss from within the room. I can barely make out the words. It sounds like some-body talking with a mouthful of marbles in his mouth.

"Let... me... out..."

It's obvious what Damon Sawyer wants. I know

the code for the door, and if I wanted, I could type it in.

I could let him free.

"Let... me... out..." A long pause. "Please..."

I shake my head and step back from the door. Not a chance. I might not know what Sawyer did to land him in that room, but I know what he'll do if he ever gets out.

I hurry down the hallway to room 912—Mary Cummings's room. As I get closer, I hear that familiar noise once again. *Click click click.* She is still hard at work on her scarf, even though it's getting quite late. She smiles up at me, and I notice how yellow her teeth are, and that three of them are rotting in the front.

I look down at the knitting needles she's working with. I don't know exactly what children's safety needles look like, but these look like legit knitting needles, made from steel. They could easily be used to take out someone's eye.

"Well, hello, dear." She blinks her watery brown eyes. They look like they have a film covering them. "Nicole, isn't it?"

I recall the name Nicole in one of the charts on the rack. Nicole must be a patient here that Mary is familiar with. I'm not thrilled about the fact that she has mistaken me for one of the patients.

"I'm sorry Dr. Beck wouldn't let you leave yesterday, Nicole," Mary says. "That must have been so upsetting."

"No," I correct her. "My name is *Amy*. I'm a medical student."

"Oh!" Mary puts down her knitting needles and claps her hands together. "Oh, how absolutely lovely! A *doctor*—your parents must be so proud!"

I settle down on the bed next to her, crossing my legs. "Actually, yes."

She tilts her head to the side and sighs. "How nice for you. Do you have a beau?"

I get asked that question a lot, but never before exactly in that way. "No, I don't."

"Well, that's a shame!" She clucks her tongue. "A pretty girl like you? You should have a million beaus."

"Um, thanks."

"I know!" Her eyes light up and she leans forward so that I can see a little bit of what could be toothpaste in the corner of her lips. "You should go out with that nice Dr. Beck. He is *such* a nice man. And so handsome. And distinguished!"

"Uh," I say. After Will Schoenfeld (and Spider-Dan), Richard Beck is the *next* most inappropriate person for me to be hooking up with on this unit. Hooking up with attendings is definitely frowned upon, even if they have sexy dimples.

"Of course," she adds, "you can't tell him that you're interested. That would look *desperate*. But you could flirt with him. Maybe put on a little makeup. A nice dress that shows off your bosom. And if you wear the right pair of shoes—"

"Mrs. Cummings," I interrupt her. "I actually wanted to ask some questions about *you*."

She clutches her chest. "About me? Oh, I am so boring. My life is over."

"Why do you say that?"

"Well, I'm almost eighty, for one thing!"

"But life expectancy is growing." Mary needs a pep talk and I'm good at that. "They say eighty is the new seventy! You could easily live to be a hundred."

"Between you and me…" Mary drops her voice. "I'm not even sure if I'm going to make it through the night."

The way she says it sends a chill down my spine. "Why do you say that? "

"Oh, I don't know." She smiles at me. "Just a feeling I have. That my time might be up."

I don't know exactly what she's talking about, if this is just her babbling, or if she has some sort of premonition. I clear my throat. "Don't you want to live for your family?"

"My husband died ten years ago." She goes back to her knitting, the needles tapping together once again. *Click click click.* "Harvey and I never had any children. The only family I've got left is my sister, and she's an old battle ax."

"What did Harvey die from?" I ask.

"Why?" She narrows her eyes. "Do you think that I killed him?"

At first, I think she must be joking, but there's an

edge to her voice that makes me think she's not. "Of course not," I say.

"Because I *didn't*." She frowns. "People fall down the stairs, you know. All the time!"

"I'm sure…"

"And I *loved* him." She tugs some of the yarn from the ball on her lap. "Even though he used to see other women, I still loved him. I would never have killed him."

Okay, now I'm starting to think that Mary definitely killed her husband.

"Anyway," Mary says, "now that Harvey is gone, there isn't much to do. I just work on my garden mostly. That's the only thing I enjoy."

"And knitting," I add.

She laughs. "No, I don't care for knitting."

The scarf trailing from the needles in her hands travels the length of the room. She has done nothing but knit since I set foot on this unit. "I would have thought you liked to knit. I mean, you're doing an awful lot of it."

She laughs again. "I'm not knitting because I *enjoy* it. I'm knitting for *protection*."

I shake my head. "What do you mean?"

She looks down at the two knitting needles in her hands. "You can't exactly bring a weapon onto a psych unit. But in case I need protection, I believe these will do nicely, don't you?"

I look down at the shiny steel knitting needles, one

in each of her gnarled hands. She's right. They could serve as weapons if need be.

I wonder if I should warn Dr. Beck that she is thinking that way.

Mary reaches into the handbag next to her chair. She digs around for a moment and pulls out another knitting needle. She holds it out to me.

"Here," she says. "You're going to need this."

My mouth falls open. "I really don't think—"

"Take it, Amy." Her hand holding the needle trembles slightly. "You're going to want it when Damon Sawyer comes at you."

Damon Sawyer. Yet another patient obsessed with him, certain he's going to try to harm us tonight. I wish I could just ignore them. I probably should. But it's hard when I keep hearing the same thing again and again.

"Damon Sawyer is locked up in seclusion," I tell her.

"Yes." Mary's watery eyes bore into me. "For now."

"Mary, I…"

"Take the knitting needle. Please, Amy. I don't want anything to happen to you."

I start to shake my head, but instead, I grab the knitting needle out of Mary's hand. She watches me as I bury the needle deep into the large side pocket of my scrub pants.

After all, it can't hurt to have a little protection.

21

HOURS UNTIL MORNING: 8

I spend the next hour with Mary,
I learn more about her life. She worked as a
secretary for thirty years for a man named Mr.
Timmerman. Mr. Timmerman liked a cup of coffee
every morning at ninety-thirty sharp, and he liked one
spoonful of sugar and one spoonful of cream in his
coffee, and to stir it once, but no more than that.
Actually, I learned quite a bit about Mr. Timmerman's coffee.

"Well," Mary finally says, her voice raspy, "I've
talked your ear off, haven't I?"

"I like listening."

"You're a very good listener," she tells me. "It's a

fine quality. You're going to make an excellent doctor, Amy."

My face flushes. "Thank you."

"Also," she adds, "will you please tell Dr. Beck that I never would have hurt that little girl? I was just taking her off the swing so the squeaking would stop. You know how annoying those swings can be, right?"

"Absolutely. I always hated swings."

She looks relieved. "Thank you, Amy. I just want to go home. Tell Dr. Beck that I'm okay to go home, will you?"

"I will," I promise. As if the attending would listen to me.

She closes her eyes for a moment, and she suddenly looks so old. She could be a hundred. "I'm truly afraid I might not make it through the night."

"Why do you feel that way?"

Mary opens her mouth as if to answer, but then she changes her mind and shakes her head. "I'm too tired to talk anymore. You should go."

She does look tired, and it's getting late. I can talk to her more in the morning. "Okay, if that's what you want."

As I stand up to leave the room, Mary reaches out to grab my arm with her spindly fingers. "Hold onto that knitting needle I gave you, Amy. You're going to need it."

This night seriously better not end with me needing to stab somebody with a knitting needle.

When I get out of Mary's room, I almost run

smack into Clint Eastwood. He is shuffling down the hallway, still holding that paper bag filled with saltines with one hand and hiking up his pajama pants with the other. He has some white spittle in the corner of his mouth.

"Nobody took my crackers!" he cries accusingly. "I still have them!"

"I'm so sorry," I say.

"I have diabetes," he reminds me. "These crackers could kill me. Why would they give these to me?"

"I have no idea. But… I'd be happy to take them for you."

Clint grumbles something under his breath. He looks like he's about to give me the bag of saltines when he gets distracted by room 912. He scratches at the gray hairs jutting out of his chin.

"Hang on," he says.

Clint shuffles into Mary's room. I don't know if he's supposed to be in there, but he seems harmless enough, and Mary doesn't seem upset about it. When she sees him, she looks up and smiles.

He reaches into the bag and pulls out a package of saltines. "This is for you, pretty lady."

Mary accepts the package of saltines. "Well, aren't you sweet!"

Clint winks at her, and the two of them grin at each other. It's so darn cute, I almost can't stand it. I let them have a little bit of privacy.

I don't even realize how late it is until I notice a lot of the lights are out in the patients' rooms. Many of the doors are closed, and it looks like everybody has gone to sleep. I suspect Cameron is sound asleep on the couch in the staff lounge. Maybe if I head over, he'll be a gentleman and let me sleep there.

But instead, I return to the nurses' station. Even though it's not required, maybe I'll write up a note on Mary Cummings. At least in the morning, I'll have something to give Dr. Beck when Cameron hands in his own novel-length masterpiece on Spider-Dan.

Ramona is sitting at the nurses' station flipping through that same magazine. This time she's looking at a page with tips on how to spice up your love life. She looks up and smiles when she sees me. "You look tired," she comments.

I am tired, but at the same time, I know I won't be able to sleep. "It's weird doing a night shift."

"Oh, that's right." She snickers. "You're at the very beginning of your third year. You haven't gotten used to the schedule yet."

"Not yet." And unfortunately, it's only going to get harder. Psychiatry is the easiest rotation of the year. I'm dreading surgery—I don't have Cameron's stamina. "I'll be okay, though."

"Don't worry," she says. "It's usually quiet here at night. Unless Mary Cummings starts acting up."

I think of Mary and her knitting needles. Instinctively, I reach for the outline of the needle in my pants pocket. It just barely fits inside.

"Have you been doing the night shift for a long time?" I ask her.

"Oh, forever." She grins. "It's nice to have your days free for appointments and all that. And I don't have a significant other to bug me that I'm always sleeping when he's awake."

"Do the patients cause much trouble here?"

She doesn't need to think about it before shaking her head. "For the most part, they're very easy. Every once in a while, we get a troublemaker."

"Like Damon Sawyer?"

Her eyes darken slightly. "Yes, like him." At those words, she sneaks a look down the hallway, in the direction of the seclusion room. The first room is still shut tight. "But that's an exception. Generally, I just pass out the meds and that's about it." She holds up her magazine. "Then I get to read all night."

I glance up at the rack of charts. "Well, I don't want to bother you. I just wanted to do a quick write-up on my patients that I saw tonight."

"No bother." Ramona gets out of her seat and pulls a chart out of the rack, then places it down in front of me. "You'll be keeping me company."

"Thanks," I say.

I sit down on one of the rolly chairs and pull the chart closer to me. That's when I realize she didn't pull Mary's chart from the rack. She saw me in Jade's room, so that's the chart she pulled for me. Jade's chart is sitting right in front of me.

It's not a thick chart, which I wouldn't expect. I don't think she's been here very long. And most of her notes are probably on the computer, which I can't access right now thanks to the maintenance being done tonight. But at the very least, her emergency room note will be in the chart. It will have her past psychiatric history and her reason for admission.

It would be so easy to look.

I place my hand on the cover of the chart. I grab the plastic cover, wondering if I should go ahead and open it. If roles were reversed, Jade would definitely look at my chart. And she wouldn't feel the slightest bit guilty about it.

I'll just take a quick peek. That's all.

I flip the cover open, but before I can even read the first sentence, the lights overhead flicker and go out.

"What the hell?" Ramona says.

The power must have gone out. It's pitch dark in here—I can't see so much as my hand in front of my face. Ramona is swearing under her breath, and I hear a chair topple to the floor. She can't see much either, obviously.

Oh my God. If the power went out, does that mean the locks on the doors stopped functioning?

Including the seclusion room?

"Ramona?" I call out.

"I'm here." I turn my head in the direction of her voice, but I can't see a thing. "Don't worry. I don't know why the power went out, but there's a generator. We should be okay."

"Ramona," I say urgently, "if the lights are out,

does that mean the locks on the doors don't work anymore?"

She's quiet for long enough that I'm starting to worry she's not there anymore. "I don't know," she finally says.

Oh no.

But before I can panic too much, the lights flicker back on. I let out a sigh of relief that I'm not going to have to spend the rest of the night in pitch blackness. But before I have a chance to celebrate the return of the lights, a man stumbles in the direction of the nurses' station. It's Miguel, except he's not wearing four shirts anymore. In fact, he's not wearing any clothing at all.

And he's covered in blood.

22

EIGHT YEARS EARLIER

J ade stormed off after I refused to even take a look at the exam. But there was no way I was going to cheat. I would rather fail.

And unfortunately, that will be the alternative. I have no chance of passing this exam anymore.

Of course, I'm not sure if the exam is the worst of my problems right now. Even if I fail the midterm, if my parents get me a tutor, I could still potentially turn things around. What is less simple to resolve is the fact that I keep seeing a little blond girl who is not actually there.

What is wrong with me? Have I completely lost my mind? I must have. Sane people don't see little girls who aren't really there.

But I don't *feel* like I've gone insane.

These thoughts are swirling through my head as I try to enjoy dinner with my family. My father is talking to my little brother, Trevor, about his upcoming baseball game. They are dominating the dinner conversation, and that's fine with me. I keep picking at my food, building a little mashed potato castle on my plate. I have eaten about three bites while we've been sitting here. I have no appetite.

"Amy." Mom flashes me a sharp look. "Will you please stop playing with your food? You're not a child anymore."

Suddenly, all the attention at the table is on me and my uneaten plate of food. Trevor, of course, has gobbled everything up in about five seconds. That kid is an eating machine—even more so since he hit puberty.

"I'm not hungry," I mumble.

Mom peers at my face, studying me in a way that has me convinced that she can see all my insides like they're on the outside. "Are you sick?"

"I'm not sick. I'm just not hungry."

"Leave her alone, Dina," my father says. "She doesn't have to eat if she doesn't feel like it."

"Are you worried about that test?" Mom asks me. "Because I can talk to your teacher—"

"It's fine." I stab a hunk of beef with my fork, but I make no effort to bring it any closer to my mouth. My mom acts like I'm still five years old, and she can solve all my problems by talking to the teacher. "I just…"

Mom raises her eyebrows. "What?"

"Well…" I dig my fork deeper into the beef.

"What if somebody was seeing something that wasn't there? What does that mean?"

My mother's eyes fly open. "Who is seeing things that aren't there? What are you talking about?"

"Nothing." I drop my eyes. What was I thinking? I never should have mentioned it. But it's been weighing on me so heavily. "I was just asking, like, *hypothetically*. It was something we were talking about in, you know… in class."

"Is it Jade?" My mother reaches out and closes her fingers around my wrist. "Did Jade tell you she's seeing things?"

I twist my arm out of her grip. "No! Of course not."

"Please tell me the truth, Amy." Her face is filled with worry. "It is Jade, isn't it?"

"Dina, leave her alone," my father mutters.

"It's got to be Jade!" my mother declares. "She's always been so troubled. And you remember her mother had those issues with—"

"*Dina*," Dad says sharply.

"Honey." Mom looks into my eyes. "If Jade is having problems, we can get her help. There are doctors and hospitals…"

"It's not like it's any secret that Jade is crazy," Trevor speaks up. "Everybody at school knows it."

Is that true? Do even the freshmen think my best friend is crazy? But she isn't. *I'm* the one seeing things that aren't there.

So that means I'm the crazy one—not Jade.

I can't let anyone know. I don't want them talking about me the way they talk about Jade. Or locking me up in some hospital.

"I really need to go study." I scrape my chair against the floor in my eagerness to get up. "Can I be excused please?"

My mother narrows her eyes at me. I'm scared that she's going to tell me no, that I can't leave. I have to stay here and discuss this further with her. But finally, she nods. "Fine. But we're going to talk more later."

"Fine," I agree, even though I can never tell my mother the truth.

23

PRESENT DAY

I can't stop screaming.

Miguel is standing in the middle of the hallway, stark naked, streaked in blood. What happened to him? Did Damon Sawyer get free? Is he currently roaming the hallways with a knife, ready to kill every single one of us?

I reach for the knitting needle in my scrub pants.

"Miguel!" Ramona cries. "Where did you get all that jelly?"

It takes me a few seconds to process her words. Miguel is not covered in blood. He's actually covered in red jelly, all over his naked body. Now that my eyes have adjusted to the light, it's very clear what the red substance is.

"I'm sorry," I mumble to Ramona, embarrassed. "I thought that was blood."

She laughs. "Seriously? It doesn't look anything like blood."

Well, maybe she's right. But she didn't have to say it like *that*.

A moment later, Dr. Beck sprints over to us, skidding to a halt when he catches sight of Miguel's naked body. His mouth drops open. "Miguel!"

"My father say I go home today," Miguel says.

Over the next fifteen minutes, Dr. Beck and Ramona piece together what went on. Apparently, Miguel stripped off all his many layers of clothing, then he urinated on the light socket, which briefly shorted out the power on the whole unit. Then he went into his dresser, where he had been stocking up on strawberry jelly for the last several days. And he went to town.

Now we need to get Miguel back into some clothing.

"Miguel." Dr. Beck folds his arms across his chest. "Please, for the love of God, put on a shirt and pants. There are *ladies* here."

Miguel shakes his head so vigorously that all his rolls of fat tremble. I should look away—I really should.

"Fine." Dr. Beck points at the remaining one of the two seclusion rooms. "Then I'm going to need you to go in here."

Miguel doesn't budge. Dr. Beck looks over his shoulder at where I'm standing at the nurses' station. "Amy, where is Cameron?"

I'm not offended that he'd prefer Cameron to me in a situation like this. If he needs to force Miguel into that room, I will be completely useless. Cameron, on the other hand, has muscles to spare. That said, he is suspiciously absent. Where did he go? Presumably, knowing Cameron, he is hiding away somewhere, studying.

"Listen, Miguel," Dr. Beck says, "if you go into the room, I'll make sure you go home tomorrow."

He's lying. He's obviously lying. But Miguel somehow buys it. He goes into the seclusion room, and before he can change his mind, Ramona slams the door shut.

Miguel realizes his mistake almost instantly. Just like in the other seclusion room, the door vibrates as he slams his body against it. "Hey!" he cries. "You lock me in!"

Dr. Beck regards the door, his face impassive. "Just for the night, Miguel. We'll talk in the morning."

"No! *No!*" The hysteria in Miguel's voice is escalating. "Help me! *Ayudame!*"

"This is for your own good, Miguel," Dr. Beck says.

"You can't!" he yells "You can't keep me in here! My father say so. He going to kill me!"

"Why would your father kill you, Miguel?" Dr. Beck asks in a calm, controlled voice.

"No! Not my father!" he cries. "Damon Sawyer!"

All three of our heads swivel in the direction of Seclusion One. I haven't heard any pounding coming from the room since the lights went out. But that doesn't mean Sawyer isn't in the room anymore. I'm sure he is still in there, plotting to get free. He must be. After all, where could he have gone?

I turn around—several patients have come out of their rooms to watch the spectacle. Spider-Dan is in the hallway, holding out his wrists, hoping to shoot a web out and miraculously save the day. Jade is by her room, a tiny smile playing on her lips. Will has also emerged from his room, one of his books still in his right hand. He leans in and says something to Jade, and her smile widens. She nods at him.

I wonder what he said.

Mary has come out of her room as well. She's left her giant scarf behind in her room, but I notice in her right hand, she is holding a knitting needle. My eyes meet hers, and she gives me a knowing look.

"Damon Sawyer!" Miguel screams. "He's coming to kill me! He's coming to kill all of us! You have to let me go!"

"Miguel." Dr. Beck is staying amazingly calm— I'm impressed. But I'm sure he has lots of experience with patients like this. "Mr. Sawyer is restrained right now. He's not going to hurt anybody. I promise you."

Dr. Beck spends several more minutes trying to calm Miguel down, but Miguel keeps screaming until his voice turns hoarse. After about twenty minutes, Dr. Beck gives up, shaking his head.

"Eventually, he'll go to sleep," he says. "And hope-fully put some clothes on."

Ramona laughs, but I just stand there. The whole incident has left me feeling shaken. Dr. Beck catches the look on my face and rests a hand on my shoulder. "He'll be okay, Amy," he says. "Don't worry."

How will that man *possibly* be okay? He thinks his father is God. He has alternated between wearing no clothing and *all* of his clothing. And he smeared his entire naked body with strawberry jelly. I'm going to hazard a guess and say this man does *not* have a bright future ahead of him.

"Get some sleep, Amy," Dr. Beck says. "Find an empty patient room and lie down for a bit. Looks like your colleague is doing that."

That's right. Throughout this entire commotion, Cameron has been absent. Even if he's asleep, which seems unlikely knowing Cam, it's hard to imagine all the screaming wouldn't have woken him up. And I happen to remember that Cam is a pretty light sleeper.

So where is he?

24

Once things have settled down on Ward D, I do a lap around the unit, looking for Cameron.

The first place I go is the staff lounge. It's the obvious place to look for him. My eyes dart from the ancient sofa to the barred window to the dusty nook behind the door that is covered in spiderwebs. But he's not anywhere in here.

My next stop is the staff restroom. The door is shut, so I knock on it—no answer. I try the door knob and it turns in my hand. But when I look inside, the bathroom is empty.

Then I start a lap around the unit, checking all the patient rooms.

I check Spider-Dan's room first. The door to his room is open, and so is the door to the bathroom. He's standing in front of the toilet, his wrists pointed at the wall. He's trying to pee/shoot out webs. But either way, Cam isn't here.

The next room is cracked open, and a man is sitting on his bed. I squint inside and notice that the man is licking his arms repeatedly. It's the most bizarre thing—almost like a cat grooming itself. I move on.

The next room has a female patient inside. When she sees me standing at the door, she scrambles to her feet. She has black tangled hair and huge glasses that give her an owl-like appearance.

"Am I going home?" she asks me.

"Oh," I say. "Um, no. I mean, I don't know."

"I need to go home." She attempts to rake a hand through her tangled hair. "My son is home. I need to see my son."

"I… I'm sorry… I don't…"

"*I need to see my son!*"

I can see the pain in this woman's eyes, but what can I do? I don't even know who she is.

"I'll see what I can do," I mumble. Even though I'm lying.

The woman gives me a dirty look, because she almost certainly knows that I'm not going to see what I can do. She goes back into her room and slams the door hard enough that the entire frame shakes.

I should tell Dr. Beck that I can't find Cameron,

but Cam would be furious with me if I ratted him out that way for stepping outside—if that's what happened.

Something not everybody knows is that Cam has a temper. He manages to do a good job of hiding it. And to be fair, he doesn't fly off the handle very often. But he acts like this good-natured guy all the time, and it's easy enough to keep that act going with friends, but it's harder to hide it from the girl that you're dating.

The first time I ever witnessed Cameron's temper was when he found out he didn't get a spot in a prestigious year-long research fellowship on the west coast. Orthopedic surgery is a competitive specialty, and doing research is—according to Cam—essential to matching in a residency spot. He and several other students in our class applied for the research position, which would have taken him to the California bay area between his second and third year of med school, and he believed he was a shoo-in. We were hanging out in his bedroom, sitting together on his bed, when he got the email. His left arm had been slung over my shoulders, and he pulled it away.

What the hell? Cam's square face had turned a shade of pink. *They didn't pick me? Seriously?*

I tried to look over his shoulder at the email, but he had already tossed it to the side of the bed. Then he leaped to his feet.

I can't believe this! he ranted. *How could they shaft me that way?*

Is it that big a deal? I said. *I mean, it's just one fellowship. There are other research opportunities.*

But this one is the best one. He started pacing his small bedroom. *I don't get it. I have the best grades in the class. It's not like you were applying for the fellowship.*

I ignored his jab because of how upset he was. *You can't let it get to you. There will be other opportunities.*

And they picked David Tobin! His voice was growing in volume as the color of his face turned a shade closer to purple. *How could they pick that asshole? I mean, what the hell is wrong with them? Seriously?*

Cam was almost shouting now, but I didn't genuinely know how upset he was until his fist flew into the wall of his room.

The plaster crunched under his knuckles, giving way to create a fist-sized crater in the wall. He yelped and yanked his hand away, while I jumped off the bed. For a moment, I wasn't sure whether to flee or see if he was okay. But the color in his face had returned to normal, and he wasn't shouting anymore. He was just cradling his hand.

I ended up having to drive him to the emergency room to get x-rays of his hand, which thankfully did not show a fracture. While I was driving him home at two in the morning with his right hand in a splint, he hung his head and said to me, *I'm sorry I overreacted like that, Amy.*

At least he was embarrassed about the whole thing and he did apologize. It wasn't the first time I saw that flash of anger. Most of the time, Cam did manage to keep his temper under wraps, but it was there. Lingering under the surface, waiting to be unleashed.

So the last thing I want to do is piss him off.

"Looking for your buddy?"

I shouldn't be surprised to see Jade standing at the doorway to the next room. 905. She is still wearing those pink sweatpants and the tank top, with no bra underneath. She looks amused by my inability to find Cameron.

"He's here somewhere," I mumble.

"Maybe he wised up," she says. "Maybe he got the hell out of here before something really bad happens."

I look up sharply. "What are you talking about?"

She shrugs. "I don't know. There's something in the air tonight. Something is going to happen. Don't you feel it?"

Do I?

"I guess you need to spend a little more time on psych units to know the feeling," Jade says.

"Yeah," I mutter.

Her blue eyes skim over my body, making me squirm. She knows me in the way that only somebody who has been your best friend since kindergarten can know you. "I can't believe you never ended up seeing a shrink."

"It was unnecessary."

"Really?" Her eyebrows shoot up to her hairline.

"Are you really going to say that to me with a straight face?"

I don't say anything to that comment.

"You know," she says, "these things don't just go away on their own. Once you're seeing things that aren't there and hearing voices, they never just go away."

"I have no idea what you're talking about," I say tightly. "Now if you'll excuse me, I have to find Cameron."

I can feel her eyes on me as I walk away. God, I wish she weren't here tonight. She knows way too much about me. And if she were to tell Cameron or Dr. Beck…

It doesn't matter. They wouldn't believe her anyway.

I continue down the hallway until I get to the end, where the two seclusion rooms are located. Miguel still hasn't quite settled down—he's belting out an off-key version of "I Touch Myself" within the room. But at least he's not screaming that Damon Sawyer is going to kill us.

As for Damon Sawyer, he is completely silent. It is, in fact, the first time I have walked past this room and not heard any sound coming from inside. He's not begging me to let him out. He's not throwing himself against the door.

But the keypad is still glowing green. He's still locked in there.

Right?

25

EIGHT YEARS EARLIER

I t's nearly midnight when someone taps on my bedroom window.

I'm still awake, of course. I'm still studying, making a desperate attempt to wrangle a passing grade in trig. It's a lost cause, but at least I'll know I tried.

When I hear the tapping on my window, I almost don't turn around. Somebody tapping on my second-floor window at midnight has *got* to be me hallucinating. But when I hear another louder tap, I turn around.

Oh my God, it's *Jade*. What is Jade doing at my window?

I abandon my trigonometry book and dash over to the window. Jade has grabbed a ladder from our garage and balanced it against the side of our house, and is now standing at the top of it, her nose pressed against the glass of my window. She smiles at me.

I wrench open the window. "Jade, what the…?"

Jade brandishes a sheaf of papers in her right hand. "I did all the problems for you. All you have to do is memorize how to do them. You're *welcome*."

My mouth drops open. "I told you. I can't…"

"Oh my *God*, Amy." She shakes her head. "You are, like, so annoying. Trigonometry is so stupid anyway—why shouldn't you get the answers? Like who cares if you actually know this stuff or not? I'm giving you an easy A! You work so freaking hard all the time. Why don't you just take the help for once?"

I fold my arms across my chest. "I'm not going to cheat on an exam, Jade. I'm not going to do it."

"You'd rather fail?"

"Yes! I'd rather fail!"

"Then you're an idiot." Jade takes the exam paper in her hand and throws it into my room. "Here. Just in case you decide to stop being stupid."

With those words, she climbs down the ladder. I watch her make her way down into the backyard, then sprint down the street, disappearing around the corner. Our neighborhood isn't terribly unsafe, but it's probably not great for her to be all alone at night. My mother would never allow me to be out of the house all by myself at this hour. But Jade's mother… well, she doesn't seem to care much about what her daughter does.

I turn away from the window. The exam paper is lying on the floor of my room, the answers to the questions filled in with Jade's spidery handwriting. How easy would it be to pick up the test and memorize the answers? Then tomorrow, all I would have to do would be to fill them in. Jade is great at math, so I'm sure she got everything right.

But I can't do that.

I snatch the papers off the floor and deposit them directly in my trash can. There. The decision has been made.

"If you don't look at that test, you're going to fail for sure."

My eyes snap up, but I recognize the voice before I even look. It's that little girl. The one with the curls and the impractical pink dress. She is standing in the corner of my room, like she was before, her blue eyes on me like a laser beam. She tilts her heart-shaped face up at me.

"Just a peek," she says. "You won't be hurting anyone."

I wipe my hands on the legs of my blue jeans, spreading two sweaty stains on my thighs. "You're not real," I say.

She smiles at me. "If I'm not real, then what does that mean for you?"

It means I'm losing my mind.

I squeeze my eyes shut as tightly as I can. I count to ten in my head, take a deep breath, then open my eyes again.

The little girl is gone.

I don't even feel relieved though. She might be gone for now, but I've seen her twice just today. She'll be back for sure. There's something very wrong with me.

What am I going to do?

26

PRESENT DAY

HOURS UNTIL MORNING: 6

Cameron must have left the unit.

It's the only possible solution. Because I have looked everywhere, and he is not here. Maybe he got sick of not having any reception on his phone, and he decided to step out at the worst possible moment. I can't blame him—I'm tempted to do the same, but I am an incorrigible rule follower. There's only been one time in my entire life when I broke the rules and did something immoral, and I paid dearly for it.

I could leave the unit and check if he's outside. Or I could slip out to finally get some service on my phone. I know the code for the keypad. It would be easy enough to leave. But technically, I'm not supposed to. And what if I open the door and a patient comes up behind me and pushes his way out? How would I explain that?

So I decide not to leave the unit to look for Cam. I'm sure he'll be back soon enough. He wouldn't risk getting a bad grade, even in psychiatry. After all, that would screw up his dream of becoming a surgeon.

In the meantime, I take Dr. Beck's advice and try to get some sleep. But there's no way I am sleeping in a patient room. The sofa in the staff lounge might be old and dirty and have visible springs poking out, but I'll get a better night of sleep there than anywhere else.

Before I go to sleep, I take my phone out of my pocket and bring it over to the window. I press it against the glass, which feels cool against my fingers. I squint down at the screen, waiting for a bar to appear. If I get any reception at all, the first thing I'm going to do is call Cam and tell him to get his butt back over here.

Please. Just one bar. Please.

But no. Nothing.

I give up. It's one in the morning—I'm going to try to get some sleep.

Except as soon as I lie down and turn off the lights, it's clear that sleep is not going to happen. I stare up at the ceiling, my brain running a mile a minute. I try to remember the tricks Dr. Sleepy tells his patients to help them sleep at night. Most of it is stuff I can't control at this point, like avoiding naps and caffeine, and getting on a regular sleep schedule. But one thing he always tells patients is that while they're lying in bed, they can do the four-seven-eight breathing method.

Now I just have to remember what the hell that is.

Okay, I remember. You're supposed to put your tongue between your upper front teeth, exhale completely, then inhale through your nose while counting to four, hold your breath for the count of seven, and then exhale to the count of eight. And do that three more times. You're supposed to make some sort of strange sound while you're doing it, but I can't be bothered by that.

Here we go…

Inhale for four. Hold breath for seven. Exhale for eight.
Inhale for four. Hold breath for seven. Exhale for eight.
Inhale for four. Hold breath for seven. Exhale for eight.

This is not working. At *all*. What I really need is some Ambien. I wish I had asked Dr. Sleepy for a prescription before leaving the clinic. In any case, I am not falling asleep anytime soon.

Where is Cameron? I can imagine him disappearing for a few minutes, but it occurs to me that I haven't seen him once since we were in the patient lounge together interviewing Spider-Dan. That was *hours* ago. It's not like him to disappear that way. Cameron might not be as big of a rule follower as I am, but nobody cares more than he does about getting a good grade in a rotation.

Whatever else you could say about Cameron,

nobody could match his energy and passion for medicine. He is truly excited about the idea of being a "bone doctor." He wants to do trauma surgery. He likes the idea of putting people back together after a terrible accident.

That's really morbid, I commented the first time he said that to me.

Why? He was truly confused. *Somebody has to do it. Don't you want to fix people?*

I do want to fix people, but not in the same way. When I was a little kid playing with Barbie dolls, the dolls were always getting "injured" and I would have to bandage them up. Jade used to complain that she was sick of playing Barbie's doctor's office. So I got what Cam meant when he said that.

However, I want to fix people without necessarily *cutting into them.* I can leave the bloody stuff to people like Cameron.

After staring up at the ceiling for about an hour, I recognize sleep is not going to happen. Instead, I decide to take a walk around the unit, hoping I can get rid of some of my anxious energy.

I pass by the two seclusion rooms. The first room is still eerily silent. After all the noise I heard there earlier and the voice begging me to let them out, it's unsettling how silent it is. I press my ear against the door, listening. But I hear nothing. Not a peep.

Not since the power went out.

"Mr. Sawyer?" I say softly. "Are you all right?"

No answer.

"Damon?" I say.

Again, there's no reply.

I'm sure he's just asleep though. He must be.

The lights were turned down in the hallway at ten p.m. to more of a mood lighting, so the glowing green keypad seems even more luminous. I could type in the code and make sure Sawyer is okay in there. Or make sure he's still in there at all. It would be easy enough to do so. Then I can put my mind at ease.

It's late enough that it's quiet on the unit right now, but as I stand there, the sound of footsteps grows louder by the second. I look off into the distance to see who's walking towards me. A shadow appears from around the bend, but before I can see who it is, the shadow vanishes.

"Hello?" I call out.

A sound echoes down the hallway. It almost sounds like a man chuckling to himself.

Before I can go investigate, I get distracted by a sound from Seclusion Two. While Damon Sawyer has gone silent, Miguel has definitely not. He is still singing to himself in the room. This time he's belting out a Britney Spears song. He apparently wants me to hit him (baby) one more time. He doesn't have such a bad voice, everything considered.

The dark hallway is filled with patient rooms. The light is on in room 906—Will Schoenfeld is still awake, probably reading. I still find that patient something of a mystery. He just seemed incredibly normal for a patient in a psychiatric unit. Like the sort of person I might be friends with if I met him in a different setting.

And as Jade noted, he's my type. Cute, nerdy, lanky, well-read. And I liked his smile, the one time I got to see it. If I met him anywhere else but here and he flashed that shy smile and asked me out on a date, I would give him my number.

Of course, I would have had no idea that he was hearing voices telling him to kill people. So I dodged a bullet there.

It occurs to me that I could borrow something from Will's John Irving collection. It would be comforting to read one of those books, and it might be enough to put me to sleep. He'd probably be willing to lend me one, and I would just return it in the morning.

The door to Will's room is cracked open, and I knock gently. I don't hear a reply, and I push it open slightly more. The room is empty, but the door to his bathroom is closed, and the light is on inside. He'll probably be out in a minute.

He's still got the stack of John Irving books on his dresser. *Owen Meany* is right on top, because that's the one he's been reading. Obviously, I wouldn't borrow that one since he's reading it right now. I remove it from the stack and pick up the second book in line. *The World According to Garp*. Another of my favorites. This one would do nicely.

I pick up the copy of *Garp* to flip through it. But when I flip open the first page, my heart stops.

This book has been hollowed out.

Someone has carved a large hole in the center of the book, leaving a space where objects can be stored secretly. Such as, in this case, a large number of multi-colored pills. I recognize them as looking similar to the ones that Ramona has been passing out.

There are more than a dozen little pills stashed away in the hollow space. A dozen pills that Will was supposed to be taking to suppress the voices in his head—the ones telling him to kill people. He claimed that the voices had stopped after taking the medications. But now it looks like he hasn't been taking those medications at all.

And then the toilet flushes inside the bathroom and the sink turns on. He's almost done in there.

He's coming out any second.

27

Oh my God.

Will is going to come out and realize that I've been going through his books and discovered his secret. He's already got paranoid schizophrenia, and now I have discovered he is not on medications. What is he going to do when he realizes I know the truth?

I slam shut the cover to the copy of *Garp* and shove it back in the pile of books. Then I balance *Owen Meany* back on top. I've got them just barely positioned correctly when Will emerges from the bathroom.

Will blinks a few times at the sight of me, like he's not certain if I'm a figment of his imagination or not. Which makes sense, considering he has been pocketing his medications since he's been here.

"Amy?" he finally says.

"Sorry," I say quickly. "I was trying to get a little

sleep, and I couldn't, so I thought I could borrow a John Irving book for the night. But I understand if you don't want to lend me one."

Will adjusts his glasses on the bridge of his nose. "Uh, sure. That's fine. Which one do you want?"

I'm tempted to ask for *Garp*, just to see what he'll say. But that would be tempting fate. The two of us are all alone in his room right now—and he's mentally unbalanced. "Maybe... *Cider House Rules*?"

"Sure."

He walks over to the stack of books. As he sorts through them, he hesitates on the copy of *Garp*. He shoots me a look, his eyes narrowing, and I hold my breath. He opens his mouth, and I'm *sure* he's going to ask me if I was looking through the book... but then he doesn't. He goes right past it and plucks one of the paperbacks out of the stack.

"Here you go," he says. "Enjoy."

"Thanks." I take the book out of his hands, and my fingers brush slightly against his. "Appreciate it."

Now that I've got the book, I recognize that I should get out of here. Nothing good can come out of lingering in this room. Yet part of me wonders if I can help this man. Maybe I can get him to confess what he's done and realize that the only way he's going to get better is to take his medications. After all, Dr. Beck mentioned that most patients with schizophrenia don't even recognize they have a problem.

"So that was wild what happened earlier with Miguel," I say. "Wasn't it?"

Will's expression is still wary, but he nods. "Yeah, it's the second exciting night in a row. Every time they lock somebody in one of those rooms, it's a big event."

"Yes," I agree. I shift the copy of *Cider House Rules* between my hands. "That definitely seems like something you want to try to avoid at all costs."

"Yeah."

"I mean," I say, "you wouldn't want to do anything to make them think you should be in one of those rooms, right?"

He takes a step back as he sucks in a breath. "Why do you think they would want to put *me* in there?"

"I don't," I amend. "I didn't mean it like that. I just mean that it seems like not following the rules in here can get you into trouble."

"He peed on a light socket. I'm not going to do that."

"Of course not." I force a smile. "But there are other important rules. Like, you want to get better, don't you?"

They say one of the negative symptoms of schizophrenia is not being able to make eye contact, but Will is making pretty good eye contact right now. He looks like he's staring me down.

"I'm going to turn in now," he says tightly.

"Are you sure?" I gesture at the chair in the corner of the room. "Because I'm awake if you feel like talking. I'd be happy to—"

"I don't," Will says abruptly.

Will is a bit of an enigma to me. Granted, I'm not a psychiatrist. But he seems like an intelligent guy who loves my favorite author and is an extremely talented piano player. If I were in that situation, and I were hearing voices…

Well, maybe that's a bad example.

"All right," I say. "I'll let you get to sleep. If you're having any trouble, I know this great breathing technique called four-seven-eight. What you do is—"

"No, thank you. I'll pass."

I force a smile. "Are you sure? Because—"

"I'm sure."

Will follows me to the door of his room, and after I leave, he slams it shut behind me. He may not be sure if I discovered his secret, but he knows I'm suspicious of *something*.

Of course, after I get out of the room, I have a real dilemma. Will has not been taking his medications. And the entire reason he's hospitalized here is to get better. Dr. Beck needs to know about this. I don't want to rat Will out, but it's not like he confided in me. I discovered his secret by accident.

Clutching the copy of *Cider House Rules* in my right hand, I walk around the circle to get to the attending physician's office. It occurs to me as I approach the office that at this hour, it might be too late and maybe I should just save this information until the morning. Then again, this is important, isn't it? What if something happens during the night?

And anyway, the light is on under the door. Dr. Beck must still be awake.

I knock gently on the door, hoping that if he is asleep, I won't have to wake him. After a second, I hear shuffling behind the door and something that almost sounds like a crash. "Who is it?" Dr. Beck calls out.

"It's Amy."

There's another long pause with a lot of shuffling. After another minute, the door is yanked open. Dr. Beck is standing there in just his scrubs, his hair slightly sticking up on the right side. I hadn't noticed when he was wearing his white coat, but he's got a decent set of biceps peeking out from under his scrub sleeves.

"I'm so sorry!" I say. "Did I wake you?"

"No…" He yawns and rubs his eyes. "Okay, a little bit. I didn't mean to drift off. But it's fine. I'm up now, anyway." He runs his fingers through his disheveled hair. "Anyway, what's up? Is everything okay?"

"Kind of…" I glance behind me. "I was just talking to Will Schoenfeld, and I discovered that…"

Dr. Beck is looking at me intently. Now I'm starting to second-guess myself. If I tell him the truth, it won't be good for Will. They may have to force him to take his medications, and whatever that involves, it won't be pretty. But actually, that's to his benefit. He wants to get better, doesn't he? You can't go through life hearing voices in your head.

"He's been pocketing his medication," I blurt out. "I found a whole bunch of them inside a book in his room."

"Shit," Dr. Beck breathes. Then he quickly adds, "Sorry. I'm tired. But… ugh. I can't believe he's been doing that."

I tighten my grip on the copy of the book Will gave me. "So what now?"

"We may have to switch to intramuscular dosing," Dr. Beck says. "I'm not the attending physician on service this week, so I'll pass it on to the primary team in the morning. If there are any problems overnight, we'll have to go to the injection route. I'm glad you told me."

"No problem," I say, even though I feel a twinge of guilt. I shouldn't though. I'm doing this to help Will.

"Anything else?" Dr. Beck asks me.

There is one other thing. I feel guilty ratting out Cameron, but I have to say something—I'm starting to freak out that I can't find him. "I don't know where Cameron went. I think he might have left the unit."

"Oh." He looks back into his office. "Actually, Cameron left a message on my machine. Apparently, he had some family emergency and had to leave immediately."

I guess that solves the mystery of what happened to Cam and why I can't find him anywhere. But it's strange that he would leave a phone message with that information. Especially when Dr. Beck is right here on the floor, and pretty easy to locate. Why wouldn't he talk to Dr. Beck directly? Also, why wouldn't Cam tell me if something happened? It's not like we're total strangers. "I see…"

"I did think it was strange," Dr. Beck admits. "I wish he had spoken to me directly about it. But he sounded pretty upset on the phone. Choked up. So he probably wasn't thinking too clearly."

Cameron was choked up? That's hard to imagine. Whenever we used to watch sad movies together and I would get tearful, he would look at me like I was out of my mind. Even when he was breaking up with me, he barely seemed upset.

"I hope he's okay," I finally say.

"Are *you* hanging in there okay?" He reaches out and rests a hand on my shoulder. "You look like you're having a tough night. I know that was kind of jarring with Miguel. I'm sorry you had to see that."

He doesn't know the half of it, but I'm not going to open up to him, even though he is a psychiatrist— or maybe *because* he's a psychiatrist. I don't want the guy judging me. And it would be very unprofessional to have that kind of talk with my supervisor for the night. I wouldn't want it to get around at school that I'm…

"I'm fine," I say. "Just tired."

He nods sympathetically. "Try to get some sleep, okay?"

I agree with him, but it's a lost cause at this point.

I say good night to Dr. Beck and trudge back to

the staff lounge, to try to read until I drift off to sleep. But when I get there, I realize I'm not alone. Somebody is waiting for me in the lounge.

It's Jade.

And she looks really pissed off.

28

EIGHT YEARS EARLIER

I don't like Mr. Riordan.

He's my least favorite teacher. Actually, he's everyone's least favorite teacher. If everyone in the school picked the teacher they disliked the most, he would be on every single list. (Well, not everyone. Not everyone has had him as a teacher. But you know what I mean.)

First of all, he smells bad. He doesn't smell like he hasn't showered or something like that, but he has this weird moldy cheese smell. Jade told me it's whatever he has for lunch, since we get to have him in the afternoon. From the second row, where I am unfortunately seated, I can always smell it emanating from him.

He also has the absolute worst combover *ever*. He has like ten strands of hair combed over his bald spot. It's seriously hard to look at.

But the worst part is he's bad at explaining math. I

could deal with the smell and his bald head if he could only explain stuff better. His voice has like two levels: monotone and yelling. Monotone is what he uses when he's explaining math problems to us. Yelling is what he does when the class gets restless because nobody understands what he's talking about because he's bored us nearly to sleep. And yet, his tests are notoriously extremely difficult.

Right now, he's passing out exams. As he walks by me, I get a whiff of that moldy cheese smell, and it's all I can do to keep from pinching my nose with my fingertips. Instead, I breathe through my mouth.

After he passes by, Jade pokes me from the seat next to mine and makes a funny face. Well, at least she's not still mad at me from last night.

When Mr. Riordan gets to the last student, he hesitates. He looks down at the test paper in his hand, then frowns at the classroom.

"Did anyone get two test papers?" he asks.

Twenty-two kids shake their heads in unison.

He presses his lips together. "I thought I had one extra, but…"

He did have one extra. And now it's lying in the garbage in my bedroom.

Jade and I exchange looks. We would both be in a huge amount of trouble if he had any idea what really happened to that extra test paper. But nobody knows the truth except the two of us.

Mr. Riordan finally gives the student the last test,

but there's a troubled look on his face. It doesn't matter though. Absolutely anything could have happened to that extra test paper. He has no idea.

And he never will.

29

PRESENT DAY

"Y ou haven't changed at all, have you?"

Jade has her arms folded across her chest, and her lipstick is slightly smeared, which makes her look like she's wearing a perpetual sneer. Although to be fair, she actually *is* sneering at me.

"What?" I toss the copy of *Cider House Rules* on the sofa. "What did I do wrong?"

"Don't act so innocent. I saw the way you ratted out Will."

I look at her in surprise. "Did you know he wasn't taking his medications?"

Jade hesitates for a split second. "No, I didn't. But that's his right if he doesn't want to take them."

"Jade..."

"No, don't you dare lecture me." She holds up her hand—her fingernails are bitten down to the quick, covered in chipped dark purple nail polish. "You don't know what it's like to be on an antipsychotic. You have no idea the way it feels to be drugged up on Haldol. And the side effects… First, you feel like a zombie half the time. And the weight gain…"

"Jade…"

"And some of the side effects never go away," she says. "The last time I was at the hospital, I met this woman and because of the meds she was on, she can't stop smacking her lips. Every two seconds, smacking her freaking lips. And it's *permanent*. She'll be like that *forever*."

She still has her arms folded, and she's glaring at me, like it's my fault that poor woman can't stop smacking her lips.

"I did it to help him," I say.

"Because you think you always know better than everyone else, right?"

I flinch. "That is not true *at all*."

Jade taps her foot against the ground. She's wearing gray socks with no shoes, and there's a hole in the big toe on the right. "What do you think Dr. Beck would say if he found out that you had your own little problem with *hallucinations*?"

I swallow. "I don't. That would be a lie."

"Oh, please, Amy. It's *me*." She taps faster now, almost like a tic. "We both know how screwed up you are. You just don't want to be drugged up like what they did to me. And Will."

"I'm not like you," I croak. "I would *never* do something like what you did. *Never*. I'm not—"

I stop myself before I say the last word in that sentence, but it's too late. Jade already knows what I was going to say.

"You're not *crazy*?" She spits at me. "Is that what you were going to say? It was, wasn't it? That's what you think of me, isn't it? I'm just your crazy old friend from high school who messed up her whole life because she's just *so* crazy."

"Jade, come on…"

"No excuses!" She stomps her foot against the ground. "When we were kids, you were my best friend in the whole world. We promised each other we would be friends for the rest of our lives, and our kids would be friends. And *their* kids would be friends. And the second shit got real, you acted like you didn't even know me. Do you know how lonely it was when I first got hospitalized? How scary it was for me?"

She's being unfair. It's not like I didn't try to be there for her, despite what she did. But she made it so *difficult* for me. And what she did…

"I'm sorry," I say. "I should have tried harder. I… I was wrong."

She stands there in the middle of the room, considering my apology. "How about after I get out of here, we can have dinner sometime?"

"Oh," I say.

"You can meet my boyfriend," she says. "We can double with you and Cameron."

The smile I manage to paste on my lips feels very fake. "Cameron and I aren't going out anymore, remember?"

"Oh, well, then it can just be the two of us." She raises her eyebrows. "What do you say, Amy?"

I hesitate just a bit too long, and Jade's expression darkens. "Oh, I get it," she says. "Never mind."

"No, I want to do it," I insist, even though I'm absolutely lying. The last thing I want is to get sucked into Jade's web again. "I'm just really busy right now. I mean, medical school is a lot of work…"

"Of course. How could I forget?"

"Maybe in a few months, when my schedule calms down. Family medicine is supposed to be pretty light. Maybe then we could…"

"Forget it," Jade snaps. "You don't want to have dinner with me. You don't want to be my friend anymore. I can take a hint, believe me."

With those words, she storms off. Part of me wants to follow her but it's better to just leave it be. The thing is, she isn't wrong. When I think back to the early days when Jade and I were kids, I have so many good memories of our friendship. But then she changed. And there was no bringing her back.

I don't want to have dinner with Jade. I don't want to meet her boyfriend. I don't want to be her friend at all, honestly. I want to steer clear of her as much as humanly possible.

Worse, I don't entirely trust her. If there's one

thing I know about Jade, she'll do anything to get what she wants. I have to protect myself.

For my own safety, I have to know exactly what Jade is capable of.

And the only way to do that is to look at her chart.

30

Technically, I'm not doing anything wrong.

Jade is my patient this evening. Yes, we do have a prior relationship. But that was a very long time ago. And it's not like Jade told me I *couldn't* look at her chart. She seemed to assume I had already looked.

It's completely quiet at the nurses' station. Even Ramona has disappeared somewhere. And of course, Cameron is gone for the night. I can't even imagine what the family emergency could have been. I hope his parents are okay. I met them once, and his dad got short of breath just from walking up the steps to their front door. He looked like a walking heart attack.

I push away thoughts of my ex-boyfriend as I grab

for the chart in the rack labeled CARPENTER. I sit on one of the stools and spend a second just staring at the chart. This is it. Once I open this, I have crossed a line.

Then again, I've crossed lines before.

I flip to the first page, where the emergency room notes are stored. Sure enough, there are several pages from her initial intake. She came in the same day Will did, but her diagnosis is different. Jade's diagnosis is right at the top, and it hasn't changed from when we were sixteen: bipolar disorder type 1.

I start reading the entire sordid story of Jade's most recent manic adventure. Apparently, she was not alone on this one. She and her boyfriend decided to rob a string of banks in the area. She would be in jail right now facing theft charges, except the two of them were armed only with beer bottles that they were pointing at the poor bank clerks like weapons, and they didn't leave any of the banks with any actual money.

A typical manic episode for Jade. And apparently, this boyfriend of hers isn't exactly the best influence. Glad I said no to the double date.

I skim through a quick summary of Jade's prior hospitalizations, and the list makes me ill. When she first got hospitalized, my mother assured me she was going to get help and it would make her better. But it *hasn't* made her better. She's been in and out of the hospital every few months since we were teenagers.

She never managed to get her bipolar disorder under control.

Mental illness is really difficult to treat.

While I'm flipping through the chart, a noise comes from around the corner of the nurses' station. It's a sickening sound, like somebody is gagging or choking. And that's when I realize how quiet it has been since I've been sitting here. Ever since they locked Miguel in Seclusion Two, he's alternated between singing pop hits and yelling about Damon Sawyer. But now the singing has stopped. In fact, there's no sound at all from the seclusion rooms.

I abandon Jade's chart on the desk. I step out into the hallway, instinctively feeling for the knitting needle that Mary gave me and being reassured by its presence. There might be better weapons at the nurses' station, like a pair of scissors, but I would look like I was nuts if I started walking through the hallways, holding out a pair of scissors. Not that a knitting needle is any better.

I step through the dark hallway in the direction of the seclusion rooms. I hear that choking sound again, coming from Seclusion Two, and now it almost sounds like someone is gasping for air.

"Miguel?" I call out. "Are you okay?"

Then something emerges from the crack under the door. A dark liquid.

It's blood. And it's leaking out from under the door.

31

"**M**iguel!" I gasp.

I don't know what happened in Seclusion Two. Maybe Miguel harmed himself. I have no idea. But he's obviously bleeding in there. I've got to help him.

I start to punch in the code for the door, but then I hesitate. What if this is a trick? Or worse, what if Miguel is inside there with a knife and when I get the door open, he's going to do to me what he did to himself. Or worse.

No, I better not open the door. Not until I have Ramona or Dr. Beck with me.

I hurry around the circle to get to Dr. Beck's office. The light is off inside, which means he might be sleeping, but I don't even hesitate to knock on the door. I pound on it with the palm of my hand until he pulls it open, looking mildly irritated. His scrubs look crumpled and he's not wearing any shoes. He was clean-shaven at the beginning of the night, but now he's started to get a hint of stubble on his chin.

"Amy." He yawns loudly. "What's going on?"

"There's blood," I gasp. "It's leaking out from under the door of Seclusion Two."

Dr. Beck takes a moment to process what I just said. "What?"

"It's all over the floor." Tears prick at my eyes. "Something must've happened to Miguel. But I wasn't sure if I should open the door…"

He blinks a few times. "Wait. You said there's *blood* on the floor?"

"Yes…"

He squints at me. "Are you sure?"

"Yes!" I wipe my eyes. "Please come look."

Dr. Beck finally nods. "Okay, yes. Of course. Let me just… Let me get my shoes on. I just…"

He seems a bit disoriented, which I guess is fair considering I woke him up in the middle of the night. But then again, he's on-call. He should expect something like this. Well, maybe not exactly like *this*.

Dr. Beck shoves his feet into his sneakers and follows me around the hall to the seclusion rooms. My heart is pounding so hard, my chest hurts. I can't even imagine what is inside that room. There was so much blood on the floor. There's no way he's all right. Poor Miguel…

We're going to have to call 911. Or actually, I guess we're inside a hospital so there's no need to call

911. I'm sure he'll have to go straight to the emergency room. If he's alive at all.

Please let him be alive. Please.

Except when we get to the room, I get the shock of my life. On the floor outside Seclusion Two, there's absolutely nothing there.

No blood. *Nothing.*

Dr. Beck turns to look at me. "You said there was blood on the floor… here?"

I stare down at the floor, which is completely clean. There isn't even a trace of blood. Nothing that could be *mistaken* for blood.

What the hell?

I bite down on my lower lip. "Maybe it wasn't right here. Maybe it was…"

But it had to be here. It was outside the seclusion rooms. I know because I was trying the code to open the door. There's nowhere else it could have been. I'm not confused…

Except where is the blood? I *know* I saw blood.

Didn't I?

"Maybe you were dreaming?" Dr. Beck's eyebrows knit together. "It's very late, Amy…"

"Maybe…"

Except I wasn't dreaming. I saw it. I know I did…

"And there was a sound in there," I recall. "Like… a choking sound. And he's gotten so quiet. Like, remember how he kept screaming and singing? He stopped doing that."

"He probably went to sleep."

I squeeze my hands together. "Can we please check on him? I'm just really worried."

"Amy." Dr. Beck shakes his head. "If he's asleep, we should just leave him alone."

It's against my character, but I push past Dr. Beck and bang my fist on the door to Seclusion Two. "Miguel! Are you okay in there? Miguel!"

"Amy!" Dr. Beck looks affronted. I can't even remember the last time I saw his dimples—he's decidedly irritated with me. "Please! Miguel has been ramped up all night and he's finally calm. I'd strongly prefer it if you don't disturb him."

I step away from the door, breathing hard. I'm never going to convince Dr. Beck to open the door, especially since the blood on the floor has magically vanished. I have not exactly proven myself to be trustworthy.

"I just feel like if we could check on him, then at least we would know that—"

Dr. Beck's lips set into a straight line. "Amy, *enough*. Do *not* bother Miguel. I want you to go into one of the rooms and I want you to go to sleep for the rest of the night. It's been a long night with a lot of excitement. You are hereby relieved from your duties."

I'm itching to tell him my other suspicions about Seclusion One. About the strange noises I heard coming from there earlier in the night that seem to have somehow ceased. But I'm getting the feeling that he's not going to take anything I say seriously. And even to my own ears, it all sounds ridiculous. Maybe he's right. Maybe I do need to lie down and get some sleep.

"Okay." My shoulders sag. "I'll go lie down."

"Good."

Dr. Beck is staring at me. He's looking at me in a way that I have never wanted to be looked at. In a way that I have always feared.

Like he thinks I've lost my mind.

32

EIGHT YEARS EARLIER

"Amy, Jade… I'd like to see the two of you for a moment."

The dismissal bell had already rung, and I was packing up my books, getting ready to head home, when Mr. Riordan approached us. His arms are folded across his checkered shirt, and he's got slight pit stains on both sides. The smell of moldy cheese emanating from his pores is almost overpowering. I freeze in the middle of stuffing a notebook into my bag.

"Now?" I blurt out.

Mr. Riordan nods gravely.

I glance over at Jade, who doesn't even look the slightest bit worried. She scratches at her elbow and slides right back into her desk. She lifts her eyes to look at Mr. Riordan with a bored expression on her face. If I didn't know she had stolen that exam right out of his desk—if I hadn't seen it with my very own eyes—I would swear she hadn't done a thing wrong.

She did steal it, didn't she? I didn't just imagine the whole thing…

God, what's wrong with me lately?

I slide back into my own desk, an uneasy feeling in the pit of my stomach. Mr. Riordan is staring at the two of us, but mostly me. His scalp is sweaty, and the strands combed over his bald skull have become frizzy. One stray lock of hair slides down onto his forehead, turning itself into bangs.

"I want to talk to you about the midterm yesterday," Mr. Riordan begins. "About one of the test papers that was missing."

Oh no.

I hazard another look at Jade, who has the slightest hint of a smile playing on her lips. I want to smack it off her. It's her fault we're here right now. It was her stupid idea to steal that test.

"Did you find it?" Jade asks in a flat voice.

"I did not." He looks between the two of us. "And I was concerned about where it went. So I asked the janitor yesterday if any students were around here after hours the day before. And he described the two of you." He leans in closer and that moldy cheese smell makes me gag. "He told me he let you into the classroom."

"He got us mixed up with someone else." Jade waves a hand. "I'm sure we all look alike to him."

Mr. Riordan is quiet for a moment. "I showed him your photos in last year's yearbook."

My future flashes before my eyes. A failing grade would have been bad, but I could have come back from that. Stealing a test from a teacher's desk is cause for suspension, at the very least. It's the kind of thing that ends up on your permanent record. *Cheating.*

I see my entire future being flushed down the drain.

Jade, on the other hand, doesn't look worried. "Come on. That guy barely speaks English."

"Regardless." His lips twist into a sneer. "I will be referring this matter to the principal tomorrow morning. You can explain to him why you were snooping around my classroom right before a test went missing."

With those words, Mr. Riordan returns to his desk and starts gathering his belongings. I want to do the same, but my body feels frozen. I watch him lean over, the buttons on his shirt straining over his gut. Of all the teachers who could catch us stealing an exam, he is easily the worst. There won't be any leniency from this man.

When I finally manage to get to my feet, my legs wobble beneath me. I'm not even sure if I can make it out of the room, but somehow I get to the door on my own steam. Jade doesn't seem nearly as shaken. She waits for me outside the classroom, studying her nails, which are coated in a layer of chipped glittery gold nail polish.

She squints up at me. "You okay, Amy?"

"No, I am not okay," I snip at her. I grab her by the arm and haul her down to the end of the hallway, out of earshot of Mr. Riordan. "We are in big trouble. You know that, right?"

Jade snorts. "What are you so worried about? You didn't look at the test. If you bombed it, then how can he claim you cheated, right?"

And then I'm quiet.

"Amy!" Jade cackles at me—it's maddening how amused she is. "You didn't! Oh my God, after that fuss you made about how it was wrong to cheat, blah blah blah, then you went and looked at the test?"

"I didn't want to fail," I mumble.

I would have failed if I hadn't rifled through the garbage in my bedroom and pulled out the copy of the test Jade brought me. At the time, it seemed like the right thing to do. But I should've gone with my gut. An honest F would have been better than what's about to happen to me.

Anyway, it's irritating that Jade won't stop laughing.

"This isn't funny!" I cry. "Jade, do you realize how screwed we are? We're going to get suspended for sure. Maybe expelled."

"Nah." She lifts a shoulder. "I doubt it."

My face grows warm. "Maybe you don't care, but I actually have plans for my life. I want to go to college and medical school. I don't want to get kicked out of high school for cheating, okay?"

"Right, and I'm just a loser with no future, so what do I care?"

Hurt fills Jade's delicate features. If it were any other time, I'd feel bad about what I said. But I don't feel bad right now. This is all her fault.

"You know," she says, "you shouldn't act so superior. You're more like me than you think."

For some reason, thoughts of that little girl pop into my head. I saw her again this morning. She was in the bathroom while I was brushing my teeth. She didn't say anything this time. She just watched me for a moment, and after I spit out the toothpaste, I looked up and she was gone.

If I tell anyone what I've been seeing, I don't know what will happen. I was looking it up on the internet last night. *What does it mean when you're seeing things that aren't there?*

The answers went from bad to horrible. It could be an issue with my vision, although that doesn't explain why the little girl was talking to me. Or I could have epilepsy. I could have a brain tumor.

Or I could be developing schizophrenia.

And if that's the case, what kind of future do I have ahead of me?

"This will blow over," Jade says. "I'm sure of it."

"I'm not so sure," I mutter.

"Look." Jade levels her gaze at me. "I told you I'd help you with the exam, and I did, didn't I? Well, now I'm telling you that this is going to be fine. Don't worry about it. I'll take care of everything. I promise."

Jade will take care of everything? What does that even *mean*? How could anyone possibly fix this situation?

I'm pretty sure my life as I know it is over, and my future is screwed.

33

PRESENT DAY

It's only after Dr. Beck has gone back to his office that I realize Jade has witnessed our entire encounter.

She's been watching from the doorway to her room, leaning against the frame, an amused look on her face. Her lipstick is still smeared, and now so is her mascara. The light is off in her room, and her face is glowing under the dim hall lights.

"So," she says, "you're still seeing things then."

"No." I shiver in my scrubs. "I'm not."

"Okay, so.... you didn't just hallucinate a pool of blood in the hallway?"

There's nothing I can say to that. She's right. I did imagine a pool of blood in the hallway. It looked so real. But now I can clearly see that there's no blood there. There isn't even anything that could be mistaken for blood.

I can't believe this is happening to me. Not again.

"And you hear things too," she says. "Don't you?"

My knees almost buckle beneath me. Since I set foot on this unit, I've been hearing noises coming from Seclusion One. Noises that nobody else seems to hear or be bothered by. So does that mean…?

"You should have gotten help when we were sixteen," Jade says. "You could have. You could've been honest with everyone."

"I'm fine," I say weakly. "Okay, I was… I was having issues for a little while. But it passed. Maybe it was… I don't know, hormonal."

"Hormonal!" Jade bursts out. "Oh, Amy. Is that really the lie you're telling yourself?"

"Keep your voice down…"

"You shouldn't be ashamed of who you are."

"At least I didn't rob a bank with a beer bottle!"

Jade's eyes widen, and for a moment, I'm scared I've gone too far. But then she throws her head back and laughs. "Oh my God, I *knew* you were going to read my chart eventually. You're so predictable!"

"Yeah, well…"

She winks at me. "If I give you a chance, you always end up doing the wrong thing."

I grunt. "I'm going to try to get some sleep. I… I must just be tired and that's why I thought I saw the blood."

"Yes, just keep telling yourself that…"

Jade is still chuckling to herself as I walk away from her, back to the staff lounge. I want to shrug off her comments, but it's hard. I was so sure I saw blood on the floor. But it wasn't there. I can't argue with that.

And I also can't argue that it isn't the first time I have seen something that wasn't there.

When I get back to the lounge, the lights are out. I frown, trying to remember whether I turned them off or not. No, I'm sure I left them on. I remember thinking to myself that I didn't want to return to a dark room, and that's why I made a point of keeping them on.

Of course, it's entirely possible Ramona came by and shut the lights off. Preserving electricity, and all that. It doesn't necessarily mean anything.

And then I see him.

The dark figure in the corner of the room. Waiting for me. And the door slams shut.

I don't even have time to scream.

34

Will's hand is on my mouth, nearly cutting off my air.

I wonder how long he's been waiting for me in this room. The best I can say is he doesn't seem to have a weapon. And when his hazel eyes meet mine through his glasses, there's no malice there. If anything, he looks just as scared as I do.

"Please don't scream," he says. "I just need to talk to you."

I stare at him, tempted to try to bite his fingers keeping pressure on my lips. Finally, I nod my head. As he pulls his shaky hand off my mouth, I eye the doorway, wondering how long it would take me to get there from where I'm standing. But Will is bigger and faster than I am—he could stop me if he wanted to.

"I'm sorry," he says. "But I needed to talk to you. In private."

"Okay…"

He glances at the closed door, then back at my face. "I saw the blood on the floor too."

That is the last thing I expected him to say. "What?"

"It was *there*." A deep crease settles between his eyebrows. "It happened just like you told Dr. Beck. The blood leaked out from under the door, and I could hear Miguel making sounds like he was... I don't know... like he was *dying* or something. Choking to death. Like someone cut his throat."

All notions of running out of the room fly from my head. I sink onto the sofa, my thoughts running a mile a minute. "So what happened to the blood then?"

"That nurse Ramona got rid of it."

I suck in a breath. "*What?*"

"She came and cleaned it all up while you were grabbing Dr. Beck," he says. "I saw her do it. She came out real quick as soon as you left, cleaned up the blood, and then she was gone before you got back and Dr. Beck could see it."

My head is spinning. "Why would she do something like that?"

Will starts pacing across the room. "I don't know. I don't know what the hell is going on here tonight. Honestly, I'm getting kind of freaked out."

I don't know what to think right now. It would be one thing if Cameron were here and told me he saw the blood. But what am I supposed to think when the only person who saw what I saw is a guy with paranoid schizophrenia who hasn't been taking his medications? And right now, Will is looking a lot more like the person that was described in his emergency room notes. His hair is sticking up, and his hazel eyes look wild.

He stops pacing and stares at me. "You don't believe me."

I play with the drawstring of my scrubs. It's time to tell him the truth. "I know you haven't been taking your medications. I found them hidden in your copy of *The World According to Garp.*"

He drops his eyes. "Oh."

"So, you know, it's kind of hard to take what you're saying at face value."

He nods slowly. "Okay, I can see why you would feel that way. But honestly, I don't think I need those medications. The voices… they got better on their own. It must've been… you know, one of those things."

"One of those *things*?"

"Look." He grits his teeth. "I *wanted* to take the medications, okay? I took them in the emergency room, but… you really feel shitty on them. I couldn't handle it. The side effects…"

I don't know what to say to that.

"I saw that blood," he insists. "I didn't hallucinate the blood, and neither did you. It was there. I mean, even if you don't trust me, why don't you trust *yourself*?"

Will is looking at me intently, searching my face

for answers. He doesn't understand, and I'm not about to explain to him anything about my history.

"I'm just…" I rub my temples with my fingertips. "I'm tired. I don't know what I'm thinking anymore."

"Well, I'll tell you something else you might not have thought about." He settles down on the sofa beside me. "That other med student—what was his name? Carter?"

"Cameron…"

"Right." He drops his voice a notch. "I heard him screaming."

"*What?*"

"Right." His eyes dart over to the door, a fearful expression on his face. "And it was *hours* ago."

"But… where?"

"I heard it from my room," he says. "And then here's the really crazy part…" He takes a deep breath. "When I came out to the hall to see what was going on, I think I saw the door to Seclusion One slamming shut."

I feel like somebody just punched me in the gut. "What? Are you sure?"

"I'm not sure," he admits. "I said I *think* I saw it. It all happened really fast. But if the door to that room was open, then…"

He doesn't have to complete the thought. If the door to Seclusion One was open, then that means Damon Sawyer got out. And I can't even wrap my head around that possibility, considering how dangerous Dr. Beck warned us he was.

"I was hoping I imagined the whole thing," Will says. "But then when he didn't show up to that whole deal with Miguel, I got worried that something happened to him."

I lean back against the couch, trying to calm my racing thoughts. "Cameron went home. He had a family emergency."

"He told you that?"

"No. He left a message on Dr. Beck's voicemail."

Will arches an eyebrow. "And do you think Cameron is the kind of person who would do that? Just leave a voicemail message and take off?"

Maybe. If something spooked him…

"Let me try to call him," I say. I leap off the couch and cross the room to get to the landline in the corner of the room. Of course, I don't know Cameron's number by heart, but thankfully, I didn't delete him from my phone in anger, although I was sorely tempted. I bring up his number on the screen, and I pick up the receiver.

There's no dial tone.

Will is sitting on the couch, watching me, his expression neutral. "The phones aren't working," I report.

"Yes," he says. "I know. They stopped working when the power went out."

Damn Miguel—why did he have to urinate on that light socket?

"Something is going on here," Will says. "Don't you think so?"

I have to admit, he's building a very strong case. But I have to remember that I am talking to a man with paranoid schizophrenia. A man who has been hearing voices telling him to do terrible things, and he has decided it wasn't necessary for him to take his medications. Of *course* he's going to think something suspicious is going on. That's part of his disease. But there's some kind of rational explanation for everything. There's *got* to be.

"I need to talk to Cameron." I check my phone screen. Naturally, there's no service.

"The only way you're going to get any service on your phone is if you leave the unit," Will points out.

He's right. If I pop out for a minute, I can call Cameron and confirm that he's fine and this is all just craziness.

"Fine," I say.

Will follows me out of the staff lounge, over to the locked door to Ward D. The hallway is so dark over here that the glowing green light of the keypad looks almost unearthly. I don't need to check the code, because I know it by heart. 347244. I've been reciting it to myself all night in case I need to get out of here.

"What are you waiting for?" Will says.

He's standing behind me, shifting his weight between his feet, which are covered in thick white socks, no shoes. His hands are opening and closing repeatedly. He looks like he can't stop moving.

It hits me that maybe this is all a trick on Will's part. What if he came to me and told me all that stuff just to get me to open the door to Ward D? Because he wants out, and he knows I'm the only one stupid enough to open the door.

But no, I don't think that's what it is. Will brought up some really good points. And anyway, he's here voluntarily. He was the one who came to the emergency room telling them he was hearing the voices. If he didn't want to be here, he didn't have to come.

I take a deep breath and punch the code into the keypad.

35

A fter I punch in the final number of the code, I expect to hear that loud alarm noise and a click as the door unlocks. But instead, all I hear is a soft buzzing noise.

I must've punched in the wrong code.

I type it in again this time, trying to steady my shaking hands. 347244. That's it. That's the code Dr. Beck typed in this morning. I could recite it in my sleep.

Except when I type it in again, I only hear that soft buzzing sound.

What is going on here?

"It's not working," I report to Will.

He rakes a hand through his hair. "Are you sure you have the right code?"

"I… I think so…" I pulled my phone out of my pocket to check the code I recorded in the notepad.

347244. I try it one more time. "I guess I have it wrong…"

"Jesus Christ," Will breathes. "This is…"

"Look," I say, "I'll go talk to Ramona. I'll ask her about the blood on the floor, and she'll tell me what the code is. I must've gotten it wrong but… I'm sure she knows it."

"And you trust her?"

Will says it in a way that makes it sound like I would be an idiot to respond in the affirmative. But I have to remind myself again that paranoia is part of his diagnosis. Of course he's going to come up with some wild conspiracy theory. When in reality, there probably is a logical explanation for all of this.

"I trust her," I say.

"Don't let her gaslight you." Will scratches at the thick stubble on his chin. "That blood was *there*. You and I both saw it."

"Right…"

He stands there for a moment, but then he gets it that I'm not going to let him follow me while I talk to Ramona. After all, if I show up with him, I'll lose all credibility. He takes a step back, holding his hands in the air. "Just let me know what you find out."

I don't answer him, but he seems to accept that and walks off back to his room. As he passes Seclusion Two, he stares down at the floor, at the exact place where all the blood was staining the tiles just a short time ago. It was everywhere, and then suddenly, it was gone.

I want so badly for there to be an answer besides just that I'm seeing things that aren't there. Maybe Ramona can give me that answer.

I start making a circle around the unit. I pass the two seclusion rooms, which are both dead silent. Of course, it is the middle of the night. Practically everyone is asleep.

When I get to the staff bathroom, a flush comes from inside. I let out a breath. That's got to be Ramona. And sure enough, after the water runs for long enough for somebody to sing "happy birthday," Ramona emerges from the bathroom.

"Amy!" She clutches a hand to her chest. "My God, you startled me!"

"Sorry," I mumble.

She squints at me in the dark hallway. "Are you all right? You look a little…"

"I'm fine," I say before she can complete her thought. I don't even want to know how I look right now. "I just… I need to ask you something."

Ramona smiles at me. She looks maddeningly perky for this hour of the night, but I guess she's used to the night shift. "Sure."

I point off in the direction of the seclusion rooms. "Were you cleaning blood off the floor in the hallway?"

"*Blood?*" She looks like she's about to choke. "Absolutely not!"

Oh God. I really did imagine it.

Unless she's lying.

"There was some strawberry jelly I noticed on the floor," she says. "Quite a bit, actually. So I did grab the mop to clean all that up. Miguel really made quite a mess, didn't he?"

"Strawberry jelly?"

"Yes." She tugs at the collar of her flower-printed scrubs. "That stuff got everywhere, didn't it? But I think I got the last of it, thank goodness."

Strawberry jelly. Could that really have been *strawberry jelly* on the floor? It certainly didn't look like it. And I was *sure* that I saw it flowing from underneath the door.

Didn't I?

"You thought that was *blood*?" Ramona bursts out laughing. "Oh, Amy, honey. You need to get some sleep."

A wave of dizziness washes over me. She's right. I do need to sleep. But I have a feeling that if I try, I'm just going to lie awake, staring at the ceiling.

"Do you…" I shift between my sneakers. "Could you tell Dr. Beck that there was something on the floor that you cleaned up?" I want him to know that I didn't completely imagine the incident—that I'm not insane.

Ramona squints at me. "You want to wake up Dr. Beck in the middle of the night and tell him that I cleaned up some strawberry jelly from the floor?"

Well, when she puts it that way…

"Listen," I say. "I need to get some fresh air."

She nods sympathetically. "Yes, I agree."

"But when I tried the code for the door to the unit, it didn't work!" I glance over my shoulder. "Could you help me get out? I'll be right back."

That's a lie. As soon as that door opens, I'm gone. At this point, I would rather flunk out of medical school than come back here.

Ramona tilts her head to the side. "Oh, Amy, I wish I could. But when the fuse blew, the doors reset. The passcode doesn't seem to work anymore. And the phones went out too. Unfortunately, we may be stuck here until the morning."

My stomach sinks. "There's no other way? I mean, we have to have a way out. What if there's a fire?"

"Believe me, I'm not happy about this," Ramona says. "But with the computer system down for the night undergoing maintenance, I'm not sure what we can do. We just better hope there isn't a fire, right?"

I don't love that answer. But she's got a point. If the phones are down and the code on the door reset, what can we do besides wait for the morning crew to arrive?

I just hope we make it till then.

36

I consider not saying anything to Will about my conversation with Ramona, but I suspect he's pacing his room, stewing about the blood on the hallway floor. I owe it to him to ease his mind. So as soon as I'm done talking to Ramona, I head over to his room.

Before I knock, I glance over at the room next to his. Room 905. Jade's room. I haven't seen her since she berated me for telling Dr. Beck about the blood in the hallway. I wonder what she would think about Will's theories.

I have a feeling she wouldn't think much of it. After all, she knows he's off his medications.

I've barely knocked on the door when Will pulls it open, as if he were standing behind the door, just waiting for me. He looks down at me with his blood-shot eyes, and I remind myself that Will himself is not entirely benign. This is a man who has been hearing voices for God knows how long, and those voices have been telling him to kill people. He's paranoid and coming up with conspiracy theories in his head. Although he looked fine at the beginning of the night, as the hours tick by, he's looking increasingly disheveled.

He's becoming unraveled.

And while he's not exactly muscular like Cameron, he's got at least half a foot of height on me and quite a bit of strength as well. Even without a weapon, he could easily overpower me.

I need to be careful.

"Hey," I say. "I talked to Ramona."

"I heard."

Of course he did. I would be surprised if he *weren't* creeping around the hallways, listening in on conversations. "So it sounds like it was just strawberry jelly. Nothing to worry about."

"You've got to be kidding me." He shakes his head. "*Strawberry jelly?* That was *blood*, Amy. We both freaking saw it! She was lying to you."

"Why would she lie?"

"I don't know." He rakes both hands through his hair, and I can see how much he's shaking. "Listen, Amy…"

"What?"

Will stands there for a moment. He seems to be struggling with some sort of internal conflict. "Nothing. Never mind."

"You should go to sleep," I tell him. "I'm going to do the same."

He snorts. "You really think you're going to be able to fall asleep?"

It seems incredibly unlikely. "Well, in that case, I'll just read the *Cider House Rules* the rest of the night." I pause. "I would have loved to read *Garp* tonight if you hadn't defaced it."

Will's lips turn down. "You have to know, I never would've done that if I didn't have a good reason."

Of course, he had a good reason. He didn't want to take his pills and get better.

"Good night, Will," I say.

He gives me a long look. "Promise you'll be careful."

"Of course I will."

I turn around to leave, but Will lingers in the doorway to his room. He's watching me walk away. It's only as I'm about to round the corner that I turn around for a moment to see if he's still standing there.

Except for some reason, instead of 906, it looks like it's the door to room *905* swinging closed. Jade's room.

But I must have imagined it. After all, why would Will be going into Jade's room?

37

EIGHT YEARS EARLIER

I've got a test tomorrow in American history, and I really should be studying for it, but instead, I'm sipping on peach iced tea and watching television.

I mean, what's the point? I'm going to get kicked out of school anyway, whether or not I ace this exam tomorrow. So I may as well enjoy a little Netflix instead of learning all the details of World War I.

"Amy?" My mother is suddenly standing over me, peering down at me through her half-moon glasses. "Are you all right?"

Well, let's see. I got caught cheating and I'm probably going to get expelled. Also, I'm seeing this little girl who doesn't actually exist and who keeps urging me to do bad things. But other than that, I'm doing absolutely fabulous. Thanks for asking, Mom!

"I'm fine," I say.

"Did you ever connect with Jade?" she asks me.

"Kind of," I mutter, not taking my eyes off the television.

A deep crease burrows between her eyebrows. "Amy, is something going on with Jade? If there is, you can tell me. I can help."

"Nope."

She settles down beside me on the couch. "The teenage years are a really hard time. A lot of girls struggle. And it can be a time when mental health issues come to the surface…"

I look up sharply at the mention of mental health issues. "What do you mean?"

"Amy…" Mom rubs a finger along her jaw. "I never told you this before, but Jade's mom… She has struggled a lot with her mental health. And these sorts of things can run in families. So I worry that Jade…"

"Jade's fine," I say, a little too sharply.

It's not a lie. I mean, she has definitely changed a lot in the last couple of years. Her behavior has been increasingly bizarre. But Jade isn't the one who's hallucinating. That's me.

"Are you sure there isn't anything you want to tell me?" my mother presses me.

I don't want to tell her any of the things going on with me. Part of me is hoping that I'll go to bed tonight, and when I wake up, everything will be better again.

I can't tell her the truth though. I don't want her to look at me the way she looks at Jade. If she finds out I'm the one hallucinating, will she still love me as much? She's always told me how proud she is of me and my good grades. She won't be proud of me anymore when she knows the truth.

"I don't feel like talking," I say. "I need some fresh air."

Before my mother can protest, I grab the remote and flip off the television. I pick up my bottle of iced tea and head outside. I wait a bit at the front door to see if my mother will follow me, but she doesn't. I'm not sure whether or not to be disappointed.

The winter has finally come to an end and it's turned into one of those really pretty spring days. The sun has dropped on the horizon, and the whole sky has turned shades of red, orange, and yellow. See, even if I'm crazy I can still enjoy a nice sunset.

Until I hear the loud honking.

I rotate my head just in time to see Jade pull up in her mother's old Dodge, which is a couple dozen miles away from falling apart completely. One of the side view mirrors is literally hanging on by a single wire, and there isn't one portion of either the front or back fender that doesn't have a dent in it.

"Amy!" she calls out.

I just stare at her, clutching the bottle of iced tea in my right hand.

"Amy!" She leans on the horn loud enough to get a dog barking next door. "I need to talk to you."

"I have nothing to say to you."

"I know you're mad at me." She tucks a wayward

strand of blond hair behind her ear. "But I fixed everything. I made it right again."

I try not to roll my eyes, but it's hard. "I'm sure."

"I did! I swear to you, Amy."

Jade's blue eyes flecked with yellow are leveled at me. She's not smiling like she's making a joke. She means it. Except I don't know how she could've fixed any of this.

"How?" I finally say.

"Get in the car." She nods at the passenger's seat. "I'll show you."

Every fiber of my being is telling me not to get into Jade's Dodge. But at the same time, I must admit that I'm curious. When Jade is determined to do something, she's very good at making it happen.

So I open up the passenger side door, climb into the car, and before I've even got my seatbelt buckled, she zooms away.

38

I decide to go to the patient lounge this time to try to sleep, if only because the couch looks a little more comfortable. There are fewer springs visibly sticking out of the cushions. Maybe I'll be able to sleep there.

There are plenty of empty patient rooms available with perfectly good beds and even blankets folded on top of them. But I'm not spending the night in a patient room. I'm *not*.

The patient lounge has a bathroom inside of it, and I make a pit stop there. But when I flip on the lights in the bathroom, I almost pass out. I don't know what happened to me in the last few hours, but I look *terrible*. My hair has come partially loose from its pony-tail, and the stray strands are wild and frizzy around my face. My eyes are just as bloodshot as Will's, and there are dark purple circles underneath. No wonder Dr. Beck and Ramona seemed so concerned.

If I were to fall asleep in one of the rooms, I could easily be mistaken for a patient. All I'm missing is the wristband.

I get a jolt of fear at the thought of having that laminated bracelet around my wrist, revealing my name, medical record number, and date of birth, and declaring me to be a patient of the hospital. For one dizzying moment, I wonder if I've got it all wrong. What if…?

No. Stop it, Amy. Stop worrying—you're fine.

I lift my left wrist. There's no wristband there. I take a few deep breaths, forcing myself to calm down. I'm fine. I'm going to be *fine*. I just need to get through the rest of the night.

After I empty my bladder, I splash some water on my face, although it doesn't help. What I need more than anything is some sleep. And to get out of here.

I wish Cameron hadn't left. I don't believe Will's paranoid theory about him vanishing into one of the seclusion rooms. I'm sure he just had a family emergency and left. That's by far the more logical explanation.

But at the same time, why didn't he tell me he was leaving? He knew how freaked out I was. Why would he leave without even saying goodbye?

There are plenty of negative things I could say about Cameron. But he's not the kind of person who would do that.

I step out of the bathroom and make my way to the sofa. Thankfully, there's a folded blanket lying on the side of it. I shake out the blanket, which is more of a quilt and not even long enough to cover my entire five-foot-four frame. But it's better than nothing.

I curl up on the sofa. And to my surprise, my eyelids start to droop. I might actually fall asleep. It's a small miracle.

Except just as my eyes have started to drift closed, I hear footsteps.

At first, I can almost ignore it. But then they start getting louder and louder. Until I'm convinced that there is somebody right outside the room. And then the footsteps stop.

I scramble off the sofa, clutching the quilt. I stare at the closed door to the lounge. "Hello?" I call out.

No answer. Of course.

I creep across the room to the door. I press my ear against the door. I hear only silence.

I place my hand on the doorknob. My fingers linger there, while I work up the nerve to twist the knob. I count to three in my head, then I push it open.

The hallway right outside the lounge is completely dark, except for the glowing light from the keypad to the locked exit. I squint into the black corners, but I don't see any hovering figures, waiting to pounce. I don't see anything.

"Hello?" I call out one more time. I clear my throat. "Mr. Sawyer?"

No answer.

There's nobody out here. Nobody I can see, anyway. Or should I say, nobody who wants me to see him. I slam the door shut, wishing to God there was a lock on it. I dart back across the room to the sofa and bury myself under the quilt.

I'm never going to fall asleep. It's impossible. No matter how tired I am, there's just no way.

And those are my last thoughts before I drift off.

39

HOURS UNTIL MORNING: 4

When I open my eyes, somebody is standing over me.

It's a silhouette of a man. His outline is visible in the moonlight coming through the window. I clutch the quilt to my chest, almost too terrified to scream.

And then I realize who it is.

"Mr. Ludwig?" I say.

Spider-Dan is standing over me, apparently watching me sleep. This man is the craziest person on Ward D, with the possible exception of Damon Sawyer. I squirm on the couch, my fingers feeling around for the knitting needle that is still lodged in my pocket.

"Don't worry," Spider-Dan says in his monotone. "I won't let him hurt you."

That's when I realize that Spider-Dan is perched in a superhero pose, his fists punched into his hips, and his legs spread apart. He has a determined expression on his face.

"What are you talking about?" I yawn. I can't believe I managed to fall asleep. "Won't let who hurt me?"

Spider-Dan does not budge from his pose. "Damon Sawyer. I won't let him get to you."

"Um," I say. "Thank you. But I think I'm okay. I don't think he wants to hurt me."

I'm proud of myself for thinking logically. A few hours ago, a statement like that would have freaked me out. But now that I have a couple of hours of sleep under my belt, I can be more realistic. Damon Sawyer is locked in Seclusion One. He's not going to hurt anyone.

"Yes, he does," Spider-Dan insists.

I stretch on the sofa, and a joint cracks in my neck. "Why do you think that?"

"Because he told me so."

"What?" Any good feelings I gained from my nap instantly disappear. Yes, this man is delusional. I mean, I can't trust anyone who thinks he can shoot webs out of his wrists. But he's being awfully specific. "What are you talking about?"

"He came to my room," Spider-Dan explains.

"He was looking for you, but I didn't tell him where you are. I won't let him hurt you."

"Wait." Any possibility of ever falling back asleep has officially left the building. "He was specifically looking for me?"

"You're Amy, aren't you?"

Oh my God. I am officially creeped out. How could Damon Sawyer be looking for *me*? He doesn't even know who I am! I just came here for the first time earlier in the evening! Why would he be looking for me?

And why isn't he locked in Seclusion One?

"He's locked up," I tell Spider-Dan.

"No, he's not." He gives me a meaningful look. "He got out earlier tonight."

Oh my God. Oh my God, oh my God, oh my God.

I jump off the couch, tossing the quilt aside. Maybe I'm overreacting—certainly Spider-Dan is not a credible source. But I heard the same thing from Will. Not to mention all the blood on the floor, which I'm still not entirely convinced was strawberry jelly. And the noise inside Seclusion One has gone suspiciously silent.

But before I can think about it, an ear-piercing sound breaks into my thoughts.

It's a woman screaming.

40

I have two choices when I hear the screams. Either I can hide or I can see what's going on.

I decide to check it out. It's an uncharacteristically brave choice on my part, but I need to know what's going on. And the screams sound disturbingly familiar.

It's very clear where the noise is coming from. Several patients have gathered in the hallway to watch the show, which consists of Mary Cummings standing outside her room and screaming at the top of her lungs. All the veins are standing out in her neck.

"Damon Sawyer!" she screams as spittle flies from her lips. "Damon Sawyer!"

It takes both Dr. Beck and Ramona to restrain her. For a woman of almost eighty years old, she sure has a lot of energy. She's got one of those steel knitting needles gripped in her right hand, and Ramona has to wrestle it loose. It clatters to the floor and rolls away.

"Damon Sawyer is going to kill all of you!" she screams at her audience. "He'll do it! He's going to kill every single one of you!"

I remember Dr. Beck described this very behavior at the beginning of the shift. Sundowning, he called it —when, in the evening, an elderly person becomes confused and agitated. Well, now I'm seeing it in action.

"Mary." Dr. Beck is speaking through his teeth as he and Ramona back her into her room. "You need to calm down, Mary. Please."

"I will not!" Mary shrieks. She addresses the crowd surrounding her. "He's going to do it! We need to stop him! He's evil! An evil, sadistic man!"

"Ramona." Dr. Beck turns to look at the nurse. "You pulled the IM Ativan?"

Ramona nods. "Let's get her in the bed first."

"No!" Mary howls. She looks wildly at the crowd, and her eyes finally rest on me. "Amy! Amy, you've got to stop him! Please!"

I back up, not sure what to say. I look around for help. Clint Eastwood is standing nearby, his bushy eyebrows bunched together, clutching the paper bag of saltines for dear life. My eyes briefly pause on Will and Jade, standing at the periphery of the crowd. And strangely, Jade's hand is resting on Will's shoulder.

"No!" Mary is screaming so loud, her vocal cords are straining. "Please no! Please don't do this!"

But Dr. Beck and Ramona have managed to ease her back into the room. Ramona kicks the door closed behind her, and just like that, the show is over.

Most of the patients shuffle back off to their rooms. Jade and Will are still standing at the periphery of the crowd. Jade's eyes meet mine for a split second, and she pulls her hand off Will's shoulder.

That was awfully strange.

Will and Jade walk back to their rooms. He disappears inside 906, and she goes into 905. But even after their doors are closed, I keep looking in that direction. It's strange how the two of them seemed to have some kind of familiarity with one another. Ward D doesn't have group sessions, and neither of them have been here even a full week. So there's no reason why they would have become friends during such a short period of time.

And when I discovered Will wasn't taking his medications and told Dr. Beck about it, Jade was the one who yelled at me. She accused me of betraying him. Except I never quite understood why she cared so much about a complete stranger.

I think back to what I read in Jade's chart. She was going from bank to bank, robbing them with a beer bottle. But she wasn't alone. According to the chart, she went on her crime spree with her boyfriend. Who presumably came to the hospital at the exact same time she did.

The same night Will was admitted to the emergency room.

Oh my God.

Will is Jade's boyfriend.

41

EIGHT YEARS EARLIER

I have no idea where we're going.

Jade is driving way too fast. She's going too fast, and she's got the radio blasting at a deafening volume. I wonder what Mrs. Carpenter would say if she knew Jade was driving so fast in her car. Then again, I doubt Jade's mother would care.

Jade's mom has struggled a lot with her mental health.

And these sorts of things can be hereditary.

I squirm in my seat, adjusting the seatbelt, which might be the only thing that keeps me from flying through the windshield if Jade crashes into another car or a tree. I look out the window, watching as she flies through the residential neighborhood. This doesn't look familiar to me at all.

"Where are we going?" I ask for the tenth time.

"Quit asking. We're almost there."

I take a swig from my peach iced tea. My right

temple throbs faintly. I should never have gotten in the car. Soon the sun will be down and my mom is going to *freak out* when I'm not home. I had no idea we would be going this far.

But then the Dodge abruptly skids to a halt. She pulls up in front of a white house that looks like it has seen better days. The outside is made of wooden panels, and the paint is badly chipped. The lawn in front of the house is all sparse patches of dying grass. I get this awful sinking feeling in my chest. I should never have come here.

"Here we are!" Jade announces.

Uh….

"Where are we?" I crane my neck to get a better look at the house. "Whose house is this?"

Jade winks at me. "You'll see."

Jade climbs out of the car and I reluctantly follow her. Except she doesn't go down the walkway to the front door. Instead, she walks down the driveway to the back entrance. There's a screen door flapping in the wind and she yanks it open, then pulls open the inner door as well. I watch as she steps inside the house.

"Come on, Amy!" She waves for me to follow her. "In here."

I shouldn't follow her. This is a mistake. I should get out of here and run home.

Jade gestures more vigorously. "Come *on*."

"All right," I say. "But just for a minute."

I step through some wayward grass that has

grown into the pathway to the back door. I climb the three steps and pass through the entrance to the kitchen. And that's when I realize whose house this is.

My mouth falls open. The peach iced tea I have been holding in my right hand drops to the floor, spilling brown liquid all over the grimy kitchen tiles, intermingling with the droplets of crimson. And I realize at that moment that I will never ever be able to drink peach iced tea ever again. That I will become ill at the very thought of it.

"Ta-da!" Jade says, and she bursts into giggles.

Oh no. This is worse than I could have imagined.

42

PRESENT DAY

Dr. Beck and Ramona emerge from Mary's room about ten minutes later, looking worse for wear. Ramona's hair has come nearly undone from her bun, and Dr. Beck has a long red scratch on his forearm.

"Jesus," Dr. Beck declares. "That's the worst I've ever seen her."

I stare at the closed door to Mary's room. "Is she okay?"

Dr. Beck nods. "She's finally calm, thank God. I don't think she'll give us more trouble the rest of the night. But starting tomorrow, she should be on a higher dose of Seroquel at bedtime. We don't need another episode like that."

I chew on my lower lip. "Should I check on her? She and I were talking a lot earlier, and she trusts me."

"Leave her alone," Ramona says. "She's drifting off to sleep."

"But—"

"I know you're eager to help, Amy," Dr. Beck says. "But when they get like this, there's no reasoning with them. She won't even know who you are."

That's not true. She saw me in a crowd and was calling out my name. She knew exactly who I was.

Ramona picks the steel knitting needle off the floor and holds it up. "My God, I thought she was going to stab me in the eye with this thing. These are *not* the children's safety needles we approved. How the hell did she get this?"

Of course, it doesn't surprise me at all that Mary somehow managed to get her hands on a real knitting needle and make the switch. She was resourceful like that. Too bad it didn't pay off in the end.

Dr. Beck scribbles a quick note which he stuffs in the chart, then he heads back to his office, leaving Ramona and me behind. Ramona has Mary's chart open, and she is writing her own note.

"Ramona," I say. "Can I ask you a question?"

"Sure," she says without looking up.

"Are there any… couples among the patients on the unit?"

She stops writing and looks up at me this time. "Are you asking if anyone is *hooking up*?"

"Well…" I glance across the hall, at rooms 905 and 906, right next to each other. The perfect proximity for a booty call. "I was just wondering about Carpenter and Schoenfeld…"

"Oh!" She laughs. "Yes, those two are definitely an item."

Wow. Jade lied right to my face. Well, she technically didn't lie, but she omitted a piece of very important information. She even suggested Cameron and I get together with her and her "boyfriend" without bothering to mention who her boyfriend was.

For all I know, it was Jade's idea for him to cut that hole in his book and hide his pills inside.

Of course, Will lied about it too. When I was asking him questions, I specifically asked about relationships, and he told me he wasn't involved with anyone. *This isn't exactly an ideal time in my life to be getting involved with a woman. I need to get myself together first.*

Neither of them wanted me to know they were together.

I remember when I was talking to Will in his room, it looked like there was something he wanted to tell me. Well, now I know what it was. Except why would he hide that from me?

One thing I do know for sure:

It must have been Jade's idea.

43

There's no chance of going back to sleep, so I might as well get my questions answered.

I march over to Jade's room. I pound on the door with the palm of my hand. I have to pound on it quite a few times before Jade finally pulls the door open. She has an amused look on her face. I try not to picture the way my reflection looked in the mirror.

"Hello, Amy," she says. "What brings you to the neighborhood?"

I push past her into her room without asking permission, but she's the one who closes the door behind me. She still has that amused twist on her lips, although most of her makeup has rubbed off by now.

"You never told me Will was your boyfriend," I say.

For a moment, she stands there in stunned silence. Then she laughs, throwing her head back so that I can see the fillings in the back of her mouth. Jade never got through a dentist appointment without needing a cavity filled. "Oh, Amy…"

"Don't deny it." I put my hands on my hips. "He is, isn't he?"

She smiles and shrugs. "What can I say? You figured out my little secret. But it would have been hilarious if we had a double date and I brought him along."

I grimace. "Yeah, I'm sure."

"And he's cute, isn't he?"

"He's *troubled*." I frown. "Will not taking his medications—is that your doing?"

She lifts a shoulder. "Why should he take them? He's *so* much more fun off the medications."

"So he's better off hearing voices telling him to kill people?"

"Oh, come on! He's not actually going to do it."

"You don't know that."

In fact, it's hard not to look at Will differently now that I know he's not taking the pills that keep him from hallucinating. Without those pills, what is he capable of? He told me he heard Cameron scream and then he disappeared. But I can't take anything he says at face value.

What if *he's* the one who made Cameron disappear?

"Maybe you should be careful around Will," I say. "People who hear voices… You can't trust people like that."

"You should know, shouldn't you?"

Jade is staring at me, that same sneer still on her lips. She's never going to listen to anything I have to say. She wouldn't listen when we were sixteen, and she won't now. Jade never wanted to be helped. She never believed she had a problem, and that's why she never wanted to get better.

"I think Will might be extremely dangerous," I say. "I think we all might be in danger tonight. But if you don't want to listen, that's up to you."

For a split second, Jade's composure slips. "You... you really think he could be dangerous?"

"I really do."

She looks like she's thinking about it. "I don't believe that."

"Just be careful around him, Jade," I say. "Okay?"

Her eyes drop. "You should go, Amy."

Even though I'm worried about Jade, I do what she asks of me. After all, I'm not going to convince her right now. Eventually, she might realize I'm right.

I only hope she realizes it in time to save her life.

44

HOURS UNTIL MORNING: 3

"Do you think Mary is all right?" I ask Ramona.

She is back to her magazine at the nurses' station, flipping through the pages. There's a full-page photograph of a very handsome twenty-something man on the page she's looking at, and it's a tribute to how much time I've spent studying in the last two years that I have absolutely no idea who this famous heartthrob is.

"She's asleep," Ramona says. "Leave her be. You want her to get all ramped up again?"

I hover over her. "Yes, but if we gave her a bunch of Ativan, shouldn't we be checking on her?"

Ativan is a sedative. I remember from pharmacology class that it can cause respiratory depression— meaning it can cause a person to stop breathing— especially in the elderly. It was *on the flash card*. For all we know, Mary has stopped breathing in there.

"She's fine." Ramona gives me a sharp look. "Dr. Beck's instructions were to leave her alone. You don't want her getting agitated again and then we have to give her more Ativan, right?"

No, I don't want that. But I could still check on her and make sure she's breathing. I don't even have to wake her up. I could just go in there, make sure her chest is moving up and down, then leave.

But Ramona is looking at me like she doesn't want me to do that.

"Okay," I finally say. "I guess I'll try to get back to sleep then."

"You do that."

I make it about halfway back to the staff lounge when I realize I won't be able to live with myself if I don't check on Mary. I really like Mary, and I want her to live till the morning. So I'm going to check on her, whether Ramona wants me to or not.

I can't let Ramona know about it though. I'm already in enough trouble with her and Dr. Beck. I'm about one infraction away from a phone call to the dean. So I've got to be sneaky about this.

I continue on the circle around the unit, making sure to take a path that will not circle past the nurses' station. I keep walking until I reach room 912. Mary's room.

I'll just go in there for one second and make sure she's breathing. Then I can leave.

I try to be as quiet as possible as I push down on the handle that controls the door. The door cracks open, and it's completely dark inside. As quietly as I can, I slip into the room.

Mary is wrapped up in the covers of her bed. But there are a lot of covers, and it's hard to see if she's breathing or not. I creep across the room and over to the bed. I lean over, to look down at Mary and…

She's not in the bed.

What the hell?

I yank the blankets off the bed, not bothering to be quiet anymore. I saw a lump on the bed, and I realize now that it was the scarf Mary had been working on. It was lying on the bed, and it looked like the form of a sleeping woman.

"Mary?" I call out.

No answer.

The bathroom door is ajar and it's dark inside, so it doesn't seem likely she's in there, but I check anyway. I search inside the bathroom and I even check under the sink as if she could be hiding there. But she's not in the bathroom. She's not anywhere.

My heart is pounding as I come out of the bathroom. But not as much as it is when I realize there's a silhouette in the doorway to Mary's room. A man is standing there, waiting for me to emerge from the bathroom. And when I do, he shuts the door, closing us both inside.

It's Will.

45

"Don't come near me, Will. I mean it."

Will's eyes look like dark hollows in the dim moonlight. Despite my warning, he takes a step toward me. I take a step back and stumble into the bathroom door.

"Will…" I say. "What did you do to her? What did you do to Mary?"

He stops abruptly. Looks over at Mary's bed and frowns. "What did *I* do? What are you talking about? What do you think I did exactly?"

"I have no idea." My voice is a hoarse gasp. "You obviously did something to Mary. And… and Cameron… and Miguel…"

"Me?" He clutches his chest. "Are you serious? I came here to talk to you because I don't know what the hell is going on. Why would you think *I* did this?"

He takes another step forward and I slide along the wall toward the window. Not that I'm escaping from a window on the ninth floor, but it somehow makes me feel more secure. "I know everything, Will."

"Everything?" He shoots me a baffled look. "What do you know? I don't understand." He frowns at my trembling hands. "Would you just relax? I'm not here to hurt you, for Christ's sake."

Yeah, right. "I know about you and Jade. That she's your girlfriend. You lied to me."

His jaw looks like it's about to become unhinged. "Me and *Jade*? You mean that psycho chick in 905? You think she's my *girlfriend*?"

"Don't lie."

"I'm not!" He lays a hand on his heart. "I swear on my life that Jade is *not* my girlfriend. I hardly even know her!"

"Is that why she had her hand on your shoulder when we were in the hallway before?"

He frowns. "She looked upset about Mary. What was I supposed to do? Push her away?"

"And I saw you disappear into her room…"

"I assure you," he says, "that never happened. Jade is… She's somebody to stay away from. So that's what I've been doing. I don't even know her last name. I swear."

Will's eyes are wide and earnest behind his glasses. He actually looks like he's telling the truth.

"I'm sorry," I say. "It's just very hard to believe you after you lied about those pills. I mean, you haven't taken any of the antipsychotics you've been prescribed. How can I trust you?"

"Look, I didn't take those pills because I don't need them."

"Oh really? You think you don't need any treatment for hearing voices?"

"No, I don't," he says firmly. "Because… I don't hear voices."

I snort. "I see. So they just went away on their own, is that it?"

"No, I…" He licks his lips as he takes a breath, carefully measuring his next words. "They never went away because I never heard them in the first place. I was never hearing voices. I… I lied about it."

Okay. This is the absolute last thing I expected him to say. "Excuse me?"

"I lied, okay?" He scratches at his stubble. "I read a bunch of stuff about how a paranoid schizophrenic is supposed to act, then I went to the emergency room and read the script. And they put me here."

I stare at him. "Why on earth would you do something like that? Are you out of your mind?"

"No, I'm *not*. That's the whole point." He drops his voice so I have to strain to hear. "So here's the thing. I'm not an Uber driver. I'm a reporter. This former patient of Ward D came to me with this story about how he felt patients were mistreated here. But, you know, it's hard to get a straight story out of a lot of the patients here, and I didn't want to print a bunch of patient hallucinations. So I thought the best way to get my story would be to experience it firsthand."

I open my mouth, but I don't even know what to say. He lied about being a paranoid schizophrenic? That's pretty… I don't even have words for it.

"In a few days, I was planning to say the voices went away," he says. "Like I took some illegal drug and that triggered it, and now I'm fine. That was my plan, anyway. But it's not working out like I thought it would."

"Gee, you think?"

"Even before tonight, I had some issues to write about." He looks back at the door to Mary's room, still shut tight. "The seclusion rooms here… I don't know how ethical any of that is. They should at least have windows on the doors so staff can check on them regularly. I didn't see it happen, but you should've heard that Damon Sawyer guy screaming his head off when they locked him in there. And Miguel was screaming to get out too… At least, until…"

I study his features in the moonlight. Can I believe anything he's telling me? It seems like such a wild story. Who would pretend to be hearing voices, just to get a news story?

"I didn't want to tell anyone the truth about me, obviously," Will says. "But enough is enough. Between Cameron disappearing and that blood on the floor and now Mary…" His shoulders heave. "And, well, you're the only person here that I trust."

"I wish I could say the same," I mumble.

"I know, I know." He sighs. "I wish we had

internet access, because I could look it up for you and prove who I am. Will Schoenfeld. I write for *The Daily Chronicle*. I've been there for two years. My dream is to work for *The New York Times*, but you don't get there by doing fluff pieces."

"You do it by pretending to have schizophrenia?"

He sinks onto the bed. "Obviously, I wish I hadn't done that. And I'm paying for it right now. Amy, you have to know that something really bad is happening right now on Ward D."

He's right about that part. Something terrible is going on here tonight. I have no idea what it is, but I'm starting to be seriously worried that I might not make it through the night here. I'm not sure Cameron has.

"You don't trust Ramona?" I ask.

"Absolutely not. I mean, *strawberry jelly*? We both know that was blood on the floor."

He's right. Out of everyone I have spoken to, he's the only one who is willing to concede that the blood wasn't a hallucination. "What about Dr. Beck?"

He hesitates. "I'm not sure. But either way, he doesn't believe anything is amiss here tonight. So he's not *helping* the situation."

"So suppose I *do* decide to believe you," I say. "What do we do about it?"

"Here's what we need to do." The whites of his eyes glow in the moonlight. "We survive the night."

46

W ill says the only way to get through the night is to stick together. His reasoning is that if we're not alone, we will be safe. I'm still not entirely sure if I trust him. Then again, most of his plan includes going back to his room and reading John Irving books for the rest of the night. It feels like the sort of plan that I can get on board with pretty easily.

"I still can't believe you defaced your copy of *Garp*," I say when we get back to his room. "It's hard to look at."

"I know." He pulls a frown. "But I didn't have a choice. I tried taking the medications—you know, for authenticity—but I couldn't think straight on them."

Jade always complained about how hard it was to be on antipsychotic medications. Not that I thought she was making it up, but I'm beginning to realize what she has gone through over the last eight years.

How hard her life has been because of her illness.
Although I'm still baffled as to why she would make
up a lie about Will being her boyfriend.

"So," I say, "was anything you told me about
yourself true?"

"Sure. The best lies stay close to the truth."

"Like what?"

"Well," he says thoughtfully. "I really did used to
drive for Uber when I had my first crappy online
paper job and my salary couldn't pay the bills without
a side gig. Also, I do live alone, and I'm single. And
also, John Irving *is* my favorite author."

"Have you read all his books?" I've now looked
through the entire stack on his nightstand, which
also includes *A Widow For One Year* and *Avenue of
Mysteries*.

"Of course." He taps the frame of his glasses.
"You think I got these thick lenses because I don't like
to read?"

"I always loved to read too." I flip through his
dog-eared copy of *Owen Meany*. "Whenever we were
assigned to read a book in school, I would always
finish it after two days, even though we were only
assigned to read like two chapters."

"That just makes you a nerd," he says. "I, on the
other hand, was a reading *renegade*. In class, while the
teacher was teaching a lesson, I would be reading a
book under my desk. I actually got detention for
reading. My teacher was always saying, 'Will, put that
book away!'"

Despite everything, I have to giggle. "You're right. I was never a reading renegade."

"That's how I always knew I wanted a career that involved writing," he muses. "Every time I would read something really great, it made me want to write."

The passion in his eyes is unmistakable. He's being completely honest. I would bet my life. "Will, tell me the truth. What do you think is going on here?"

His hazel eyes cloud over behind his lenses. "Honestly? I don't know. But I do know one thing. Sawyer has been a problem ever since he got here. They had him isolated from everyone else even before they locked him in seclusion. And ever since they locked Sawyer in Seclusion One, I've heard loud noises coming from that room. But then after the power went off—nothing."

"So…?"

"I think he must have gotten out." He shudders. "When the power died, the locks must have turned off as well. And he took advantage."

I clasp a hand over my mouth. "You think so?"

"I hope I'm wrong. Because from what I've heard, that guy is seriously disturbed."

When I close my eyes, I can picture Mary Cummings screaming his name. *Damon Sawyer is going to kill all of you!* And then Spider-Dan's insistence that Sawyer had come to him and said he was going to hurt me.

Why would he want to hurt *me*?

I shiver.

"Don't worry." Will reaches out and places his hand on mine. "There's no way in hell I'm letting him near you. Like I said, let's stick together and we'll be fine. It'll be morning before you know it."

I want so badly to believe him. I remember my first impression of Will when I came into his room at the beginning of the evening. Despite his diagnosis, I thought he seemed like a nice, normal sort of guy. A cute guy. The kind of guy I might agree to go out to dinner with, if it ever came up. But appearances can be deceiving.

Can I trust him?

"Don't worry," Will says again as he squeezes my hand. "I won't let anything happen."

But I have a terrible feeling that Will can't protect me from Damon Sawyer. Nobody can.

Just like nobody could protect me from myself when I was sixteen years old.

47

EIGHT YEARS EARLIER

I can't rip my eyes away from the man duct taped to a chair in the middle of this tiny kitchen. His hands and legs are bound with the dull gray tape, and there's a piece holding his mouth closed. His face is dripping with sweat, and one of his eyes is swollen closed. And there's blood on his scalp, intermingled with the sparse strands of hair combed over his bald spot.

"Mr. Riordan," I breathe.

Mr. Riordan groans at the sound of his name. His one eye that isn't swollen shut is bloodshot, and he turns it in my direction. There's desperation in his gaze.

"The door wasn't even locked!" Jade reports gleefully. "I mean, who doesn't even lock their door? It was so easy. Of course, all he's got is a bunch of crap in here that's not even worth stealing. So maybe he's hoping somebody will break in and, I don't know, clean his house or something." She snickers. "Is that what you were hoping, Mr. Riordan?"

He doesn't answer, and Jade kicks him in the shin with her Doc Marten. In response, he groans loudly.

"What did you do, Jade?" I manage.

She smiles pleasantly, like there isn't a bloody man tied up two feet away from us. "I just told him if he didn't do what I said, I was going to stab him in the eye. He was *really* cooperative after that."

"You can't possibly think this is going to solve anything," I choke out. "I mean, as soon as you let him go, we're going to be in so much more trouble."

"Right." She bobs her head. "Except we're not going to let him go. We're going to kill him."

At Jade's words, Mr. Riordan's good eye flies wide open. He starts struggling against the duct tape, although it doesn't do much good. The whole display just makes Jade laugh.

"We'll make it look like a burglary." She looks around the kitchen, her eyes scanning the surfaces. "Well, we won't have to take much. Just mess things up a little bit. Be sure not to touch anything you don't take with you, okay? We have to be careful about fingerprints."

"Jade…"

"I mean, it's not like anybody is going to even miss him. I don't think he has any friends. *Definitely* no girl-friends."

Enough of this. I can't let Jade think this is actually going to happen. We are *not* going to kill anyone under any circumstances. I grab her by the arm and pull her aside. "This is really stupid, Jade. We are not going to do this."

"Not with *that* attitude."

"Jade!" I sneak a look at Mr. Riordan, who is struggling harder now against the restraints. But Jade tied him up good and tight. Despite how awful he's been to me, I want to cry at the sight of what she did to him. "Seriously, you parked right outside. We're going to get caught. And even if we didn't, I'm not going to kill anyone. No way."

"Right." She snorts. "Isn't that what you said about cheating? But you looked at the test, didn't you?"

She has a point. "That's different. This is really bad, Jade. If you think I'm going to help you kill somebody, you have seriously lost your mind."

Jade's finely plucked eyebrows shoot up. "Well, I wouldn't be the only one then, would I?"

For a moment, it's like time is standing still. I stare at her, her words ringing in my ears. "What?"

"Don't think I don't know," she hisses in my ear. "I know about that little girl you keep seeing everywhere. You're always talking about it. *Did you see her, Jade?* Nobody sees her, Amy. Nobody sees her but you."

I open my mouth but all that comes out is a squeak.

"There's no little girl, Amy," she says. "You think you're so superior, but it turns out you're even crazier than I am. And if you don't help me, I'm going to tell everyone."

No. *No.*

"What do you think will happen to you?" She smirks at me. "What do you think they'll do to you when they find out you're seeing things?"

That faint throbbing in my right temple has turned into a jackhammer. I squeeze my eyes shut for a moment, and when I open them, I realize we are no longer alone. We have a guest in the kitchen.

It's the little girl in the pink dress.

"Amy…" The little girl is calling my name. I want to run over to her and wring her neck, except she's not even real. "Amy…"

I turn my head in the direction of the little girl. "Shut up," I tell her.

"Amy, she's right," the girl pipes up in her little girl's voice. "You have to kill him. It's the only way."

"No…" I whisper.

She smiles at me, tilting her heart-shaped face up to look at me. "Kill him, Amy."

"Shut up!" I scream.

Jade takes a step back, startled by my outburst. Even Mr. Riordan has quieted down and paused in his battle with the duct tape. I look in the corner of the room, and the little girl has vanished again.

"Amy," Jade says. She reaches out and attempts to touch my shoulder.

"Stop," I croak.

"Amy, this is the only way. You see that, don't you? You don't want that asshole to ruin our lives, do you?"

I find myself shaking my head. No. I don't want that.

"Well, then." Jade walks over to the kitchen counter and picks up a carving knife, already stained with droplets of blood. "Do you want to do the honors or should I?"

I know at that moment, my life will never, ever be the same.

48

PRESENT DAY

HOURS UNTIL MORNING: 2

I didn't do it.

I didn't kill my trigonometry teacher. Obviously.

I didn't let Jade do it either. When she tried to hand me that carving knife, I ran out of Mr. Riordan's house and out to the main road. I hitched a ride back to my own house, found my mother, and burst into tears as I told her everything.

Well, not everything. I didn't tell her about the little blond girl. But the little girl disappeared soon after that. And I never saw her again. I never saw anything that wasn't really there ever again.

Until tonight.

No. That's not true. The blood on the floor was *real*. Will saw it too.

After my mother called the police, thankfully in time to save Mr. Riordan, Jade had a psychiatric evaluation and received her bipolar diagnosis. It was what saved her from kidnapping and attempted murder charges. The next time I saw her, she was right here, on Ward D. She was pumped up with Lithium, lying in a messy hospital bed, staring up at the ceiling vacantly.

I tried to talk to her. I apologized for turning her in and explained that I did it for her own good. I was trying to *help* her. I babbled on for the better part of an hour while she didn't say a word. It was so hard to see my best friend pumped full of drugs that made her like a zombie.

At least, I blamed the drugs at first. But then when I was getting ready to leave, Jade finally rolled her head in my direction. The seething look in her eyes was unmistakable.

I will never forgive you, she said to me. *Never.*

Even so, I stupidly believed she would get over it. Jade and I had fought before, but we always made up. I came back a few more times, but most of the time, she didn't say a single word. On the final visit, she sat up in her bed, her purple-rimmed eyes filled with venom.

If you come back here again, Amy, I will kill you.

And that was my last visit to see Jade.

But I try not to think about any of that as I sit in

Will's room now, attempting to lose myself in a book —something I used to find easy to do.

I haven't had much time for fun over the last two years. It's been mostly studying the Krebs cycle, loads of pharmacology flashcards, and the intricate details of the celiac plexus. And of course, occasionally hooking up with Cameron. But I always made time to read. Whenever I pick up a book, it's like an escape. For an hour or two, I get to be part of the book world instead of my own much more boring world.

It's not easy to escape the world that is around me right now. There is a very real chance that a psychotic man is currently doing laps right outside the door. But Will is sitting on his bed reading, and I'm on the chair next to him, also reading, and every five or six minutes, we both look up to make sure everything is okay. And while I am in this room, reading this book, it feels like everything will be okay. After all, only a few hours remain until morning.

And then there's a knock on the door.

Will's eyes snap up. He looks at the door, then over at me. He puts his index finger to his lips, then he calls out, "I'm not decent! Come back later!"

Jade's voice flits under the door. "Will, I know Amy is in there. I'm coming in."

I inhale sharply as the door swings open. Jade peeks her head inside, and our eyes meet across the room.

"Amy," she says, "can we talk?"

I place my book on my lap, but I don't budge from the chair. "Sure. Talk."

"Outside?"

Will shakes his head emphatically. "I'd rather talk in here," I say.

Jade frowns. There's something in her expression that throws me off. She doesn't look like her usual smart-ass self. She actually looks...

Frightened.

"*Please*, Amy," she says. "Just for a moment."

Will is still shaking his head, but despite everything, I still am not entirely sure I can trust him. After all, I've known Jade almost my entire life, and I've known him for less than twenty-four hours. Yes, my gut is telling me I can trust Will. But it's not like my gut hasn't been wrong before. I dated Cameron, after all.

"I'll be right back," I tell Will. "Five minutes."

There's a wary look in his eyes as he stares up at Jade, then back at me. "Five minutes."

I slip out of the room, leaving my book behind on the chair. After I leave the room, Jade closes the door to Will's room behind us. She doesn't want him to hear what she's about to say to me.

As soon as we are clear of the room, Jade wraps her fingers around my arm and pulls me over to the nurses' station, where Ramona is waiting. They are wearing equally concerned expressions on their faces.

"Are you okay?" Ramona asks me. "Did he try to hurt you?"

"No, of course not," I say.

"I was so worried!" Jade squeezes her hands together, and to my surprise, her eyes spill over with tears. "I couldn't find you, and when I realized you were with him, I was so scared he was doing something terrible to you."

"Not even a little bit." I give her a hard look. "He did tell me that the two of you aren't really dating though."

Jade's eyelashes flutter. "He said that? Seriously?"

"Yes…"

Jade reaches out and takes my hand in hers. "Will and I have been dating for *three years*. I swear it. I don't understand why he would say something like that. Well, I *do* understand, actually. He's always been a compulsive liar. What other nonsense did he tell you?"

I open my mouth but I'm not sure what to say. Will told me a lot of things, but none of them felt like lies.

"He loves to make up jobs for himself to seem more important," Jade says. "Like that he's a pilot. Or a teacher. Or a reporter. Even though all he's done since we've been dating is occasionally drive an Uber, and most of the time he doesn't even do that. His parents have been giving him money to keep him afloat, or else he'd end up on the street."

I can only shake my head.

"You didn't believe him, did you?" Jade squeezes my hand. "Don't feel bad if you did. God, I can't even tell you how many of his lies I fell for over the years.

But after I talked to you, that was the first time I got scared that he could be dangerous."

"I... I don't know if he is..." I stammer.

"How could you say that?" Jade bursts out. "You're the one who convinced me! He's done some terrible things here tonight. That's why I got Ramona and told her everything."

"I don't think he's done anything wrong," I say. "He... We think that Damon Sawyer got out of the seclusion room..."

"Mr. Sawyer is still in Seclusion One," Ramona says. "I checked on him about twenty minutes ago. He's sound asleep."

I remember Will's response when I asked him if we could trust Ramona. *Absolutely not.*

But that's a moot point if I can't trust him.

"Will is a very smooth talker when he wants to be," Jade says. "Don't feel bad that you fell for it."

"You don't understand." I look between the two of them. "Will isn't dangerous. I know what I said to you, Jade, but—"

"Amy," Ramona interrupts me. "There's something you need to see."

I told Will that I would be back in five minutes, but I'm not sure I'm going to make it. Still, I have to see what Ramona wants to show me. Although I get a horrible feeling in my stomach when I realize where she's leading me.

Mary's room.

"I saw him slip out of her room not that long after

her episode of agitation," Ramona tells me. "And then later I came in to check on her, and this is what I found."

She throws the door open to room 912. It looks about the same as it did when I checked in here earlier. Mary is gone, the blankets are still on the bed, and the scarf is arranged in a way that almost looks like a body. But then Ramona flicks on the lights.

Oh my God.

There's blood all over the bed. I didn't even see it when the lights were off.

I cover my mouth with both hands. I think I might be sick. I lean forward and gag a bit—it's a good thing I didn't manage to eat much for dinner tonight.

Jade's hand is on my back. She rubs my back in circles, which sort of helps. But not really. The only thing that would help at this point is to *get the hell out of here*.

I straighten up, looking away so I don't have to see all the blood on Mary's bed. I don't know what happened to her, but there's no way she's okay. Not with all that blood soaking the sheets.

"Where is she?" I gasp.

"She's lying down in a clean empty room," Ramona says. "She'll be all right, thank goodness, but she told us Will attacked her with a weapon."

I breathe a sigh of relief that at least Mary is going to be okay. I still can't believe Will would have done anything like that to her, but I don't believe she'd lie about that.

"Will has always been off balance," Jade says softly. "But I'm scared now he's really lost it. I'm scared of what he's going to do next."

"We need to talk to Dr. Beck about this," Ramona continues. "We need to make sure Will can't hurt anyone else."

Ramona and Jade are both staring at me, waiting to hear what I have to say. Five minutes ago, I trusted Will. I trusted him, even though I hardly knew him. And now I realize he has tricked me. All along, he had me just where he wanted me.

I wipe my lips with the back of my hand. "What do you need me to do?"

When I get back to Will's room, he sets down his copy of *Owen Meany* and stares up at me. "That was more than five minutes."

"I know. I'm sorry."

He presses his lips together. "What did they say to you?"

Of course, I knew he would ask me that. I have to play this very carefully. "She was feeling anxious about everything that happened. She just wanted to talk to me."

"That's it?"

"That's it."

He narrows his eyes at me. The diagnosis in his chart is paranoid schizophrenia, but he claimed it was a lie. That he was faking it. But in retrospect, everything he has done or said since we've been here has been incredibly paranoid. He has created an entire conspiracy theory. When, in fact, he is the most suspicious person of all.

"Your hands are shaking," he notes.

"Is that so surprising?" I retort, as I try to get my shaking hands under control. It's not easy. "I mean, given everything that's going on here…"

"Yeah, but they weren't shaking before you went out to talk to Jade." He hops off the bed, keeping a distance of a few feet between us. "What did you talk to her about? Tell me the truth."

"I did."

"I don't believe you." Now his own hands are shaking as he tugs at the hem of his worn T-shirt. "Look, I know this whole thing is crazy, but I swear to you, Amy, everything I've told you has been true."

I don't know what to say to that. It's not true, anyway. From the moment we first talked, he's been lying to me. And he knows it.

"You've got to believe me." His eyes are wide. "I need you on my side here. I can't trust anyone else. If we don't stick together…"

There's a knock on his door. We both jump and turn to look at the door. Without waiting for an answer, the door swings open. Dr. Beck and Ramona are standing in the doorway. There's a syringe jutting out of the pants pocket of Ramona's scrubs.

"Hello, Will," Dr. Beck says. "Do you have a moment to talk?"

All the color drains out of Will's face. He backs up against the wall. "Oh no. *No.*"

"Will…" Dr. Beck steps into the room, his face creased in concern. "There's no reason for you to be scared."

"Please," Will says. "I… I don't want to cause any trouble…"

"A little late for that," Ramona tuts.

Dr. Beck walks over to the nightstand, to the pile of Will's books. He sorts through them and when he gets to the copy of *Garp*, he flips it open. He frowns at the hollowed-out center with the pills hidden inside.

"Oh, Will," he murmurs. "This is so incredibly disappointing. Don't you want to get better?"

"I'm fine." Will squirms. "Really. I… the voices just went away on their own. I don't hear them anymore. So I'm fine."

Dr. Beck cocks his head to the side. "And what happened to Mary Cummings, Will?"

Will's mouth falls open, and he shakes his head. He looks like he's about to pass out.

"We don't have to talk about it now," Dr. Beck says. "But in the morning, the police will be here, and believe me, we're going to get to the bottom of it. In the meantime, we have to make sure you don't hurt anyone else."

"I would never…" Will chokes out.

"We can't exactly take you at your *word*, Will," Ramona says.

That's when Will sees the syringe in her pocket, and intense panic fills his face. Like I did in Mary's room, he looks over at the window, wondering if escape could be possible from the ninth floor. But like me, he realizes it's futile.

"Amy." He appeals to me instead now, the same way Mary did in her last moments. I get a sick sense of déjà vu. "Please tell them. I didn't do anything to Mary. I didn't hurt anyone. *Tell them.*"

But I don't say a word.

Dr. Beck nods at Ramona and the two of them close in on him. Dr. Beck goes for his right arm and Ramona goes for the left. Will fights like crazy, but between the two of them, they managed to wrestle him to the ground. Even when they've got him pinned, he's still screaming and struggling.

"It's just a mild sedative, Will," Dr. Beck grunts. "This would be so much easier if you could just stay still."

It takes both of them to keep him restrained, which means Ramona can't get to the syringe in her pocket. She looks over her shoulder at me. "Amy, can you grab the syringe? Just inject it right in his deltoid."

My stomach drops. "You want *me* to do it?"

"Amy, no!" Will screams. "Please! I didn't do anything! You have to believe me!"

It would be easy enough to do. A syringe is sticking out of Ramona's scrub pants, and all I would have to do is jab it in his upper arm. Two people are holding him down, so it shouldn't be that hard to do.

Except then I hear a snicker from behind me.

I rotate my head, and that's when I notice Jade standing just outside the door. Her hands are folded across her boobs, and she has a smirk on her lips. I have known Jade for a long time, and I know that look.

That's when it hits me. She's not afraid of Will at all. She was lying to me. She was lying to Ramona and Dr. Beck. She is *enjoying* this.

"Amy?" Ramona says.

I swallow a hard lump in my throat. "I... I don't think..."

"Oh, for God's sake," Ramona grumbles. She throws the weight of her knee onto Will's arm, then she grabs the syringe with her left hand. She pulls off the cap with her teeth, then plunges the needle into Will's deltoid.

It doesn't take effect instantly, so Ramona and Dr. Beck have to keep him restrained on the floor. But slowly, the fight leaves his body. He stops struggling and goes limp on the floor.

"Ramona," Dr. Beck says, "please help Mr. Schoenfeld back into bed."

Will's eyelids are droopy at this point, and he needs her help just to crawl off the floor and climb back into his bed. If he were ever dangerous, he isn't anymore. But I'm not sure if I believe he ever was.

"Amy." Will's voice is slurred now. "Don't... don't trust..."

Ramona lays a firm hand on my shoulder. "Come on, Amy. Let him sleep."

She firmly guides me out of the room and shuts the door behind us. I can't help but remember that this exact same thing happened to Mary. Ramona injected her with a sedative, then we left her alone in her room. And now she's gone, and all that's left is blood on her sheets.

I have doomed Will.

And the worst part is that now there is absolutely nobody left I can trust.

50

Dr. Beck is alone at the nurses' station, writing in Will's chart. When he sees me approaching, he frowns. "I'm so sorry you had to experience that, Amy," he says.

"Yeah," I mumble.

"It's been an uncharacteristically difficult night." His shoulders sag. "Please don't think it's always like this. I don't want this to sour you on the field of psychiatry."

I manage a halfhearted smile. "I wasn't going to do psychiatry anyway, remember?"

Dr. Beck taps the pen against his page. "Yes, that's right. It was your colleague, Cameron, who was the one feigning interest."

"Dr. Beck." I sit down beside him at the nurses' station. "When Cameron left that message on your machine, how did he sound?"

"I told you. He sounded choked up. I certainly

believed he had a family emergency." He arches an eyebrow. "Why do you ask?"

"Did he sound scared?"

Dr. Beck considers my question for a moment. His eyes cloud over as he looks at Will's closed door, then back at my face. "Amy," he says quietly. "Have you ever heard of a psychiatric syndrome called folie à deux?"

"Um… no…"

"It's also called a shared psychotic disorder," he says. "Basically, it's a delusional belief, sometimes even involving hallucinations, that are shared by two people. For example, if a married couple both believed that their dog could speak English."

I blink at him. "Oh, I don't think—"

"Will has unfortunately managed to convince you that certain delusions of his were true," Dr. Beck says. "But if you think about it, you will realize that nothing he believed was rational. He was using these delusions to justify insignificant events, and ultimately, his own violent behavior."

I look down at my hands. "Oh."

"I'm afraid Will's psychosis is much worse than what my colleague from the day shift reported to me," he says. "He should really be transferred to a much more secure facility, possibly even a criminal facility given our suspicions about what he did to Mary Cummings."

"I… I see."

Dr. Beck reaches out and puts a hand on my

shoulder. "The night is almost over. Please just try to get some sleep, and this will all get taken care of. Don't worry about Will. He will get the psychiatric treatment he needs, whether he likes it or not."

With those words of wisdom, he closes the chart labeled SCHOENFELD and sticks it back up on the rack. Then he goes back to his office.

I wonder how he would feel if I asked him if I could follow him and hide in the corner of his office for the rest of the night.

But instead, I am left alone at the nurses' station. Jade has gone back to her room, Ramona is off somewhere, and Will is in a drugged slumber. Now it's just me. And the dangerous man who has quite possibly been wandering the halls ever since the power outage.

Damon Sawyer.

I close my eyes, remembering the sounds I heard from within that room when I first arrived. Those awful guttural noises. Or when Sawyer was throwing himself at the door, attempting to break it down. Or when he pleaded with me to let him out. Although the scariest thing of all was the silence. The man somehow got out of his wrist restraints. And now he may have escaped the room entirely.

Except where is he?

I had thought Damon Sawyer's chart had been removed from the nurses' station, but now I realize that it's just been pushed into the corner. There was no reason to look at it when I first got here, because I did not believe I would be seeing him. But now it's the only way to know what I'm up against.

I need to know what this man did to put him in here. I need to know what he's capable of. I need to be able to defend myself, especially now that Will is incapacitated.

I grab the chart, my hands shaking so much that I almost drop it. I pull the cover open, turning to the emergency room notes. Just like in all the other charts, he's got a note from his intake. It was written the night he came in and details the events that led to his incarceration here, as well as his mental health history.

As I start reading, a sick feeling comes over me. Oh my God. I wish I had read this from the beginning.

This changes absolutely everything.

51

D amon Sawyer is a thirty-two-year-old man with a history of schizoaffective disorder. Schizoaffective disorder is a combination of schizophrenia and a mood disorder—in this case, bipolar. In Sawyer's case, he had symptoms of schizophrenia including hallucinations, delusions, and disorganized thinking, but also mania.

I've never seen such an extensive psychiatric history. There was never anything like this in the charts for Dr. Sleepy's patients.

There are documents faxed in from multiple sources, all synthesized into a ten-page detailed history on Sawyer. I read every single sentence, my eyes locked on the chart. With every page I turn, I have a better understanding of the man locked in seclusion, and why everyone here believes him to be so incredibly dangerous.

Damon Sawyer's family history is unremarkable. His father is a businessman, and his mother is a homemaker. There was no abuse or neglect recorded to explain the fact that at a young age, Sawyer was diagnosed with something called conduct disorder.

Even though I have no internet access, I have several medical apps on my phone that don't require the internet. I check the psychiatry app, which informs me that conduct disorder is a mental disorder diagnosed in childhood or adolescence, presenting with a persistent pattern of theft, lies, and physical violence. A classic antisocial behavior pattern.

In Sawyer's case, he really liked setting fires.

Sawyer was hospitalized on and off for several years starting at age ten after a variety of physical altercations and charges of arson. Finally, at age fifteen, he set a fire that resulted in "two casualties." He claimed voices in his head told him to do it, and as a result, was committed to a psychiatric facility for the next four years.

During his time at the psychiatric facility, he received his diagnosis of schizoaffective disorder in addition to his conduct disorder. You would think after someone sets a fire that kills two people, they would be locked up for good, but he was released at age nineteen after supposedly being stabilized on medication.

In his twenties, Sawyer struggled with substance abuse. After Jade's mother's overdose, I learned how common it is for people with mental illness to also struggle with addiction. Sawyer bounced between prison and psychiatric hospitals, as he was picked up multiple times on charges of possession and dealing. But on the plus side, he didn't set any more fires.

At least, none that anyone knew about.

The note goes on to mention that Sawyer has been convicted of assault and even an attempted manslaughter charge, but due to his extensive psychiatric history, these sentences were commuted into psychiatric hospital stays. But clearly, this is a very dangerous man. In the emergency room, he had to be restrained by four staff members, although he eventually calmed down enough with medication that they thought he would be appropriate for Ward D.

They were wrong.

But none of that is what is shocking. What makes my heart drop into my intestines is the story of what brought Damon Sawyer to the emergency room in the first place on this particular occasion. When I read it, I'm certain I must've read it wrong. This can't possibly be what I think it is. But every time I read the words, they say the same exact thing.

Sawyer was with his girlfriend. The two of them were drinking beer together, and they decided it would be hilarious to go and rob a bunch of banks using their beer bottles. So they went all over town, demanding money from bank clerks while pointing their beer bottles at them.

Jade does have a boyfriend. But her boyfriend isn't Will Schoenfeld, who was never hearing voices at all and just went too far to achieve his dream to be a reporter for *The New York Times*.

No, Jade's boyfriend is Damon Sawyer.

52

I t finally makes perfect sense.

Jade is the one who helped Sawyer escape from Seclusion One during the blackout. She's been helping him with everything tonight. Including misleading the rest of us by pretending Will had been her boyfriend. I fell right into that trap.

I close the chart with a snap and push it away, like it's made from poison. Damon Sawyer, who has a list of psych hospitalizations as long as my arm, is now roaming Ward D. Damon Sawyer, who required four staff members to restrain him in the emergency room.

Oh God, what do I do?

I stand up from my seat and creep into the hallway. I look both ways, but nobody is around. The door to room 905 is closed and the light is off inside. It occurs to me that Sawyer could be hiding in that room. Maybe that's where he's been all along.

We need to survive the night.

Those were Will's words of wisdom before Jade convinced me to turn against him. He was right. I don't need to be able to fight Damon Sawyer. All I need to do is survive the night.

I knock on the door to room 906. It's not surprising that I don't hear anyone call out that I can come in. Again, I check the hallway to make sure it's empty and I let myself into the room.

The lights are out, but thank God, Will is still lying in bed. He hasn't vanished and been replaced by bloody sheets. I quietly walk to the bed, where he is out cold. I crouch down, grab his shoulder, and give him a good shake.

"Will!" I whisper. "Wake up!"

He doesn't stir. But his chest is rising and falling. So he's alive, at least.

"Will!" I press the palm of my hand into his sternum, which is how they taught us to rouse extremely lethargic patients. "You've *got* to wake up. We're in big trouble here."

He groans, but his eyelids don't even flutter. Even if I manage to arouse him just a little bit, it won't help. Ramona made sure to completely knock him out. He's useless now.

I straighten up. At this point, I have to weigh my options. And I don't have many.

I can't leave Ward D. Not without help. The code that worked at the beginning of the shift is no longer functional. The phones are down and so are the computers. My cell phone isn't getting any service.

And the only guy on the unit that I could trust is now unconscious.

There's only one thing left that I can possibly do. I have to tell Dr. Beck what's going on. I'm fairly sure he's going to think I've lost my mind, and who knows how it will impact my medical school career. I mean, he already thinks I have that folie à deux thingy going on. But at the same time, he's the boss here. If I tell him what Jade is up to and can be convincing enough, he can help me.

It's my only chance.

Will is sleeping soundly in his bed, his right arm thrown across his forehead. He is still wearing his glasses, and I pull them off and put them on the nightstand next to his stack of books. "Don't die," I instruct him. "I'm getting help."

After I leave Will's room, I walk around the circle to get to Dr. Beck's office. I'm keeping a close eye out for Ramona. After Jade, I trust her the least. She was the one who cleaned up that blood before Dr. Beck could see it, and she claimed it was strawberry jelly when it definitely wasn't. I don't know what her motivation is, but I can't trust her.

When I arrive at Dr. Beck's office, the light is thankfully on underneath the door. At least I don't have to wake him up yet again. I knock on the door, and after a minute, he pulls it open.

"Amy." He doesn't look thrilled to see me. I can hardly blame him at this point. If he has to give me a grade, it's not going to be an A. "What's going on this time?"

While I walked over here, I thought about what I was going to say. At this point, the only thing he is going to listen to is some objective evidence, not wild theories. "I'm worried about our safety in case of an emergency," I say.

He frowns. "Okay…"

"Because the phone lines are down," I point out. He can't argue with that one. "And also, did you realize that the code to the unit door doesn't work anymore? We're trapped here."

His face blanches. "What? Are you certain?"

I nod vigorously. "Absolutely certain. Ramona didn't tell you?"

"No, she *didn't.*" He swears under his breath. "That's unacceptable. What if there were a fire?"

"Exactly! That's what I said!"

"The codes must've reset when the power went out," he says. "That happened once before."

I feel a rush of relief. Finally, somebody in a position of authority is taking charge of the situation. "So what do we do?"

"Let me check it out." He smiles almost apologetically. "Sorry, it's not that I don't trust you, but…"

"It's fine," I say.

He digs into the pocket of his scrub pants and pulls out a set of keys to lock his office door. Then we make the loop around the unit one more time to get to the exit. I've got my fingers and toes crossed that this could be the last time I have to make this loop.

The keypad in the dim hallway is glowing green like usual. Dr. Beck punches in the code—the same one I've been trying. And just like during my attempts, we get that same buzzing sound in response.

"Damn," he mutters. "What a pain."

"Can you fix it?"

"Maybe…"

Although he doesn't look hopeful. The thought that he might not be able to fix it hadn't even occurred to me. After all, Dr. Beck is the attending physician. He's all-powerful.

"Maintenance fixed it last time it happened." He rubs his chin. "I'll grab Ramona and see if she has any ideas."

"No!" I gasp.

His eyebrows shoot up to his hairline. "What's wrong? Ramona has worked here longer than I have, and if anyone can fix it, she can. She's the expert."

"She couldn't though," I insist. "I already asked her."

He waves a hand. "I'm certain if we put our heads together, we can figure it out. Let me get her."

This is just great. Not only have I not found a way out of here, but I might have put Dr. Beck in danger too. I start to protest, but a wave of dizziness washes over me. It's like the events of the evening have finally caught up to me.

"Amy?" He furrows his brow. "Are you okay?"

"Yes… just a little… lightheaded…"

Dr. Beck has to help me into the staff lounge, and I barely make it to the sofa before I collapse. My hands won't stop shaking.

"You're not going to pass out, are you?" he asks.

"No," I manage.

He lets out a long sigh. "I'm so sorry. This night has been such a mess. Let me just sort out the door code, and I promise, we'll get you home in one piece. Hang in there."

I don't want him to leave me, but before I can get out the words, he is out the door. I guess his priority is making sure that we have an emergency exit. And I'm grateful that he's finally taking the situation seriously, even though I'm scared about what's out there.

What if Dr. Beck doesn't come back? What if he disappears like Cameron did?

I lean my head back against the sofa and close my eyes. The dizziness seems to be subsiding, but I still feel uneasy. A dangerous man is wandering the unit. And Jade… I don't quite understand her part in this. But she's held a grudge against me since high school.

Jade will never forgive me. I did what I had to do —it wasn't like I had a choice in the matter. I couldn't let her kill our trigonometry teacher. But she could never see it that way.

Where is Dr. Beck? Shouldn't he be back by now? The unit only takes like sixty seconds to walk around. How long has it been since he disappeared out the door?

Did Jade and Ramona do something to him? Is that why he isn't back yet?

I reach into my pocket to grab my phone and check the time. God, how did it get so late? But the night is almost over. One way or another, I'm getting out of here.

Then something makes my heart leap:

I've got a bar on my phone!

It's just one bar, but it's the most I've had the entire night. I hold up my phone, and it vibrates in my hand as a text message from Gabby comes through. This is amazing! I can call for help! I can finally get out of here!

I click on the text message from Gabby, which came hours ago, shortly after I texted her that I had arrived at Ward D, and that Dr. Beck was cute. God, my priorities were different back then. Her text message fills the screen:

> You think Dr. Beck is cute??? You perv, Dr. Beck is like eighty years old!!!!

I stare at the text message on the screen. My heart is pounding out of my chest.

Dr. Beck is like eighty years old!

So according to Gabby, who spent a week working with him, Dr. Beck is an old man. And if the attending physician on this unit is an old man, then *who the hell was just with me in this room?*

And then the bar on my phone disappears.

53

I am in even worse trouble than I thought.

When Cameron and I first arrived at Ward D, a man in his thirties wearing scrubs and a white coat introduced himself as Dr. Richard Beck, which was also embroidered on his coat. He wasn't wearing an ID badge, but I didn't think anything of it at the time. There was no reason to think he was anyone other than Dr. Beck. And it was confirmed by the nurse, Ramona.

Dr. Beck is like eighty years old!

Gabby had no reason to lie. It's very clear now that the man I have been addressing as the attending psychiatrist on the unit is not Dr. Beck. And then, of course, there's the question of where the real Dr. Beck is. Because he was the assigned psychiatrist on the call schedule. So at some point, was he ever here?

My head is still spinning, but I force myself to my feet. I hold up the phone, saying a prayer that I'll get a bar or two of reception. That's all I need and I'll be able to call 911. I step over to the window, pressing my phone against the glass the way I did earlier.

"Please," I whisper. "Please... just one bar..."

My prayers are not answered.

I can't spend the rest of the night here, praying for a bar of phone reception. I've got to figure out a way to escape. Because it's beginning to be clear that I do not have any friends on Ward D. Not anymore.

Except how can I get out of here when the doors are all locked?

I think back to the events of the evening. I remember how things took a turn when Miguel peed on the light socket. It blew out all the lights on the unit. At the time, I thought it was done on purpose by whoever is pulling the strings, but now I'm not so sure. Maybe that really was just Miguel accidentally blowing out the lights. I don't believe any of it is related to the landline phones going out, which I think was done purposefully, but the power outage was real.

If the power goes out again, will the door lock disengage?

It's worth a shot.

There are a bunch of mugs lined up by the sink. I pick up one that says "If you're happy and you know it, thank your meds." I turn on the sink and fill it up with lukewarm water. Then I walk over to the light socket.

Here goes nothing.

I pour the water directly over the light socket,

trying my best to get it right inside. Right away, sparks fly. I crane my neck, looking up at the lights overhead. They flicker for a moment.

And then they go out.

If I ever had a chance, this is it. I grab my phone out of my pocket and turn on the flashlight function. I shine it around the room until I locate the door. And then I make a run for it.

The door to the unit is directly on my left. All I have to do is grab the handle and get the hell out of here. But before I can do it, I find myself hesitating. I find my eyes drawn in the direction of the seclusion rooms. Notably, to Seclusion One.

Don't you want to see what's inside?

I shine my flashlight in the direction of Seclusion One. The keypad that usually glows green has gone dark. Is this when Damon Sawyer escaped? Or is he still in the room, ready to pounce when I open the door?

And then a terrible thought hits me.

When anyone leaves the unit, the door alarm sounds off. It's like a siren—you can hear it every-where. And I haven't heard that sound once since I first entered Ward D.

Cameron supposedly had a family emergency and left the unit. But if that were true, we would have heard that deafening siren noise emit from the door. Which means…

Cameron never left.

If he had gone through that door, I would have

heard the siren. So that means he must still be here. Since I have searched everywhere else, that leaves one remaining place where he could be. And if he is in there—if Damon Sawyer somehow grabbed him and pulled him inside—I owe it to Cameron to try to rescue him before it's too late.

I can't leave here without seeing what's behind this door. It will only take a second.

I reach for the handle, and it turns easily in my hand. The locks have disengaged like I hoped they would. I yank the door open, shining the light on my phone into the dark space.

As I stare inside the room, my legs tremble beneath me. Oh no. Oh my God.

I never should have opened the door to this room. I should have made a run for it while I still could.

54

The stench of blood fills Seclusion One.

A couple of my friends are taking their surgery rotation right now, and when they discuss the surgeries they saw, they never mentioned the smell of blood. But this room is thick with it—an acrid, metallic smell that assaults my nostrils as I stare into the small dark space.

There's death in this room.

I should run. The second I smell the blood, that should be my cue to run for it while I still can. But I am frozen in place, my phone glued to my palm. I want to look away, but I can't. All I know is I will never forget it, not until the day I die. I will never stop seeing this room, even when I close my eyes to go to sleep at night.

The beam of my flashlight first rests on the bed. There's a woman there. A small woman of around eighty years old. She is staring up at the ceiling, a drop of blood in the corner of her mouth. She is so still.

It's Mary. Mary Cummings.

She's finally joined her husband.

I move the beam of light away from Mary's dead body. But that's a mistake. Because the next thing the light illuminates is a figure lying in the corner of the room. A male with the frame of a football player, dressed in blue scrubs. And when the beam hits his eyes, they are staring ahead at nothing.

I clasp my free hand over my mouth. "Cameron," I whisper. "Cam…"

He's dead too. I don't even have to check. I was mad at him for the way he broke up with me, but I didn't want this for him. I wanted him to suffer just a little bit, then go off and live his life and be a surgeon or whatever he wanted. But that's never going to happen now.

I almost drop the phone, but when I lower the light beam, I realize there are two more bodies on the floor of the room. The carnage is not over.

The first is a woman. I don't recognize her, but she is just as still as Mary and Cameron. She's lying face down on the floor, her arms and legs splayed out around her body. She's dressed in only her underwear.

And there's one final body.

This one is a man. He looks like he was in his seventies, with a bushy white beard. Like the woman,

he is also in his underwear. I notice a bruise blos-
soming on his shoulder from where he tried to bash
the door down. As I shine my light on his head, I can
make out the deep indentation in his skull.

"I thought he was dead the first time," a voice
from behind me speaks up. "But he wasn't. He got up
and he kept trying to get out of the damn room.
Fortunately, the second time I hit him in the head, I
had better results."

I turn around, raising my phone in the air like a
weapon. And there he is. Standing right in front of
me. The man who spent the whole damn night
pretending to be Dr. Beck. Pretending to be taking
care of all these patients when, in fact, he was nothing
but an imposter.

And then the lights flicker back on. The generator
has kicked back in.

My chance to escape is gone. I should have run
while I could. I'll never get another chance like that.
He'll make sure of that.

"You're more resourceful than I thought you
were." His gaze lifts to the fluorescent lights overhead.
"If you hadn't been so damn curious, you actually
might have gotten away. Respect, Amy. Truly."

I take a step back. "Stay away from me…"

"Why are you so afraid?"

"I don't know who you are, but I know you're not
Dr. Beck."

"You're right—I haven't even introduced myself."

He smiles at me and those dimples pop. He really is handsome—I can see why Jade fell for him. "My name is Damon. Damon Sawyer. And it's very nice to finally meet you, Amy. I've heard *so* much about you."

55

I have to hold onto the wall to keep from passing out.

All this time, I thought the monster was in Seclusion One. I thought he was roaming the halls, hiding in dark corners. But all along, he was right in front of me.

Footsteps echo from down the hallway, growing closer. Bile rises in my throat when Jade and Ramona round the corner. Now it's three against one, not that I had any chance against Damon Sawyer even on his own.

"You found her!" Jade's face breaks into a smile. "Where was she?"

Damon turns to look at her, and the affection on his face is unmistakable. "She was checking out the seclusion room. Admiring our handiwork."

"What do you think, Amy?" Jade's blue eyes

flecked with yellow rest on my face. "And you thought I would never do anything significant with my life…"

"I never said that," I mumble.

Jade comes up right beside me, her eyes boring into me. "No, you never said it. But you *thought* it. Didn't you?"

She's not entirely wrong. "Jade…"

"You disappointed me though, Amy," she muses. "I always thought of you as being very smart, but you never saw any of this coming. You believed *me* over that geeky reporter, even though you know I'm a brilliant liar." She looks over at her boyfriend with admiration. "And worst of all, you trusted *him*."

Damon clutches his chest. "Hey, are you saying I'm not trustworthy?"

"You did put on an excellent performance," she concedes. "I guess those psychology books you were always reading paid off."

"Well, thank you."

Jade winks at me. "Damon really is wonderful, Amy. I wish you could have known him in a different context. Of course, that couldn't happen because you didn't want to have anything to do with me outside of here."

"I… I'm sorry," I manage.

She ignores my feeble attempt to apologize. "We met in such an interesting way too. What do they call it—a meet-cute? Damon was my mother's drug dealer. You know how she was always hooked on pills? Well, he used to bring them to her."

I'm not sure I would call that a meet-cute, but I'm not about to contradict her.

She smiles distantly. "And he was the one who brought her the cocktail she OD'd on. She had no idea what she was putting into her system. Damon was so clever about it."

Damon grins, showing off his dimples. "You're very welcome, babe."

My mouth is open. "You were the one responsible for your mother's overdose? How could you do that?"

The smile vanishes from Jade's face. "The woman used to burn me with her cigarettes. Do you think I feel any regret about giving her exactly what she deserved?"

I remember the way Mrs. Carpenter smashed that ashtray against the wall. The suspicious marks on Jade's arms. She begged me not to tell anyone. I should never have listened.

I made a terrible mistake. I should have helped my friend, even when she asked me not to. There's a small part of me that feels like I deserve everything that's about to happen.

But no. These people are monsters. Whatever created them has already happened. I can't let them hurt anybody else.

I back against the wall, trying to figure out my next move. Three of them and one of me. I don't like those odds. If only Will were still conscious, I would have a fighting chance. But without him…

I've got to buy myself some time. One thing I

know about Jade is that she's a talker. I could probably keep her talking until the sun comes up.

"I don't understand," I say. "How… how did you manage this? Why didn't anyone recognize you?"

"It was surprisingly easy," Jade says. "The real Dr. Beck wasn't working on the unit this week, so most of the patients had never seen him before."

Damon jerks his head in the direction of the room full of dead bodies. "And we managed to take care of most of the people who did recognize me."

Of course. Miguel and Mary were both convinced that Damon Sawyer was roaming the hallways long before anyone else was. Lucky for him, neither of them were terribly trustworthy. I'm guessing if I opened the door to Seclusion Two, I would find Miguel's body in there.

"As soon as the dayshift staff left," Jade says, "I opened the door to the seclusion room. It was almost pitifully easy for me to get that code. Just as easy as it was to give you the wrong code. And once Damon was out, we took care of the real Dr. Beck and Ramona."

My eyes are drawn to the woman that I believed was Ramona all night. She's looking down at her nails critically, but when she notices my attention, she looks up and smiles. "My name is Nicole," she says. "I actually *am* a nurse."

"Before you went berserk," Jade points out.

Ramona, who is actually Nicole, shoots her a look. "You asked for my help and you got it."

Nicole. That was the name of the patient Mary had mixed me up with. I remember Mary saying something about how Dr. Beck wouldn't let her leave.

My eyes go to the ID badge clipped to Nicole's scrubs. The photo is tiny and blurry, and while it looks somewhat like Nicole, any other middle-aged woman with brown hair could likely have passed.

"Don't pretend you were doing us a favor," Jade snaps at Nicole. "Your brother was trying to have you *committed*. We did you a big favor letting you in on our plan. How about a little *gratitude*, huh?"

Nicole screws up her face. It doesn't look like any expressions of gratitude are forthcoming.

"*Anyway*." Jade rolls her eyes as she turns back to me. "We had to get rid of your buddy Cameron, because let's face it, he's a big guy and the two of you together would be difficult to take on. But when we had the element of surprise, he was fairly easy to take down." She snickers. "He should have spent more time at the gym and less time studying."

"Don't you dare make jokes about him," I snap at her. "Cam was a really good guy. He didn't deserve that."

"Oh really? Didn't he dump you to study for an exam?" Jade retorts.

"Plus he was kind of an obnoxious kiss-up," Nicole adds.

Jade whips her head around to glare at Nicole. "We don't need your opinion on every little thing."

"Will you shut up, Jade?" Nicole shoots back, her

eyes flashing. "The whole night it was like you got to call all the shots. I told you that Amy was getting suspicious, and did you listen? Of course not! You're always talking and never listening. Frankly, I don't blame Amy for not respecting you! You always—"

I don't know what Nicole was going to say next, but she never gets a chance. Damon removes what appears to be a paperweight from the pocket of his scrubs and bashes it against her skull with incredible force. Nicole stops speaking mid-sentence, and a second later, she crumples to the floor. A little pool of blood starts to form around her head.

I take another step back, my mouth hanging open. I can barely breathe.

"Jesus Christ," Damon comments. "She was really beginning to annoy me. No wonder her brother wanted to have her committed."

Jade's expression has not changed. If her boyfriend's act of violence has disturbed her in the slightest, it doesn't show on her face. "Don't worry, Amy. That was part of the plan all along. The only people who are going to survive the night are me and Damon. Nicole was just a third wheel."

I look between the two of them, trying to figure out if there's any reasoning with either one of them. Jade—well, I've tried it before. I've tried to talk her out of doing something terrible. And it didn't work. But on the other hand, she was my best friend. We've known each other our whole lives. She wouldn't really hurt me if it came down to it.

Would she?

Now that I know who Damon really is, I notice the crazed glint in his brown eyes. Even his hair has taken on a wild edge, sticking up every which way instead of neatly combed like it was at the beginning of the shift. When I first found out about the man locked in the seclusion room, it sounded like they were describing a wild animal. And when I look at Damon Sawyer, that's what I see. A man who would smash a paperweight into a woman's skull and kill her just because she was being *annoying*.

No, there's no reasoning with this man. It's Jade or nobody.

"Jade," I say, "whatever you're planning, you don't have to do this. It's not too late to turn things around."

"You really think that?" She nods in the direction of Seclusion One. "You really think it's not too late?"

She has a very good point.

"You always thought you had all the answers," she says. "You always thought you were better than me. Well, tonight *I'm* calling the shots for a change."

"I'm not better than you." My voice breaks. "I don't think that. I never thought that."

"Of course you do!" Jade bursts out. "You always did! You were the one who got all A's and were the teacher's pet, and I was the crazy one. You never had any idea what it was like to be me."

Damon grins. "Maybe you should've dropped a few more hallucinogens in her peach iced tea."

I feel like Damon just slugged me. For a moment, my entire world is crashing down around me. "*What?*"

Jade drops her eyes, but Damon just laughs. "Come on, Jade. She's going to die—you should at least tell her what you used to do to her. It's *funny*."

"You didn't!" I cry.

Jade lifts a shoulder. "You are always drinking those peach iced teas. It was so easy just to drop a little something in there if you went to the bathroom or… you know."

"Oh my God." I clutch at my cheeks. "I thought I was *losing my mind*. That was you drugging me all along? How could you do that to me, Jade?"

"It wasn't that big a deal." She juts out her lower lip. "You were such a square. It probably helped you loosen up a little. It certainly didn't make you any nicer though."

I can't believe it. When I started to see that little girl everywhere, I thought my brain was broken. I had never been so terrified in my life. But it was really just my best friend slipping drugs into my freaking drink behind my back.

But any relief is short-lived. I'm still stuck in this locked unit with two extremely dangerous people and no way out.

"Anyway." Damon looks down at his watch. "We better get going with this. The sun will be up soon."

My heart sinks. "Get going with *what*? What are you going to do?"

Jade ignores my question. "You're right, Damon.

Should I go grab the paint thinner?"

Paint thinner?

Damon tosses the paperweight, splattered in Nicole's blood, between his hands. "Honestly, anyone who is dumb enough to leave a can of paint thinner on a psych ward is just asking to have the whole place burned down."

I remember looking through Damon's chart. The history of arson when he was a child. He had an affinity for setting fires. *Two casualties.*

"No," I breathe. "You're not going to do that…"

He winks at me. "Weren't you the one who said this place was a fire hazard?"

I start to move towards him, but I've barely taken a step when Damon raises the paperweight over his head. I remember the way the marble smashed into Nicole's skull and I freeze.

No. Not now. It's not the time.

Jade goes back behind the nurses' station and she pulls out a bucket. She starts humming to herself as she splashes the caustic material all over the floor. She drenches the floors with it, and for good measure, she pours a bunch of it on Nicole's body.

"You can't do this," I croak. "You can't kill all these people because you're mad at me. That's not right."

"Oh, get over yourself." Jade sneers at me. "This isn't about you. Damon and I wanted a fresh start, so what better way to get it than to burn down the psych unit and pretend both of us went up in flames?" She smirks. "Although when I saw your name on the call list for this week, I did get excited about the idea of having a little fun with you in the process. We were going to do it last night, but we decided to move our plans just for you."

"It's true," Damon confirms. "Jade made me wait a whole extra night. She must really hate you."

A sweat breaks out on my palms as I imagine the entire unit going up in flames. I imagine the temperature rising as flames lick at my feet. I've heard being burned to death is a terrible way to die.

But hope is not lost. The two of them are going to need to leave the unit if they don't want to burn down with it. As soon as they're gone, I can short out the light circuit again. And then I'll be able to get out.

Except then I see Jade crouched on the floor, going through Nicole's pockets. My heart sinks when she pulls out a syringe—the same kind Nicole plunged into Will's arm earlier.

"We're not completely heartless," Jade says. "You're going to sleep through the whole thing. We'll put you to sleep, and then you're going to wake up dead."

No. Oh my God, *no*.

"Damon," Jade says, "how about you hold her down and I'll inject her?"

He winks at me again. "That sounds like a plan."

"Please." Tears fill my eyes. "Jade, you can't do this to me. *Please*."

She frowns at me.

"We were best friends," I remind her as I swipe at my eyes. "Doesn't that mean anything to you?"

"Best friends," she repeats mockingly. "Please, Amy. You should have seen the look of disgust on your face when I suggested the two of us go out to dinner. You didn't even bother to come to my mother's funeral. I mean, yes, I'm the one who killed her, but *you* didn't know that. Is that how you treat a best friend?"

"I'm sorry!" I cry. "I was terrible to you, and I admit it. But I want to change. I want to get to know you. I want to be best friends again."

Jade's eyes soften. Maybe this will work. Maybe she really will rethink what she's about to do and change her mind.

But then Damon bursts out into loud laughter. "Jade, you aren't seriously falling for this bullshit, are you?"

If we ever had a moment, it's now broken. "No. Don't be stupid." She looks up at the clock on the wall. "Let's do this."

There's no way to stop this. It's just me versus the two of them. They're going to knock me out, then they're going to burn down Ward D. And there's nothing I can do about it. I might have a chance if it were just Jade, but I don't have a chance against Damon. His upper arms are bulging with tight muscles—he's very strong. After all, he killed Nicole with one blow to the head.

There's no way out.

56

I back away down the hallway, knowing there's nothing behind me besides the door with a lock I can't open. Damon has put the paperweight back in the pocket of his scrubs, and he's coming at me with nothing but his bare hands. Which is enough, unfortunately.

"Don't make this harder on yourself, Amy," Jade says. "Believe me, you do *not* want to be awake when this place starts to burn down. We're doing you a huge favor."

"We're very nice people," Damon adds.

"Please," I whimper. "Please don't do this."

My head is spinning. Between the two of them coming at me and the fumes of the paint thinner, it's hard to think straight. I hit something solid and almost stumble. I have backed up into the door to Ward D. The green keypad is glowing, taunting me. I could've left when I had a chance and I didn't do it. I will pay for that stupidity for the rest of my life, which will be exceptionally short.

Jade grips the syringe in her right hand. "Okay, grab her arms."

"No!" I cry.

Damon starts to reach for me and I brace myself, vowing to fight as hard as I can against him, even though Will was bigger and stronger and he couldn't successfully fight him off. I may be doomed, but it doesn't matter. I'm still going to fight.

But the offensive move never comes. Out of nowhere, Damon's face morphs into a mesh of white lines. He screams and claws at his cheeks.

"Go web!" a voice yells out.

I stare at the scene unfolding in front of me. It takes me a moment to figure out what just happened, and when I do, I can't quite believe it. It's Spider-Dan. He came out of freaking nowhere and dropped a web constructed out of *dental floss* onto Damon's face. And now he is tightening the web, cutting off Damon's airway.

Spider-Dan is stronger than he looks. Also, you *can* make a spiderweb out of dental floss, apparently. I can't believe it—Cameron was right.

Thanks, Cam.

"Stop that, you lunatic!" Jade screams.

She tries to lunge for Spider-Dan with the syringe, and if I've ever had a moment, this is it. I jump at Jade with all my might and knock her down, the syringe flying from her fingers. Spider-Dan and

Damon are tussling on the floor, and I'm coming at Jade with everything I've got.

I've never been in a fight before though. I'm willing to bet Jade has, and on top of that, she is freakishly strong. The syringe has flown off across the hallway, but she is still able to overpower me and put her weight on top of me. I'm starting to wish I were one of those med students who gorged myself when I was nervous instead of starving myself. I could use an extra twenty or thirty pounds right now.

"You are not getting out of here alive," Jade hisses in my face, bits of spittle flying into my eyes. "You're not going to run off and live your dream life and have your dream job while I rot away in a mental institution for the rest of my life. It's not fair!"

There's a gasping noise coming from next to me. Spider-Dan is on top of Damon, tightening the web around his neck. Jade doesn't even seem to notice though. She is completely focused on me. She claims I wasn't her target tonight, but I don't believe that.

"Whatever else happens," she says, "it all ends tonight for you, girlie."

And then her hands wrap around my neck.

57

I can't breathe.

The weight of Jade's body is crushing my abdomen, and her fingers are crushing my windpipe. I reach out and try to claw at her, attempting to scratch her in the face, but she's got leverage on me, and with each breath that I don't get to take, it gets harder and harder.

I'm starting to see spots in my eyes. My arms go limp at my side, and I realize how easy it would be to just give in. It's not a good thing that I'm thinking that way, but I don't know if I have the energy to fight this woman.

I stopped her once before though. Maybe I can do it one more time.

If only I had a weapon.

Mary's knitting needle! It's still in your pocket—stab her with it!

I grasp around with my right hand, and my

fingers close around the cold steel needle. All of Jade's attention is focused on my face, which feels like it's turning blue. In another few seconds, I don't know if I'll be able to think straight anymore. I've got one chance to do this right.

As hard as I can, I jab the knitting needle right into Jade's rib cage.

I hit the money spot. She screams and rolls off me, clutching her side. I've still got the needle in my hand, and I climb on top of Jade, using the weight of my body to hold her down. And then I take the knitting needle and bring the pointed end right close to her cheek.

"If you move one inch," I say, "I swear to God, I will put this knitting needle right through your eye."

Jade's face is bright pink. There's a sheen of sweat on her forehead. "Yeah, right," she chokes out. "You don't have the guts to do something like that."

I bring the needle closer so that it is almost touching the white of her eye. She squirms. "Try me," I say through my teeth.

I hazard a look over at Spider-Dan and Damon. To my utter shock, Spider-Dan has gotten the better of Damon Sawyer, who is now lying unconscious on the tiled floor. The dental floss has made deep indentations on his skin. I have to say, that was a very well-made web.

"I told you I would protect you, Amy," Spider-Dan tells me.

"You did," I acknowledge. "Thank you so much. I can't thank you enough."

"All in a day's work for your friendly neighborhood Spider-Man," he says. His voice is still monotonic, but I could swear I hear a touch of pride as well.

Before I can figure out exactly how to respond, I hear pounding at the door to Ward D. A man's voice rings out: "Everything okay in there? We heard shouting."

I almost laugh at how completely not okay it is in here.

"We're locked in!" I shout at the door. "Please help us!"

The man yells back that he's getting somebody to come open the door. As relieved as I feel, I don't ease up my grip on Jade or the knitting needle. I don't trust her for one second. That's how quick she'll turn on me, so until that door is open, I'm keeping my eyes on her.

"It's over then," she croaks. "It looks like you won."

I just shake my head. At least five people are dead on this unit, including the boy that I used to think I loved. Five lives cut short. And it's at least partly my fault. I could've done more for Jade. How can I call myself a doctor if I can't even try to heal my best friend in the entire world?

It might be over. But I definitely have not won.

58

I don't release the knitting needle or my grip on Jade until I hear the alarm sound and the click that signifies the door to Ward D is now unlocked.

As soon as that happens, I stand up and throw the needle as far as I can. I raise my hands over my head just to be safe. There are a lot of bad things happening right here, and I don't want anyone to get any idea that I'm responsible for any of it.

Jade scrambles to her feet as well, doing her best to smooth out her blond hair so it doesn't look quite as wild. I might have been well served to do the same. Only about five percent of my hair is still in my pony-tail and the rest is hanging loose around my face or possibly sticking straight up in the air. But at least I don't have smeared makeup like she does.

A man bursts into the unit. He's a maintenance worker who I vaguely recognize from the last two years, with gray hair, a belly that hangs over his work belt, and an ID badge that says "Chuck" in big black letters. I wonder if he recognizes me. Probably not. There are so many of us students.

Chuck's eyes widen as he stumbles inside the unit. He takes in Jade with her wild blond hair and streaked mascara, me with my hands up in the air, Damon on the floor with his face covered in dental floss, and then Spider-Dan, looking quite proud of himself.

"What the hell is going on here?" Chuck barks.

He doesn't even know this is just the tip of the iceberg. He hasn't seen what's in the seclusion rooms.

"She attacked me!" Jade swipes at her eyes as she glares at me. "She's a crazy person. Thank God you came to our rescue!"

"That's not true," I say in a calm, even voice that belies what I'm feeling inside.

Chuck looks between the two of us. He's *got* to realize that she is the patient and I am the... well, I'm not a doctor yet, but I'm definitely not a patient— even though when I look down on my chest, I realize that my ID badge came off during the scuffle.

Chuck must see that I'm the sane one.

Right?

Finally, his eyes rest on me. "I know you," he says. "You're the medical student who kept forgetting the combination to your locker in the anatomy lab."

That is extremely accurate, although embarrass-ing. I had to ask Chuck to cut my lock off no less than three times during my first year. I never claimed to be good at remembering numbers.

"Yes," I say.

"What's your name, Medical Student?"

"Amy. Amy Brenner."

"Okay, Amy." He nods firmly. "I want to hear from you and you alone. What happened here tonight?"

AFTER HE HEARS an abridged version of my story and gets a glimpse of what's inside Seclusion One, Chuck calls 911.

Several other hospital staff members join us in Ward D, to assess the damage, and take Jade and Damon into custody. Damon briefly lost consciousness, but he comes around when security gets onto the unit. However, being choked with dental floss has taken a lot of the fight out of him. A nurse whose ID badge identifies her as Hazel takes me aside. "Anyone else injured?" she asks.

Spider-Dan seems... well, as good as he ever was. Then I remember Seclusion Two. "There's a patient in there too. His name is Miguel."

Much like the door to the entrance, a code isn't working on this one either. Chuck has to reset it manually, and we all step back to let him do his job. As I watch him, my stomach churns. What are the chances that Miguel is perfectly fine in there?

As soon as the door swings open, I immediately see the rest of the blood that Nicole couldn't clean up. Strawberry jelly—how could I have *ever* believed that? It's streaked all over the floor in the room, although I can't see much else because the emergency staff members have already run inside. It just showed how much Jade was messing with my head that I could have ever doubted myself.

"No pulse!" someone announces from inside the room.

Even though I knew it had to be true, I still feel a wave of sadness. One more casualty of the night. Hopefully the last one.

A few patients have wandered out of their rooms to see what the commotion is about. Even though the staff is desperately trying to keep them inside, there are too many patients and the staff is too busy with all the dead bodies. Clint wanders out, dodging a nurse who tries to step in his way. He is wily that one.

"Amy!" Clint calls out. He's still holding that bag of saltines.

I didn't even know he knew my name—it's awkward since I still don't know his. In my head, he is Clint Eastwood. I attempt to smile, but I can't get my lips to cooperate. "You should go back to your room, sir."

His overgrown white eyebrows scrunch together. "Is Mary okay?"

I don't have the heart to tell him the truth. "Yes, she'll be fine. Please, just go back to your room."

He'll never know the difference. He'll just think she got discharged. There's no reason for him to know she's dead.

"Okay." He digs around in the bag of saltines and pulls out one of the little packages. "When you see her, will you give her one of these?"

I accept the package and drop it into my scrub pocket. "Of course."

As Clint obediently shuffles back to his room, a terrible thought occurs to me. I look over at room 906 —one of the few patients who has remained in his room. I grab Hazel, who is lingering in the doorway of Seclusion Two. "You need to check on the patient in room 906," I tell her urgently. "They drugged him with something."

Hazel nods and hurries into room 906, without bothering to knock on the closed door. I hear the creaking of bedsprings within the room, and a few seconds later, the intercom blasts above us:

Code blue room 906.

I don't even need to check the handy guide on the back of my ID badge, which lists what the different code colors signify. Code blue is cardiopulmonary arrest.

Oh my God. Will is in cardiopulmonary arrest.

No, not another one. I can't take it anymore.

I step aside while the code team rushes into the room with a crash cart. I try to get a glimpse inside, but all I can see is somebody intubating him. That's not a good sign. A moment later, they have got him on a stretcher and they dash past me, with Will intubated. A nurse is blowing air into his lungs manually with a bag while they roll him along.

"Hey." Hazel grabs my arm. "Do you know what they gave him?"

My mouth almost feels too dry to speak. "I think it was Ativan," I croak. "Is he… what's going on?"

She flashes me a grim look. "He wasn't breathing."

A second later, they are out the door and gone. I'm assuming they're taking him down to the ICU. But at least he's alive. He's got a chance of surviving.

Please let him survive this night.

The police have been questioning me for over an hour.

In their defense, it's a long story with a lot of details. And while it's a very wild story, they seem to believe it. They hang on my every word and write everything I say down on a little notepad.

"You had quite a night," a tall dark-haired officer named Moreno comments.

"Yeah." My hands have not stopped shaking for the last hour. I'm not sure if they'll ever stop shaking. Good thing I don't want to be a surgeon. "Where did you take Jade and Damon?"

"To jail," Moreno says. "Don't worry—they won't be able to hurt you ever again."

Of course, that's not much consolation after all the things that they've already done. Five dead bodies on the unit. And Will down in the ICU, a tube stuck down his throat so he can breathe.

Over Moreno's shoulder, I can see them wheeling a stretcher out of the seclusion room. Unlike when they were taking Will out of the unit, there's no urgency now. All the people in that room are already dead. The stretcher has a body on it, covered head to toe in a white sheet.

As the stretcher hits a crack in the floor, something drops out from under the sheet. It takes me a second to realize what it is.

It's a package of Ring Dings.

It must be Cameron under the sheets. I should have guessed based on the bulky outline of the body —the former college football player. I clasp a hand over my mouth, my eyes filling with tears. I was such a jerk to him the last time we talked. He tried to extend an olive branch, and I shut him down.

In my defense, I didn't realize it would be the last time we would talk *ever*.

And now he's dead. He'll never be an orthopedic surgeon. He'll never be *anything*. How could this be? He was only twenty-four years old. Yes, he wasn't perfect, but he was a good guy. All he wanted was to put people back together again after they got hurt.

"You okay?" Moreno asks me.

I consider lying and trying to be strong, but instead I shake my head. "No. Not at all."

My phone buzzes inside my scrub pocket. With the door to the unit open, we seem to be getting cell reception, although I've been too busy to spend any time on my phone. Eventually, I need to tell other people what happened here, but I'm not ready for it. Not yet.

I did do one thing though when I had a spare moment. I googled *The Daily Chronicle* and brought up a list of the staff members. And there he was, third from last, along with a color photograph. William Schoenfeld, Staff Reporter.

He was telling the truth all along.

My phone buzzes again, and I pull it out of my scrub pocket. There are a bunch of text messages from Gabby that are equal parts curious, irritated, and concerned. I skim to the final message:

> Where are you??? There are like a million police cars here!

I clear my throat. "Hey, is it okay if I leave? My roommate is waiting outside and I've been up the whole night."

Moreno hesitates. "Okay, but I'm going to give you my card. After you get some rest, give me a call right away. We've got a lot to talk about."

I don't doubt that.

It's like I'm in a haze as I walk down the hallway to the elevators. Last night, I did this exact same walk in reverse. I was a completely different person back then. It feels like I've stepped into a parallel universe where my whole life has changed overnight.

When I get into the elevator, I consider stopping off at the ICU. I'm desperate to know if Will is doing okay. But Gabby is waiting for me downstairs, and I don't even know what floor the ICU is on. I'll call when I get home. I may even try to visit if I can work up the nerve to ever set foot in this building again.

The elevators are just as slow on the way down as they were on the way up. There are a handful of people in the elevator, all oblivious to what happened last night on the ninth floor. I'm sure most people know something happened, but the details will probably emerge over the next twenty-four hours. It's surreal to be in a small space filled with people who have no idea what I have just been through.

I lean against the side of the elevator, resting my head on the metal surface. I have been running on adrenaline the last couple of hours, but now the exhaustion hits me like a ton of bricks. I could sleep standing up at this point. My eyes sag shut, and for a moment, I almost start to drift off until my phone buzzes again. It's a text message from my mother.

> Are you busy this weekend? I thought I could take you to lunch tomorrow.

Lunch with my mother? Oh God, that sounds exhausting. And yet, I find myself punching in:

> Sure.

And then:

> I love you.

That may have been the wrong thing to say. Almost immediately, a text message appears on the screen:

> I love you too. Is everything okay?????

And then I tell my mother the biggest lie I have ever told her in my entire life:

> Yes.

I shove my phone back in my pocket just as the elevator doors slide open. It's the lobby.

Without thinking about it, my legs move me forward. I keep walking until I get to the entrance to the hospital. I scan the entranceway until I spot that gray Toyota all the way on the side—the one that brought me here twelve hours ago, although it feels like twelve years. Somebody is honking at Gabby, but she's not moving. She waves at me vigorously.

I walk over to the Toyota and slide into the passenger seat without saying hello. Gabby flashes me a smile. "I thought they were going to tow me away or something," she says. "There's something seriously crazy going on at the hospital. Did you see all those cop cars?"

"I guess," I murmur. Sooner or later, Gabby will find out about everything that happened last night. She'll find out that our classmate is dead. But right now, I just don't want to talk about it anymore.

"So how did you like Dr. Beck?" she asks. "He's pretty great, isn't he?"

"Yep."

"If I decide to do psychiatry," she says, "I want him to be my mentor."

As Gabby turns her key in the ignition and the engine roars to life, I dig around inside my scrub pocket, pushing aside the packet of saltines. After a second, I retrieve the crinkly plastic package that I had surreptitiously swiped off the floor of Ward D just before I left.

"Ring Dings!" Gabby exclaims. "Your favorite! Where did you get them?"

"Cam brought them," I mumble. "He, uh… he switched with Stephanie to be on-call tonight."

"Oh, wow," she sighs. "You know, I ran into him last week and he was asking me if there was any chance you would take him back. I told him absolutely not. I told him you *hated* him."

I use my teeth to rip open the plastic packaging. "Oh…"

"But I've been thinking about it, and he's not such a bad guy," she says. "I mean, he's an idiot, for sure. But he likes you a lot. You think you would ever get back together with him?"

I ignore her question as the plastic tears under my teeth. I rip the bag the rest of the way open. "Do you want one of these?"

"Sure. I never say no to chocolate cake."

I pass her one of the two chocolate cake pies as I

take a bite of my own. I close my eyes, chewing on the chocolate and cream mixed together. It's the last Ring Ding I'll ever eat.

EPILOGUE

ONE YEAR LATER

I made it through my third year of medical school in one piece.

Barely.

When the year started, the odds were against me. I didn't think that by July of the next year, I would be sitting in a Starbucks, at a corner table, sipping on an iced dirty chai tea latte. A year ago, I didn't even know what an iced dirty chai tea latte was. My boyfriend introduced me to them, and now I'm weirdly addicted. I may need to go to a support group if I ever want to quit.

I take a sip from my drink. That is good stuff. Even better than peach iced tea. Not better than Ring Dings though.

I put down my drink and raise my hand as my coffee date marches through the door. The guilty party in my addiction. Will Schoenfeld.

Will's hazel eyes light up and he raises his hand in

greeting when he sees me. He looks really cute today in his Columbia T-shirt and baggy blue jeans, with his hair just the right amount of tousled from the wind outside. You can't even tell that he spent a night in the ICU a year ago, recovering from an overdose of Ativan. We've been dating for four months now, and we recently had a talk where we asked each other if we were really boyfriend and girlfriend or if we were just casual. And we decided that yes, yes we are indeed boyfriend and girlfriend. So that's where we are right now.

"Did you order me one?" he asks as he slides into the seat across from me.

"I kind of feel like you can order your own damn drink," I tease him.

He laughs. We laugh a lot together, but that's not how our relationship started. Well, it really started that night on Ward D, but after that, Will reported on his experience for *The Daily Chronicle*, and we spent a lot of time piecing together the events of that night for his feature article. Considering he got knocked out prior to the exciting conclusion, he needed me to help him re-create everything that happened, and it helped me to work through it as well. He also spent forever interviewing all the other patients who were at the hospital that night, although he never seemed to be able to locate the original patient who was the one who inspired him to investigate Ward D in the first place.

He admitted later that he didn't need to call me

quite as much as he did. But we did have a lot in common—John Irving was just the tip of the nerdy iceberg of books and movies and TV shows we both love—and I enjoyed hanging out with him. His friendship meant a lot to me during a hard time.

He waited a long while before attempting to take that friendship to the next level. For months, I was having nightmares about that awful night. And I couldn't stop crying for weeks after Cameron's funeral. I wasn't in any mental state to be starting a relationship, and he knew it.

He waited until after his article got picked up by practically every paper in the country, and everyone was talking about that wild night in the psychiatric ward. It wasn't until the spring when he suggested maybe instead of that lunch we had planned, I might be up for dinner and then a movie. His treat.

I'm not sorry I agreed to do it.

"So how is the book coming?" I ask him.

"Really well," he says. "I'm about halfway done. I can't wait for you to read the whole thing."

"Have you revised the beginning much?"

"A little." He smiles crookedly. "Don't worry. I didn't change the dedication."

After Will's story about Ward D went viral, publishers were clamoring after him to write a book about the experience. Will asked me if I wanted to write it with him, but my life is busy enough as it is. But when he showed me the first few chapters, it came with a dedication:

To Amy. I wouldn't be here to write this book without you.

I thought it was really sweet. And also, extremely true.

Of course, we both have scars from that night. Will was in the ICU for a night and then was at the hospital for another week recovering from the pneumonia he developed. We both still have nightmares, but now it's more like once a week rather than several times a night.

Damon Sawyer survived his attack by the spider-web. (Or *floss*web, as the case may be.) He and Jade were both arrested, although ultimately, they were sent to a psychiatric hospital for the criminally insane. Their insanity defense kept them from life in prison, but I've read that some of those psychiatric hospitals are much worse than prisons. After all, they will be surrounded by people just like themselves.

I have no doubt Jade deserves to be locked up for the rest of her life, but a tiny part of me wonders if it all could have been prevented. Maybe if I had done things differently when we were sixteen, I could've saved her. I'll have to live with that guilt forever.

But I'm trying to learn to be more sensitive. I could never be a psychiatrist after everything I've been through, but I'm taking another rotation in outpatient psychiatry before embarking on a family medicine career. I've even become friends with Spider-Dan. Once his medications were adjusted, he was discharged back to his group home, and I've been visiting him a couple of times a month. Usually, we watch a superhero movie together, which is the best way to get him to smile. I've learned a lot from our friendship, and I want to do my best to treat patients with psychiatric issues in the future. I don't want anyone else to end up like Jade.

After all, there's nothing worse than losing your mind.

"I'm so excited for you." I grab Will's hand across the table. "This book is going to be huge. I can just tell."

"I could never have done it without you." He gives me a sober look as he squeezes my hand. "Really. I don't know what I would do without you."

"Then maybe you shouldn't be without me."

"I hope I never am."

And now we are grinning at each other like two idiots. I liked Cameron a lot, and I miss him every day, but my romantic relationship with him was never like this. Will is the first guy I've ever dated where I thought it might lead to something more. Like, *forever* more.

But it's still so early. Four months in. Just because I have a feeling he might be the one and I'm walking around feeling giddy half the time, I don't want to get too excited. We've got time.

"Hey." I stand up from my chair. "As a reward for making great progress on your book, I am going to go get you that iced dirty chai tea latte after all."

"Wow, you really are the perfect woman."

Will starts scrolling through emails on his phone

while I run over to the counter to buy him that drink. He always grabs me one when he arrives first, so it's only fair.

Fortunately, there isn't much of a line. I place the order and lean back against the counter, waiting for the barista to make the drink. Will is still at our table, tapping at the screen of his phone. He notices me watching him and flashes me an adorable smile before going back to his screen. Will is just so great. He makes me want to fill a spiral notebook with bad poetry about his *smoldering hazel eyes*. I could really see this working out. Marriage. Two point four kids. A golden retriever and a house with a white picket fence.

"He's too good for you, you know."

I jolt slightly at the voice. I drop my eyes, and my heart sinks.

A pretty little girl is standing in front of me as if waiting for an iced dirty chai tea latte of her own. Her blond hair curls around her heart-shaped face, and she's wearing an immaculate and frilly pink dress. Her familiar blue eyes bore into me, an unreadable expression on her face.

I hate this little girl. So much.

I avert my gaze, trying to ignore her like I always do. But she is not to be ignored. "He's probably going to dump you soon," she says.

I swivel my head to watch the barista making a drink, observing the steps with great fascination. I wonder how they know how to make all those drinks.

Do they take some sort of course to learn? Coffee 101?

"He'll dump you just like Cameron," the little girl adds. "Just like all the others dumped you."

"Shut up," I mumble under my breath.

Her pink Cupid's bow lips curl into a smile, pleased that she finally managed to get to me. "You know it's true, Amy. Will is going to break your heart just like all the others."

"Shut *up*," I say through my teeth.

"Unless you kill him first."

My jaw drops as I stare at the little girl's sweet face, still smiling up at me. I had been feeling so good just a few minutes earlier. Why? Why does she always—

"Miss?"

The barista has finished my drink and has been attempting to get my attention. I snatch the iced dirty chai tea latte out of her hands, although my own hands are shaking so badly, I almost drop it. When I look back at where the little girl was standing, there's nobody there. She's gone.

As usual.

She'll never entirely leave me though. I saw her the most when I was drinking those peach iced teas laced with hallucinogens, but even after Jade left my life, I still saw the little girl from time to time. It's been nine years, and I have never told a soul aside from Jade. I don't know if the drugs she slipped me triggered something inside me that couldn't be turned off, but that little girl is always with me. Always.

And she always tells me to do things. *Bad* things.

But I don't listen. Of course I don't.

Well, most of the time.

I did listen at that party when Cameron and I hooked up. I dropped some laxatives from the medicine cabinet into his girlfriend Jess's drink because I had my eye on Cameron for a while, and the little girl knew how badly I wanted to get him alone. I listened to her when she told me to send a damning letter to the director of that research fellowship Cam applied to because she knew I didn't want him disappearing across the country for an entire year.

I also listened to her when she told me to go back and check Seclusion One instead of making my escape from Ward D. And when she whispered in my ear to stab Jade with Mary's knitting needle. I never would have thought to do that on my own.

But I don't listen to her blindly. It's not like I would do absolutely anything she tells me to do. I mean, I would never *kill* anyone just because the little girl told me to. Even though it feels like more and more, that's what she's been telling me to do. But I wouldn't do it.

After all, I would have to be insane to do something like that.

THE END

ACKNOWLEDGMENTS

A lot of people read this book before I published it, and I need to thank all of them!

Thanks to my mother for reading it (twice) and effusively telling me, "OMG THIS IS THE BEST BOOK EVER!!!" Thank you to my father for giving feedback as a practicing psychiatrist, none of which involved women's shoes (this time). Thanks to Jenna, Maura, Rebecca, and Beth, for being a totally supportive writing group! Thanks to Kate for the great suggestions. Thank you to my other beta readers, Pamela and Mark. Thank you to Avery for cover advice. Thank you to Val for your eagle eyes.

As always, I want to say a huge thank you to all my readers out there. I seriously could not do this without your support, so you are awesome. Yes, all of you.

Manufactured by Amazon.ca
Bolton, ON

34160595R00188